Kingspeak

D1297173

Daniel Lieske

CARACAL™

ISBN: 978-1-5493-0295-4

Library of Congress Control Number: 2018931085

www.lionforge.com

10 9 8 7 6 5 4 3 2 1

Contents

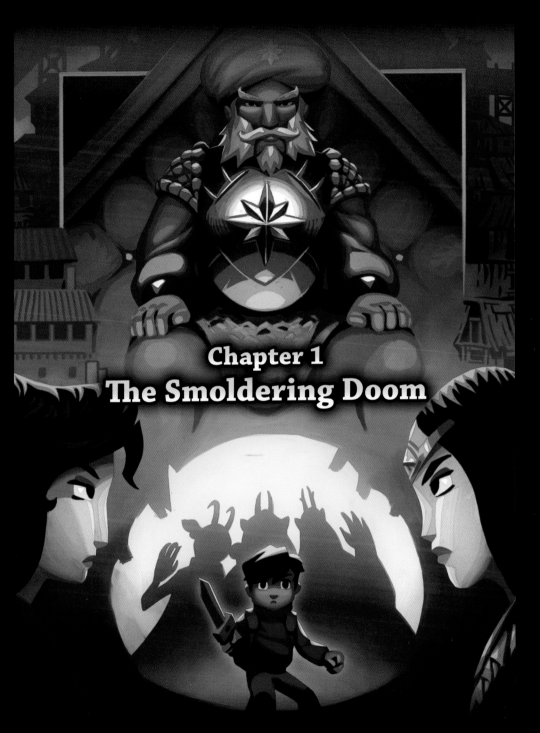

Chapter 1
The Smoldering Doom

Visibility below three hundred feet!
Speed to two knots!
Rudder two points port!

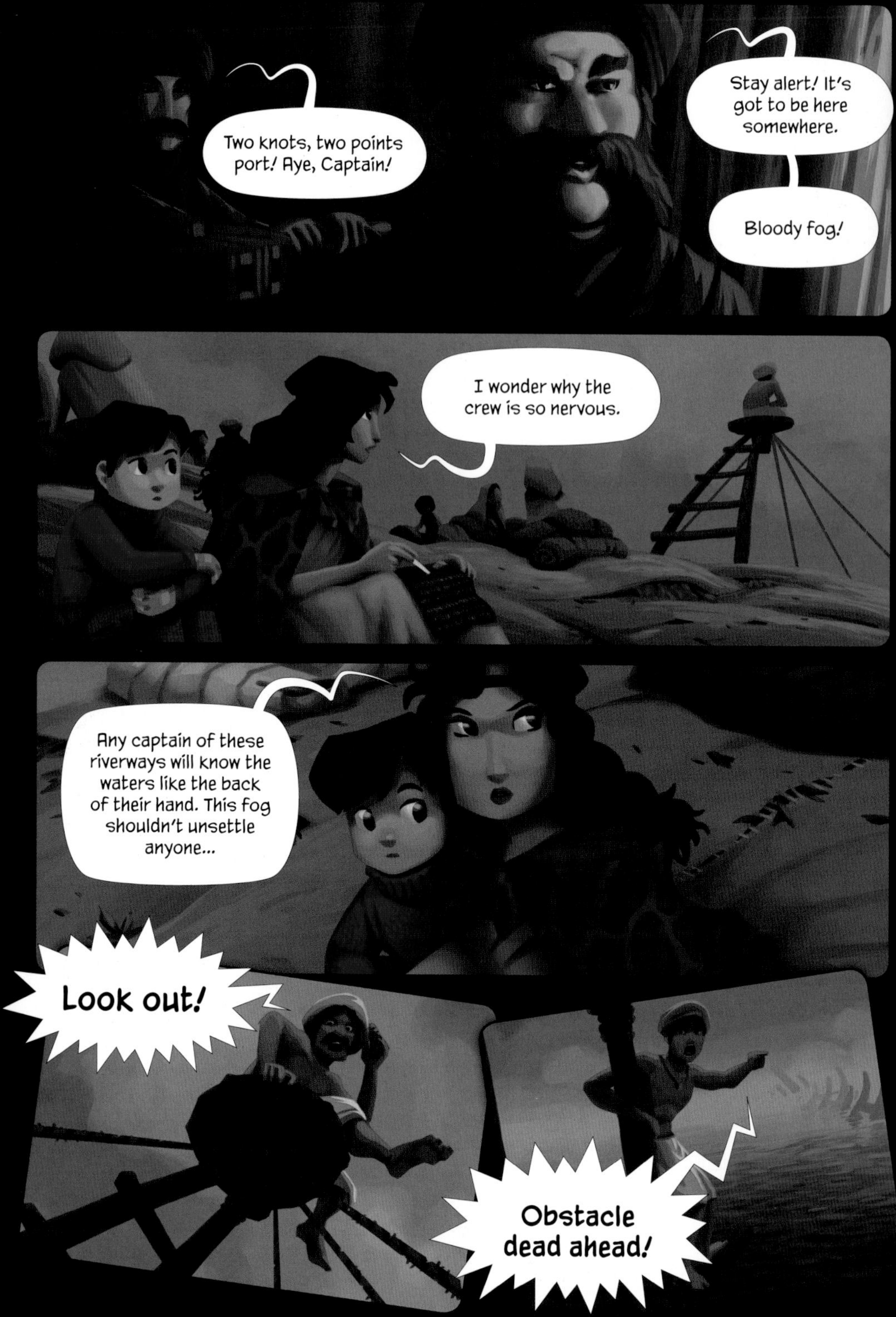
Two knots, two points port! Aye, Captain!
Stay alert! It's got to be here somewhere.
Bloody fog!
I wonder why the crew is so nervous.
Any captain of these riverways will know the waters like the back of their hand. This fog shouldn't unsettle anyone...
Look out!
Obstacle dead ahead!

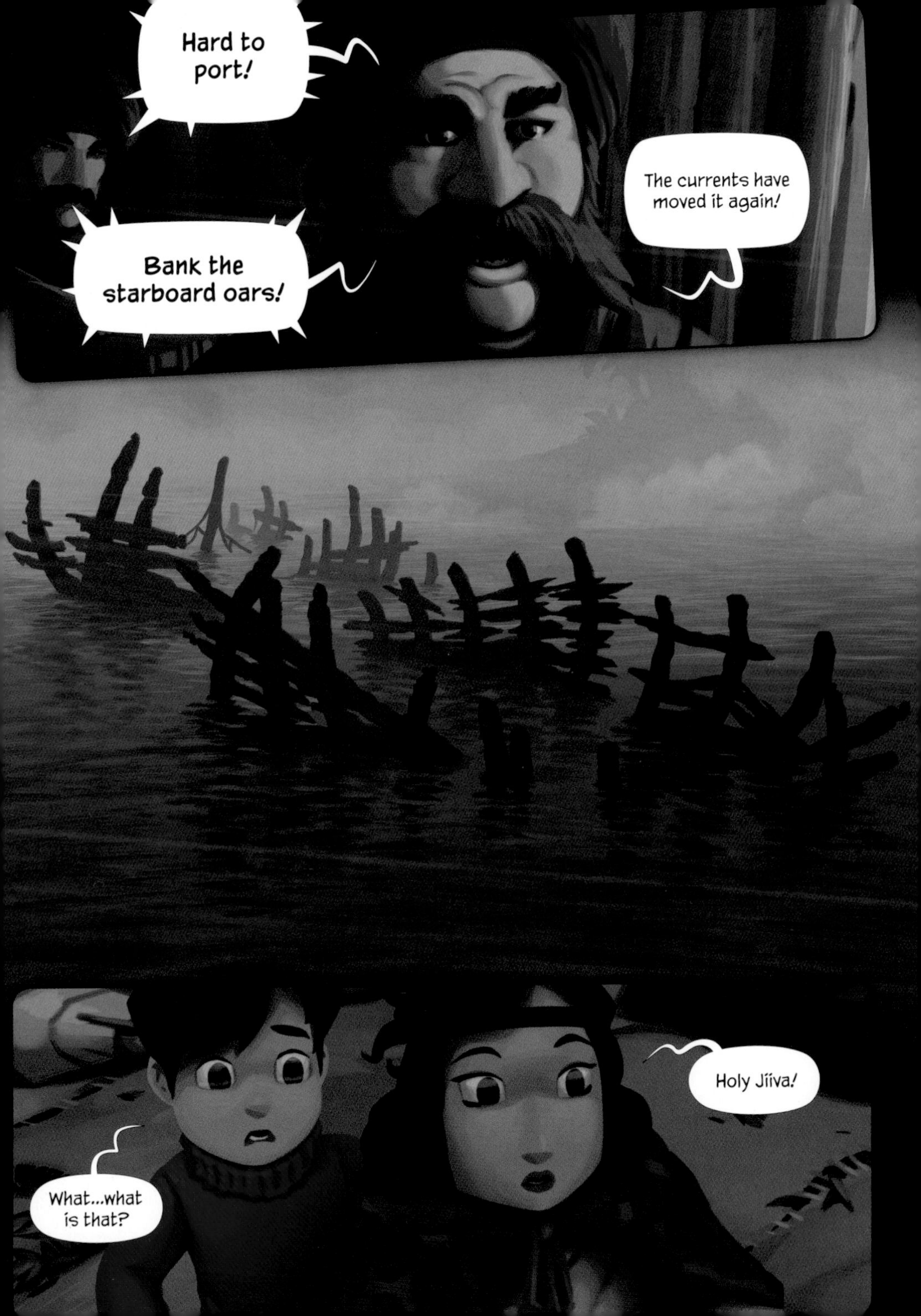
Hard to port!
Bank the starboard oars!
The currents have moved it again!
Holy Jiíva!
What...what is that?

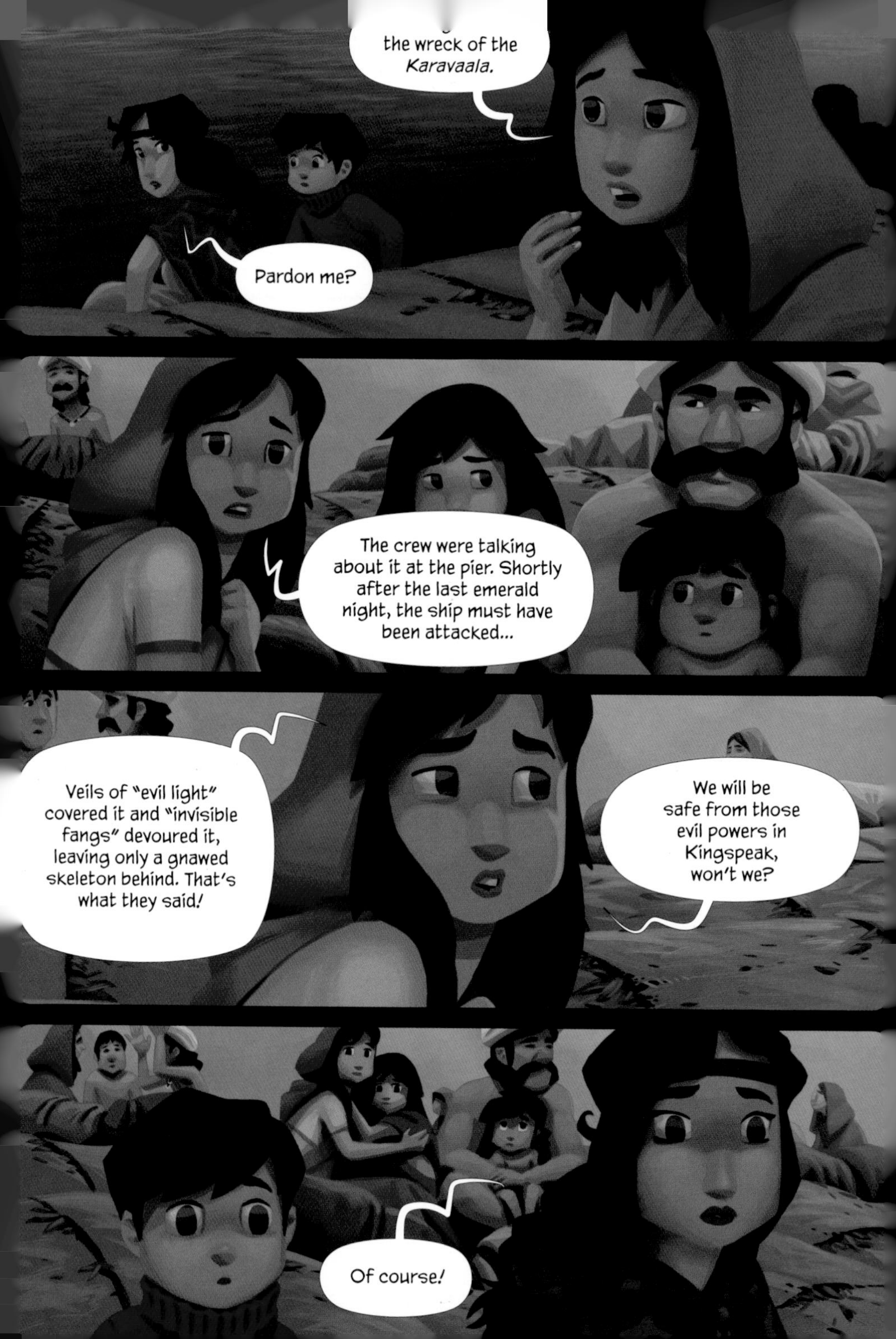
the wreck of the *Karavaala.*
Pardon me?
The crew were talking about it at the pier. Shortly after the last emerald night, the ship must have been attacked...
Veils of "evil light" covered it and "invisible fangs" devoured it, leaving only a gnawed skeleton behind. That's what they said!
We will be safe from those evil powers in Kingspeak, won't we?
Of course!

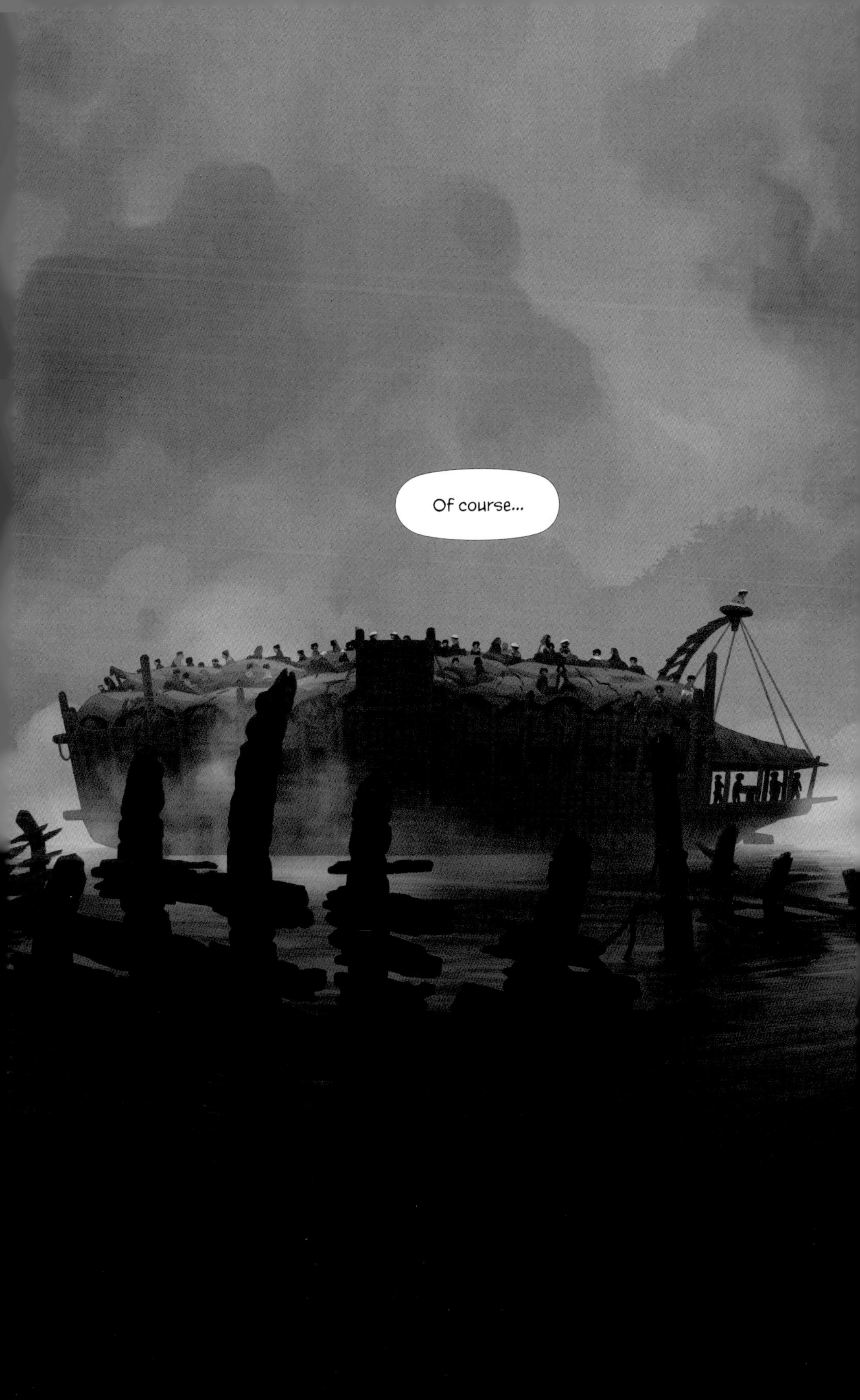
Of course...

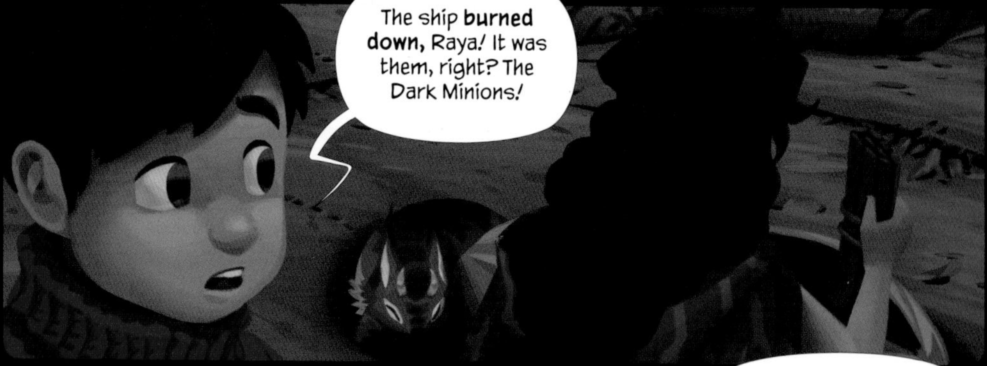
The ship **burned down,** Raya! It was them, right? The Dark Minions!

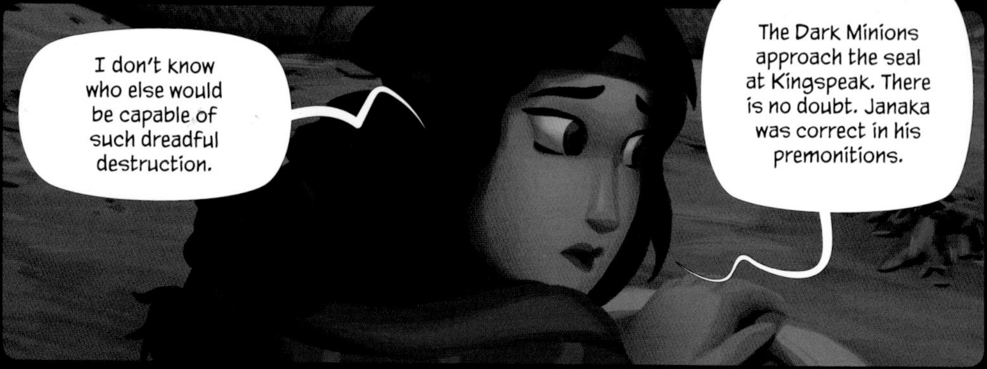
I don't know who else would be capable of such dreadful destruction.
The Dark Minions approach the seal at Kingspeak. There is no doubt. Janaka was correct in his premonitions.

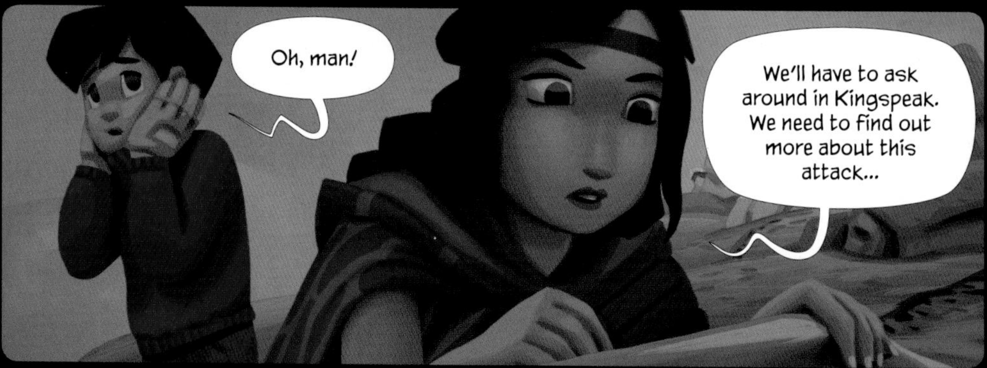
Oh, man!
We'll have to ask around in Kingspeak. We need to find out more about this attack...

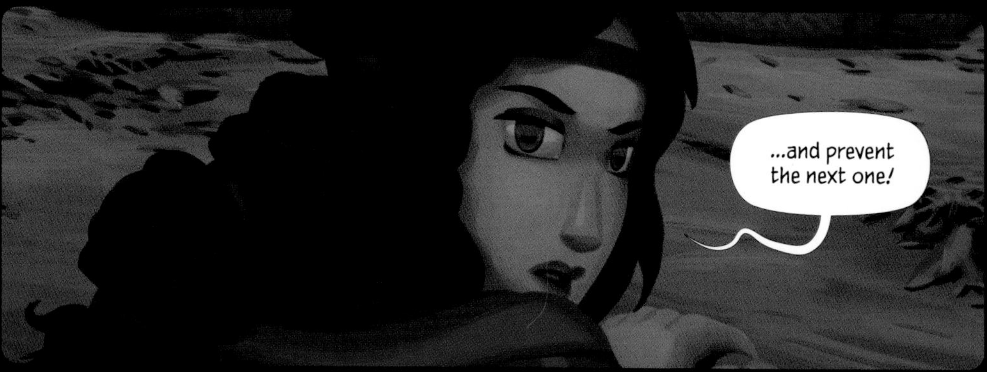
...and prevent the next one!

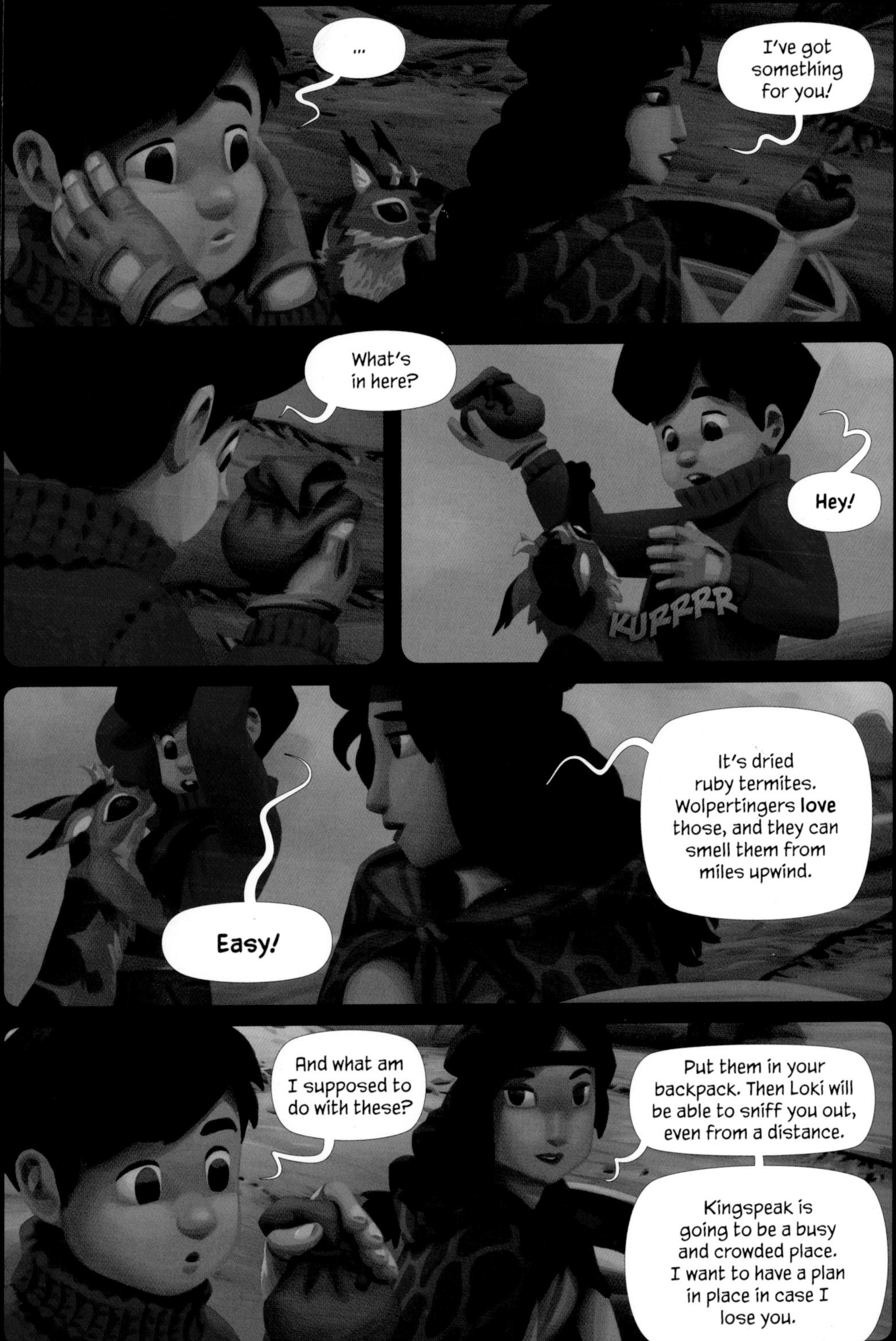
...
I've got something for you!
What's in here?
Hey!
KURRRR
It's dried ruby termites. Wolpertingers **love** those, and they can smell them from miles upwind.
Easy!
And what am I supposed to do with these?
Put them in your backpack. Then Loki will be able to sniff you out, even from a distance.
Kingspeak is going to be a busy and crowded place. I want to have a plan in place in case I lose you.

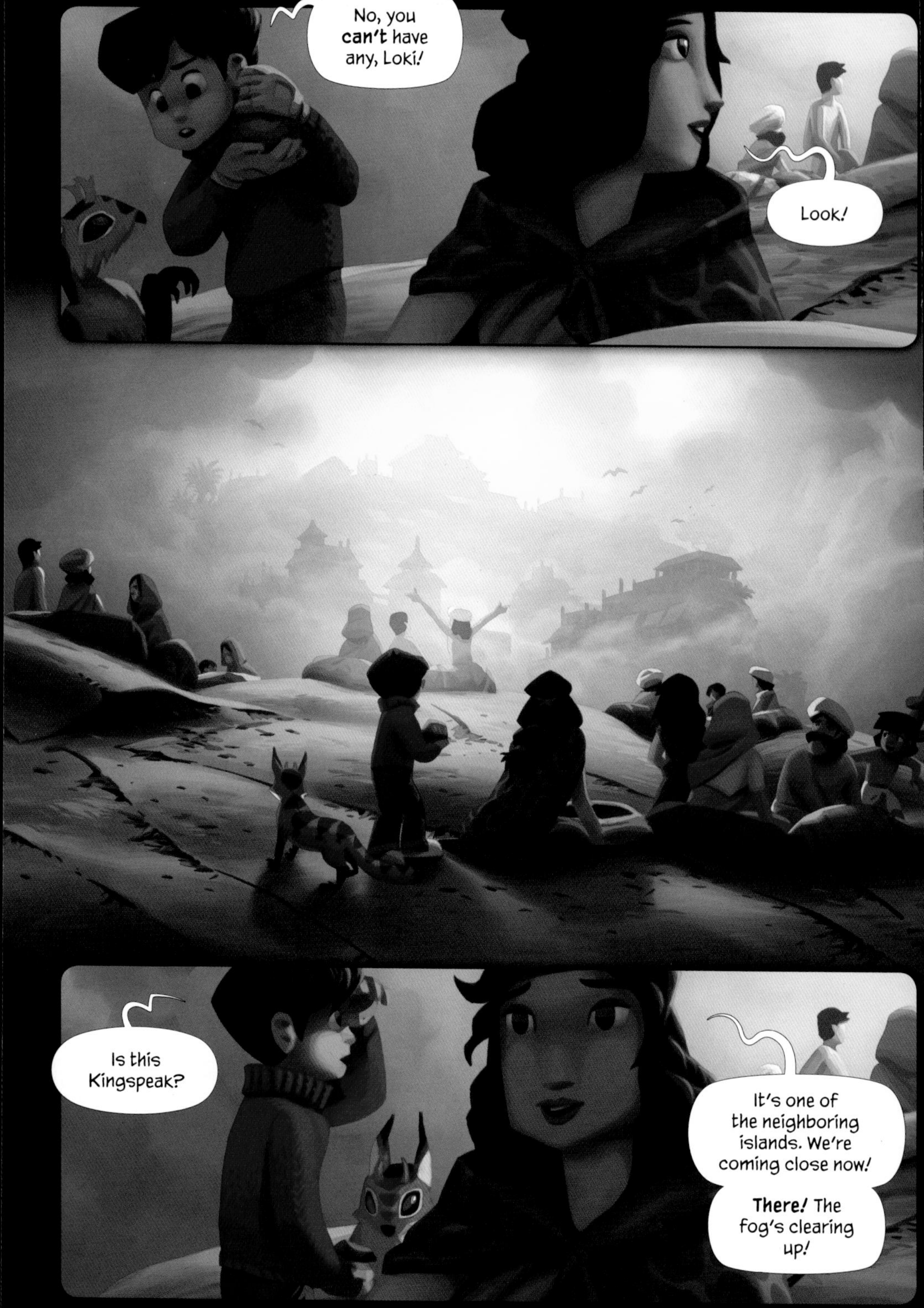
No, you **can't** have any, Loki!
Look!
Is this Kingspeak?
It's one of the neighboring islands. We're coming close now!
There! The fog's clearing up!

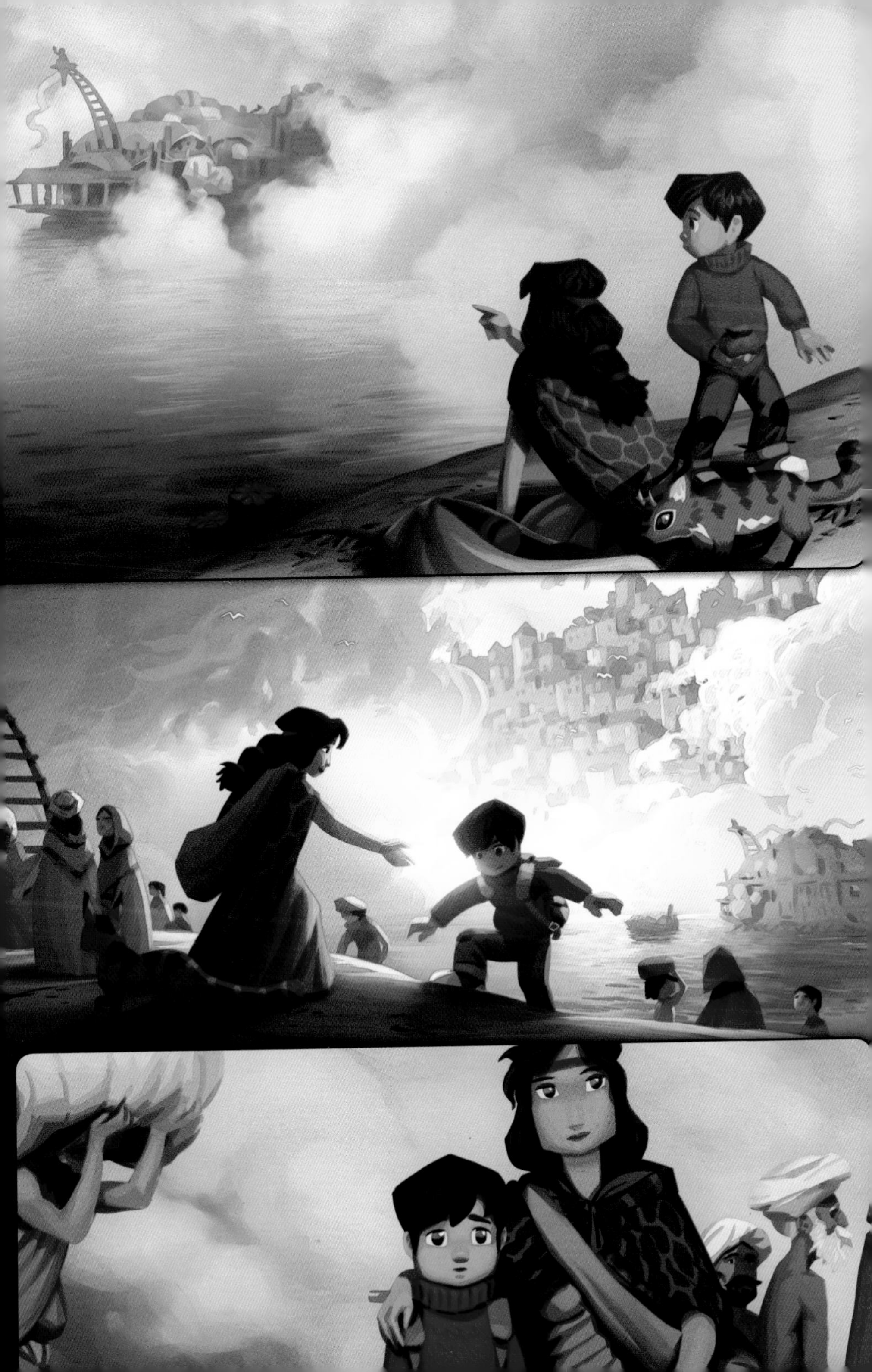

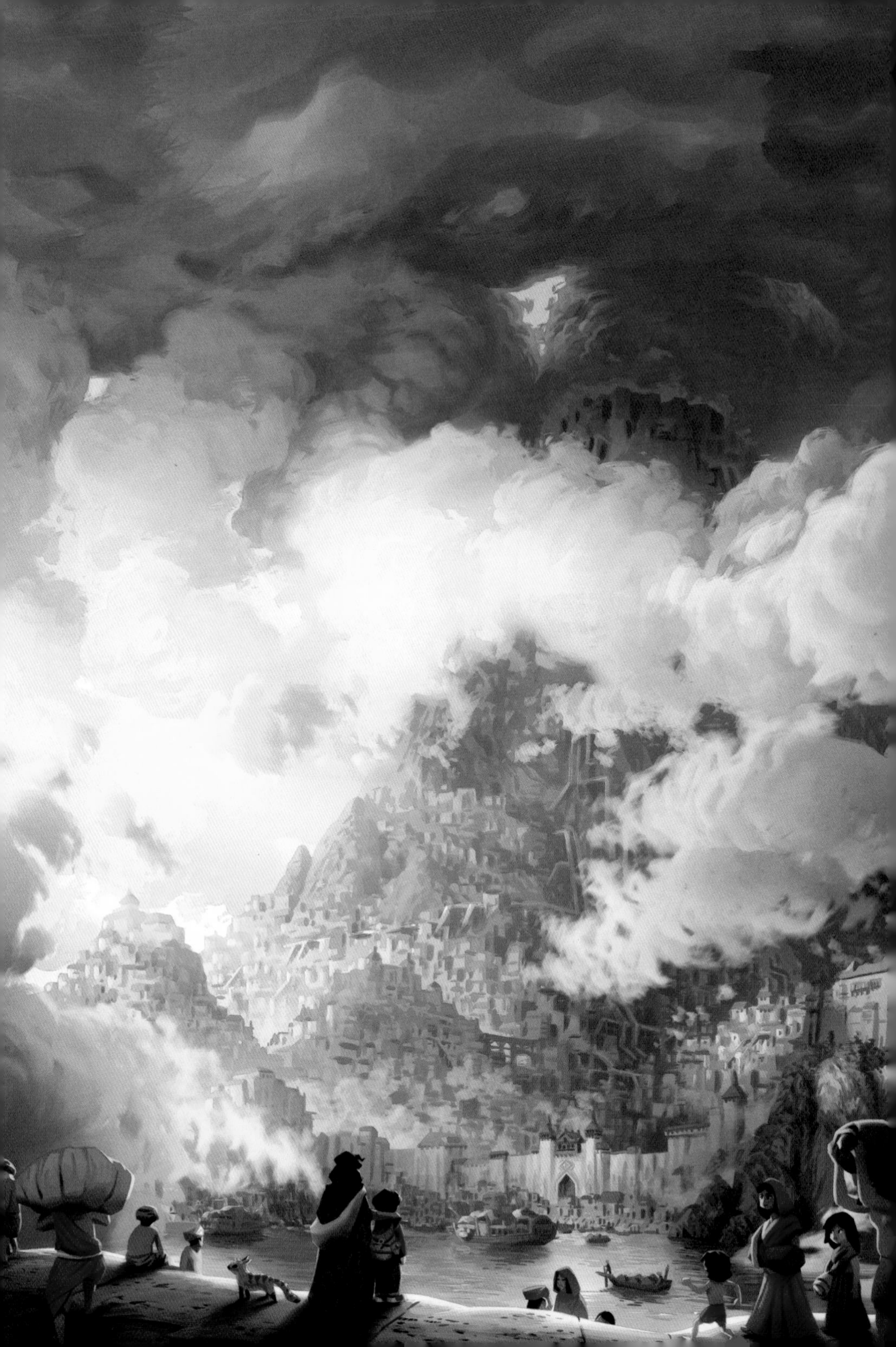

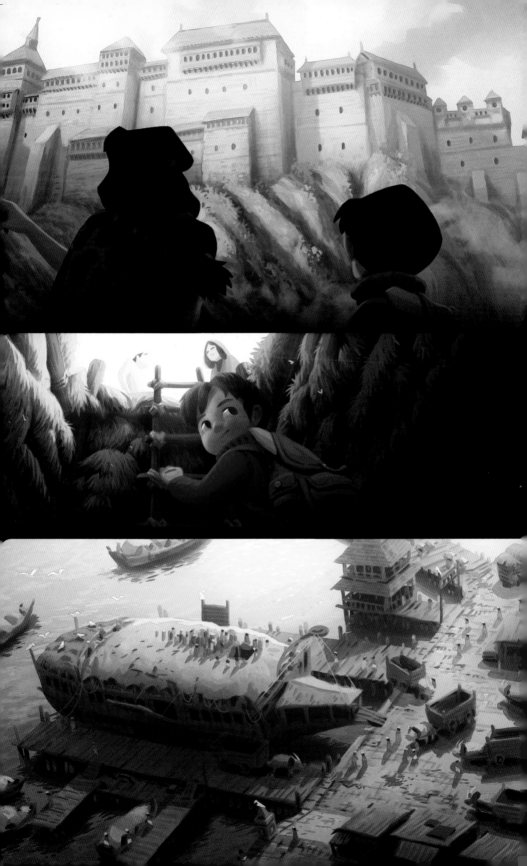

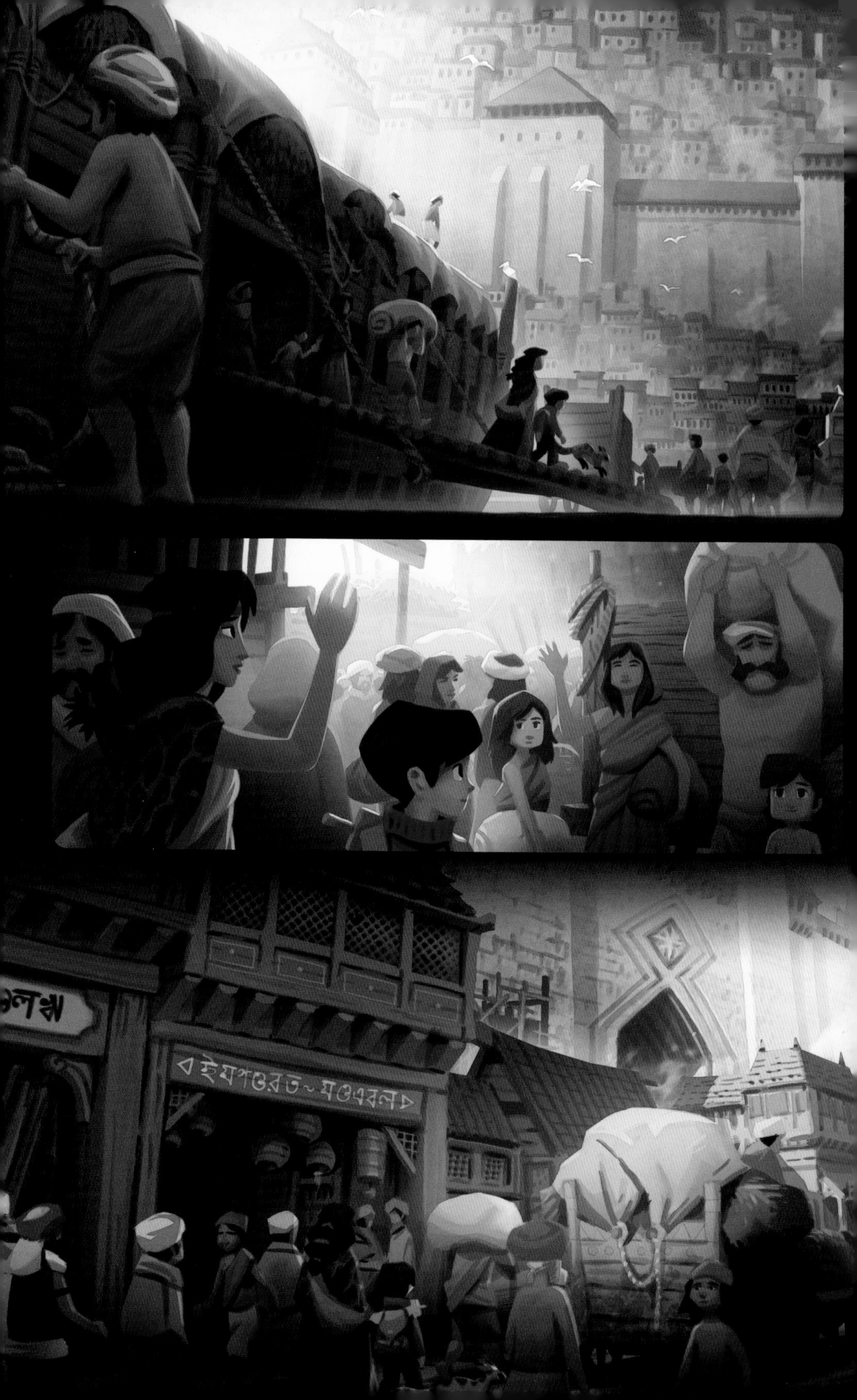

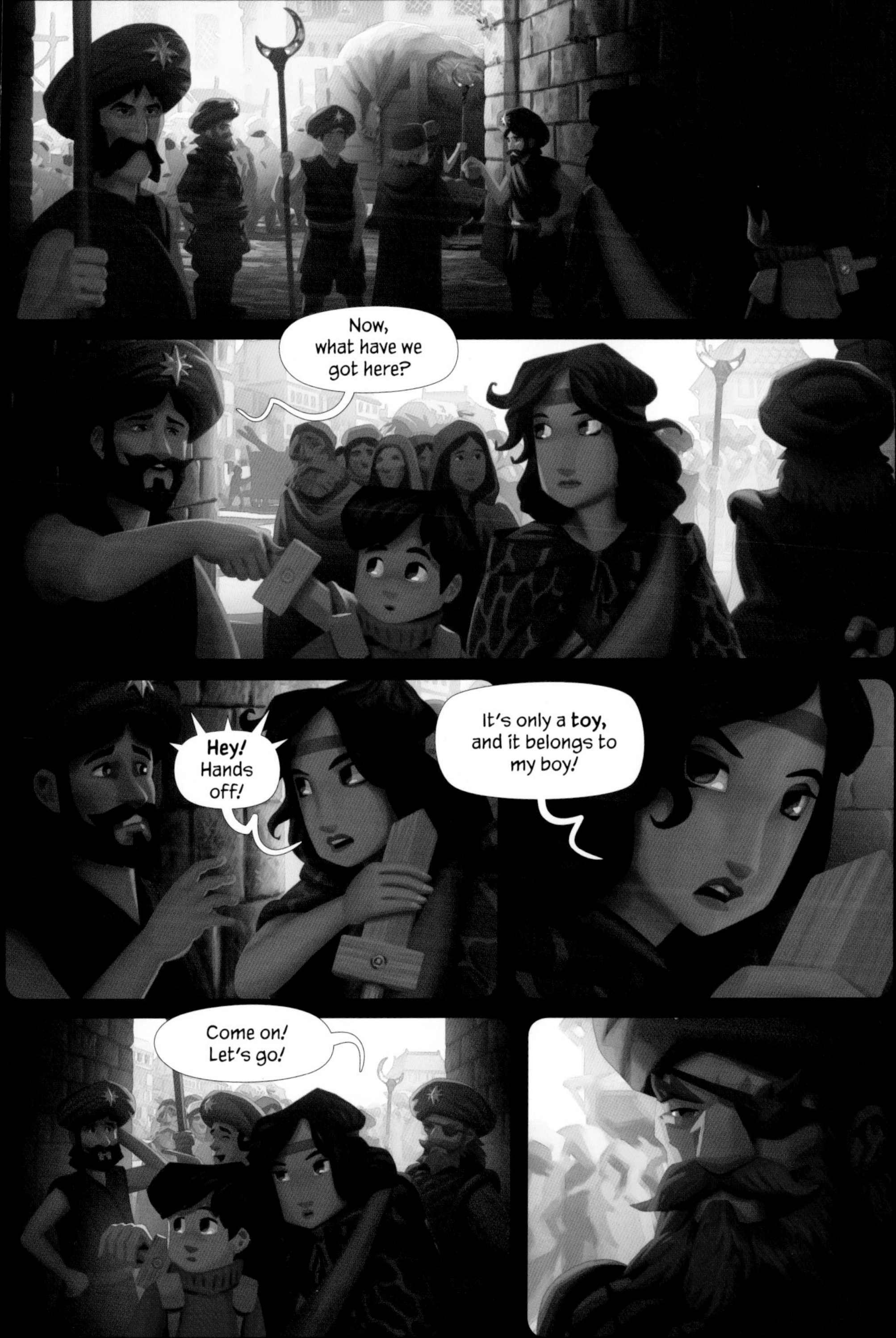

Now, what have we got here?
Hey! Hands off!
It's only a toy, and it belongs to my boy!
Come on! Let's go!

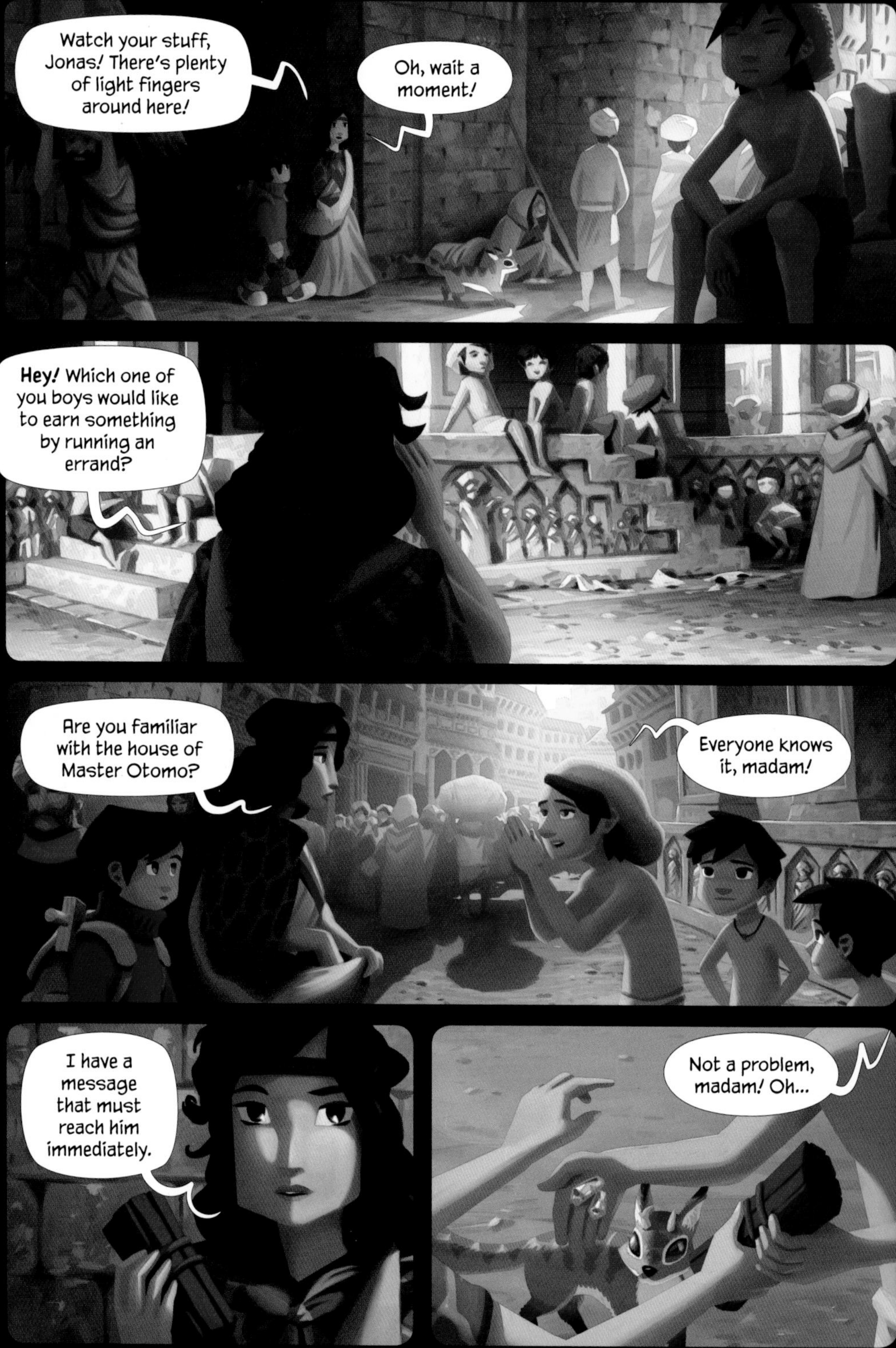

Watch your stuff, Jonas! There's plenty of light fingers around here!
Oh, wait a moment!
Hey! Which one of you boys would like to earn something by running an errand?
Are you familiar with the house of Master Otomo?
Everyone knows it, madam!
I have a message that must reach him immediately.
Not a problem, madam! Oh...

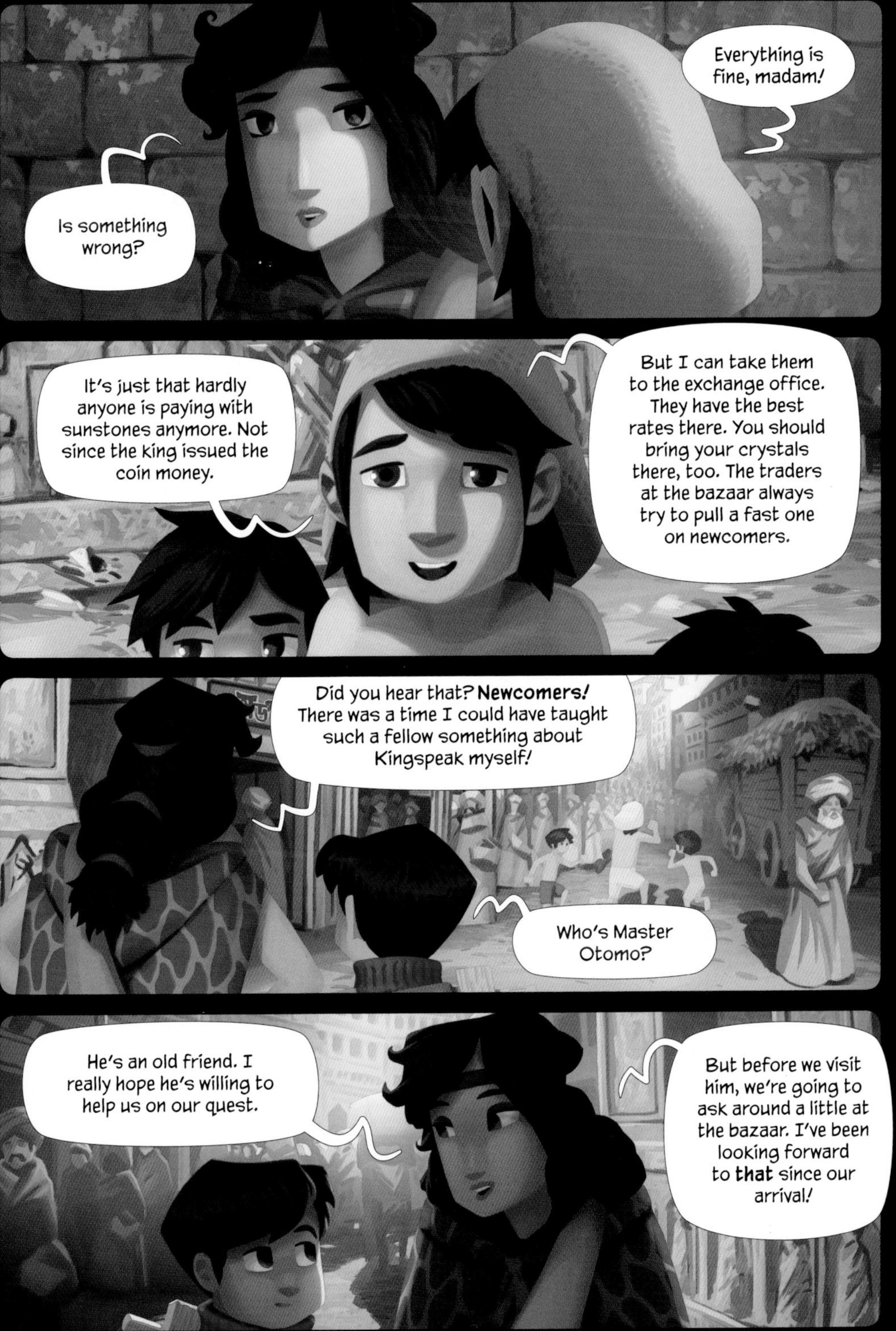
Everything is fine, madam!
Is something wrong?
It's just that hardly anyone is paying with sunstones anymore. Not since the king issued the coin money.
But I can take them to the exchange office. They have the best rates there. You should bring your crystals there, too. The traders at the bazaar always try to pull a fast one on newcomers.
Did you hear that? **Newcomers!** There was a time I could have taught such a fellow something about Kingspeak myself!
Who's Master Otomo?
He's an old friend. I really hope he's willing to help us on our quest.
But before we visit him, we're going to ask around a little at the bazaar. I've been looking forward to **that** since our arrival!

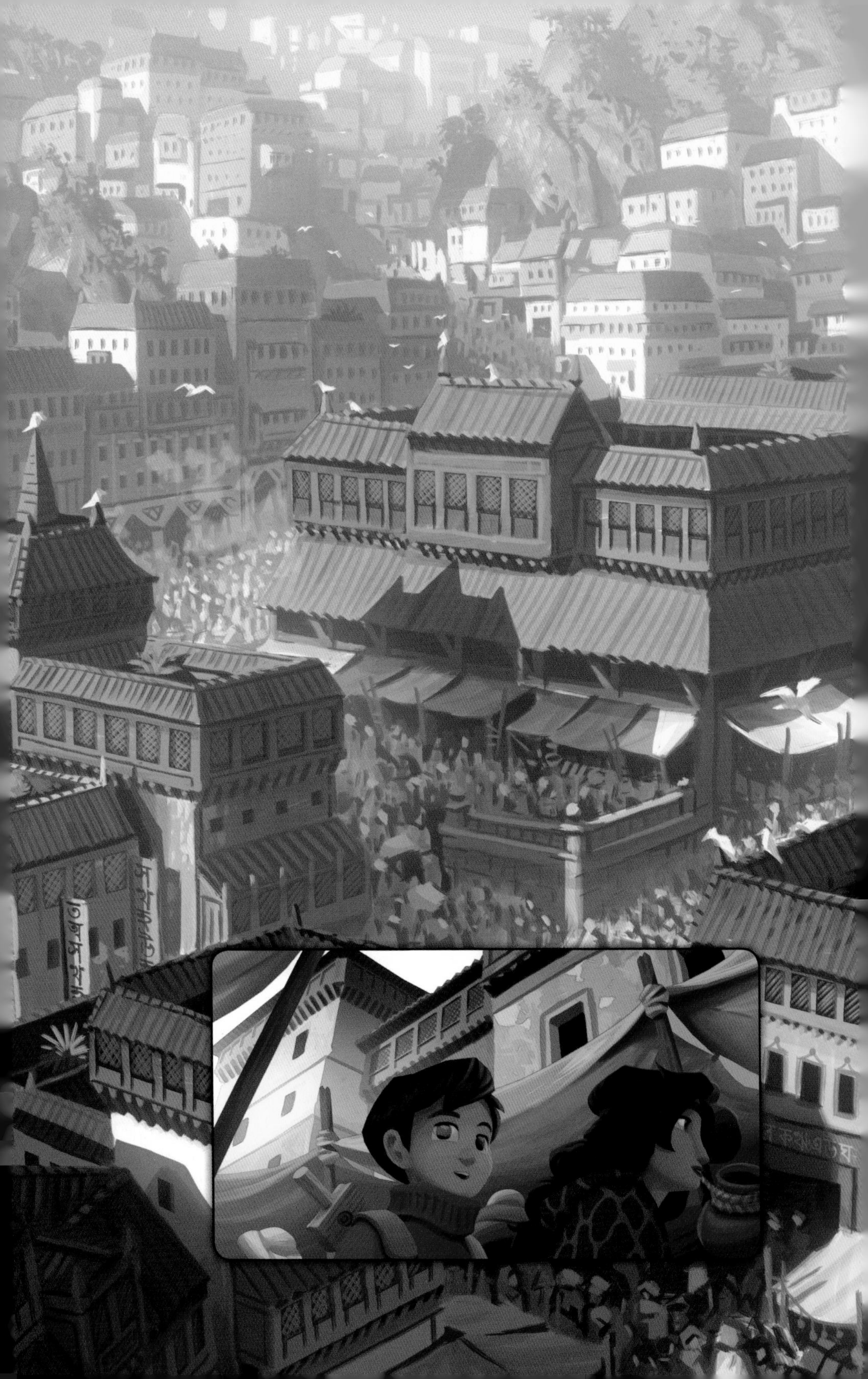

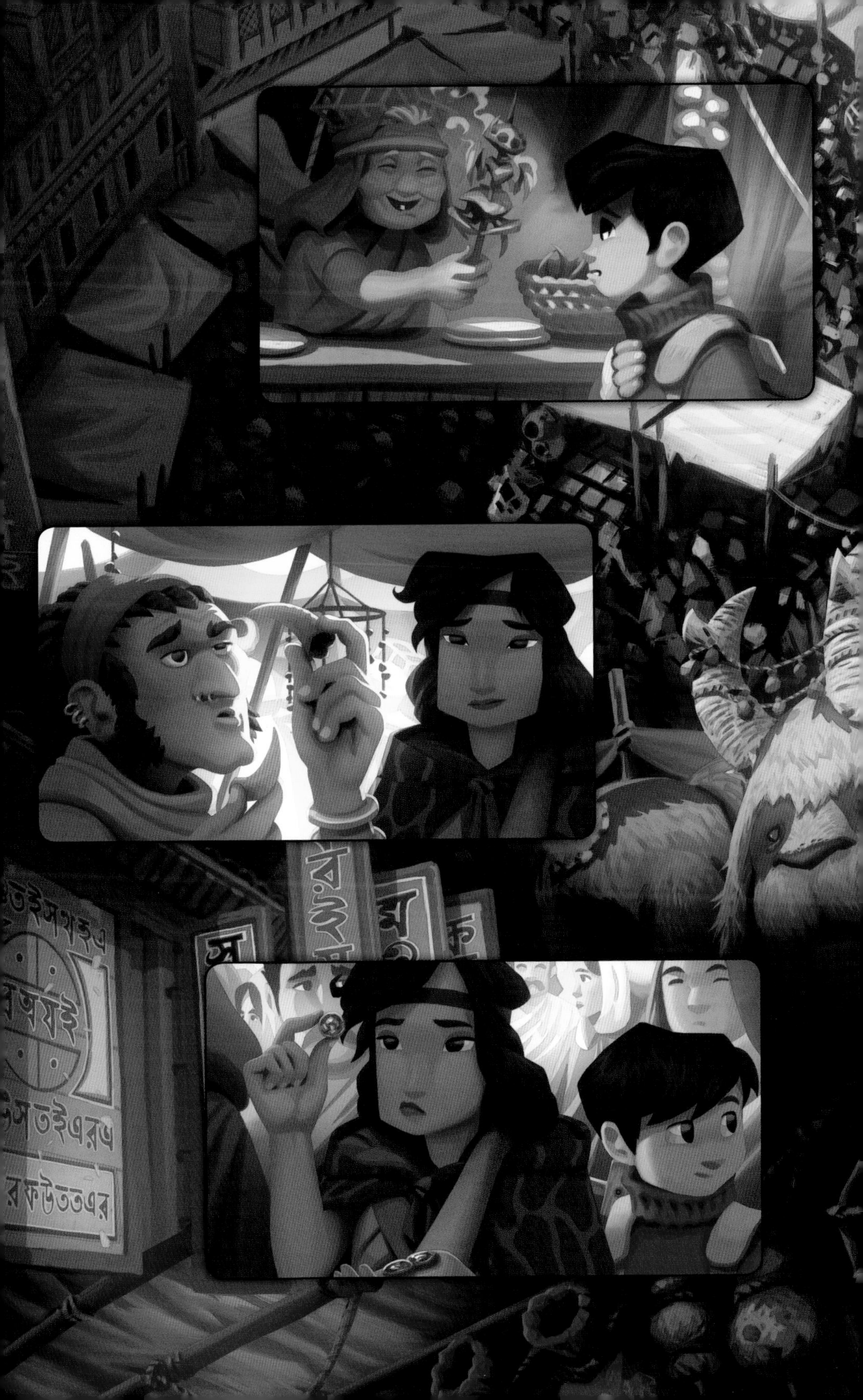

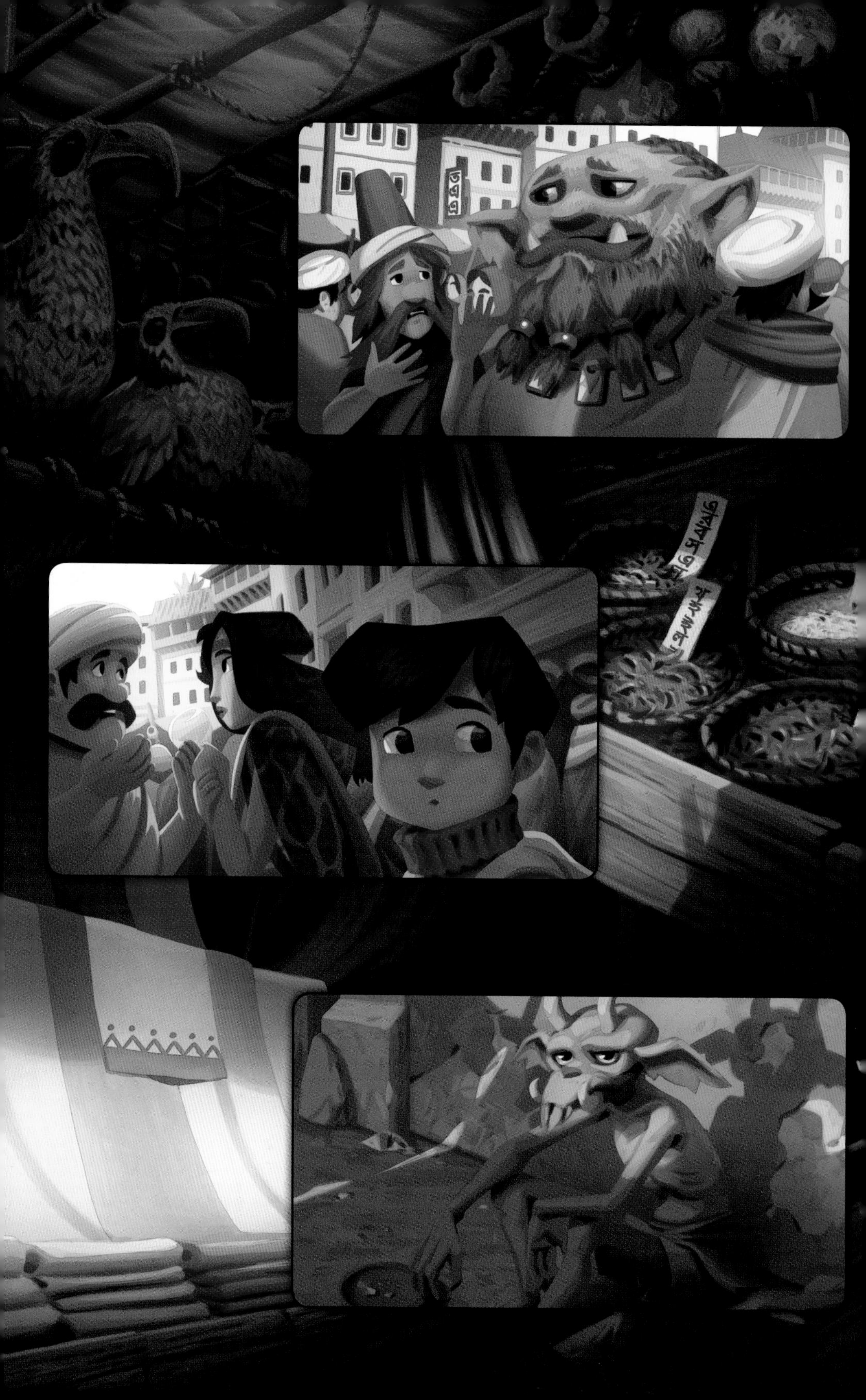

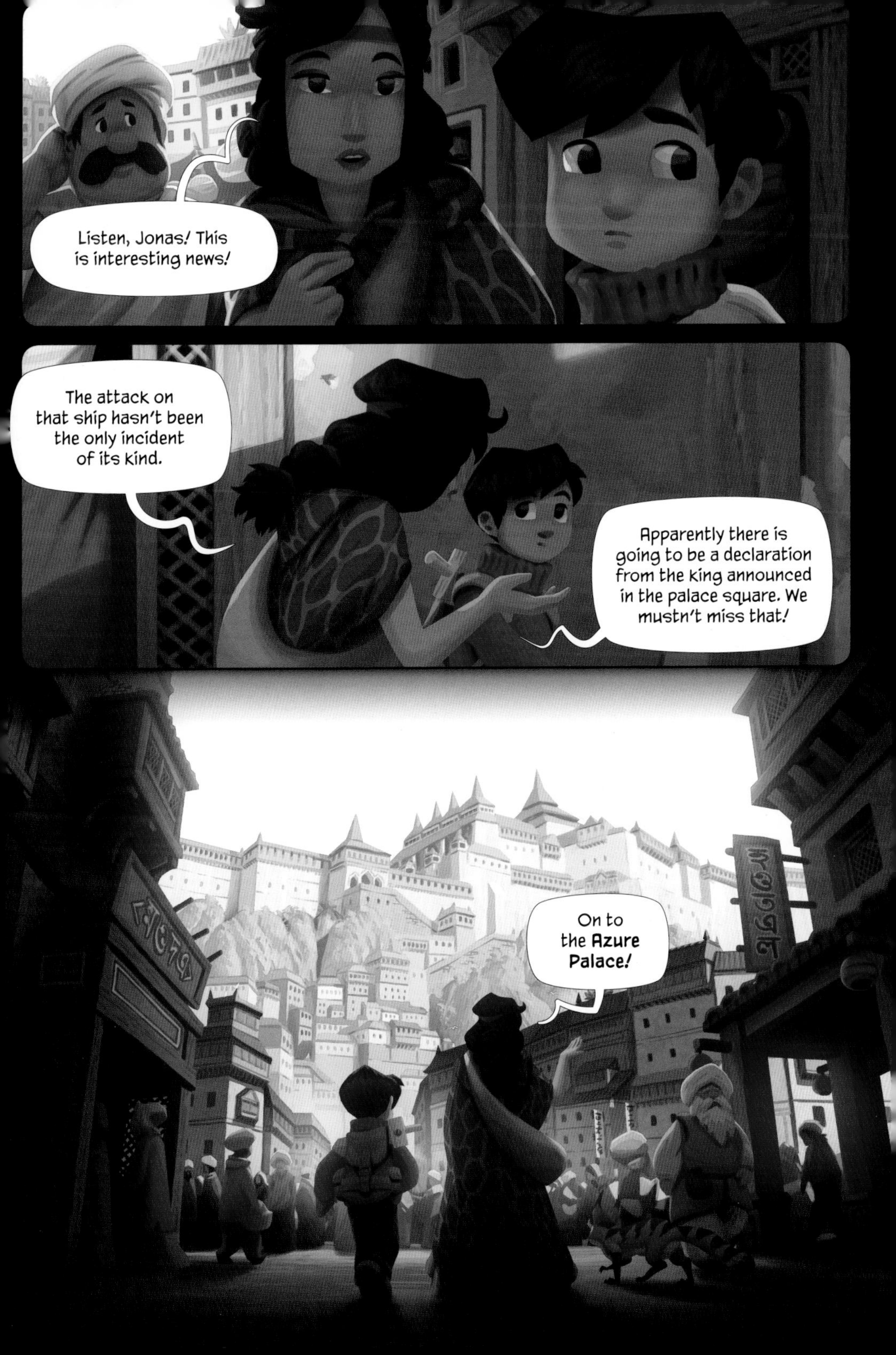
Listen, Jonas! This is interesting news!
The attack on that ship hasn't been the only incident of its kind.
Apparently there is going to be a declaration from the king announced in the palace square. We mustn't miss that!
On to the **Azure Palace!**

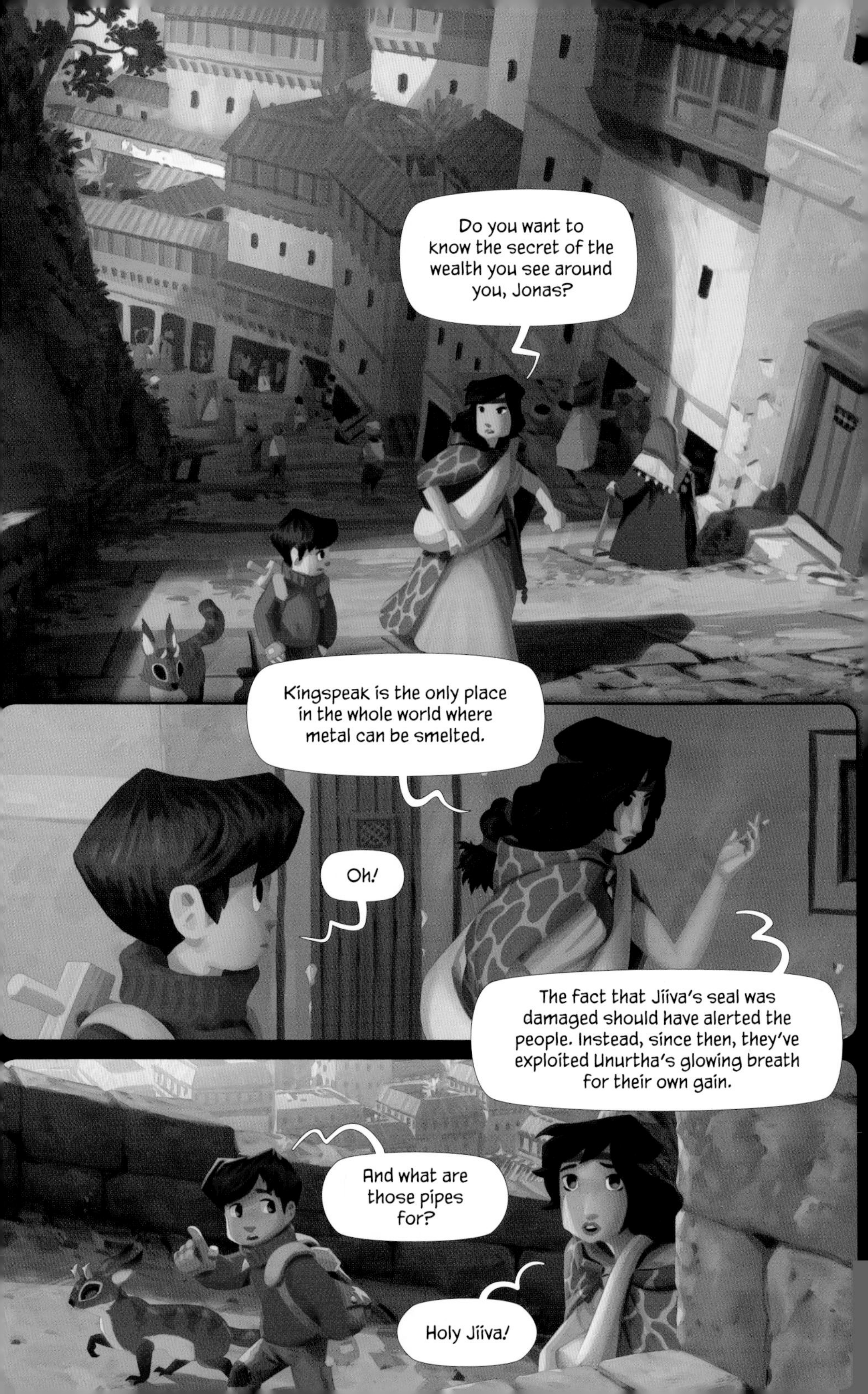
Do you want to know the secret of the wealth you see around you, Jonas?
Kingspeak is the only place in the whole world where metal can be smelted.
Oh!
The fact that Jiíva's seal was damaged should have alerted the people. Instead, since then, they've exploited Unurtha's glowing breath for their own gain.
And what are those pipes for?
Holy Jiíva!

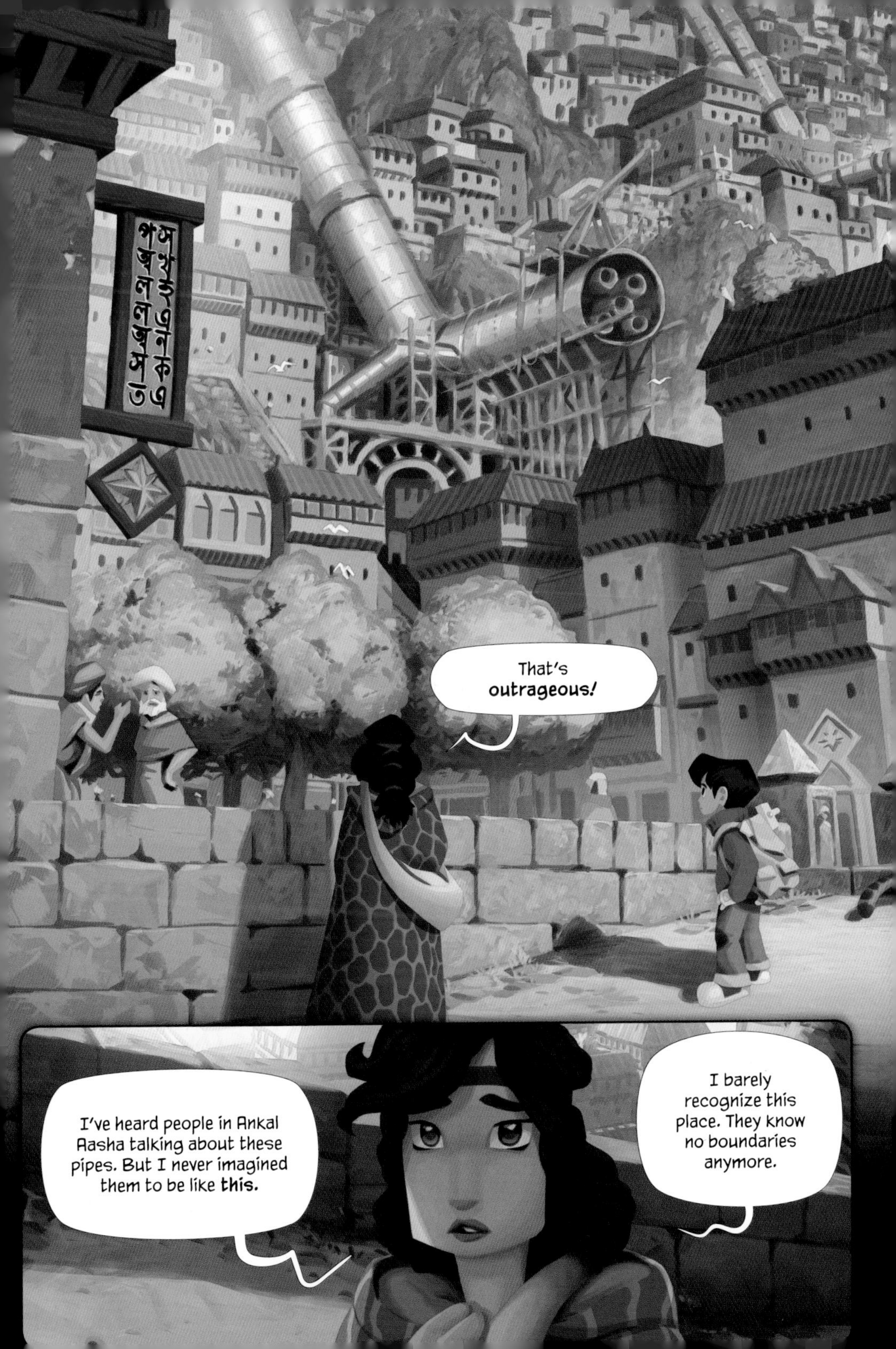
That's outrageous!
I've heard people in Ankal Aasha talking about these pipes. But I never imagined them to be like this.
I barely recognize this place. They know no boundaries anymore.

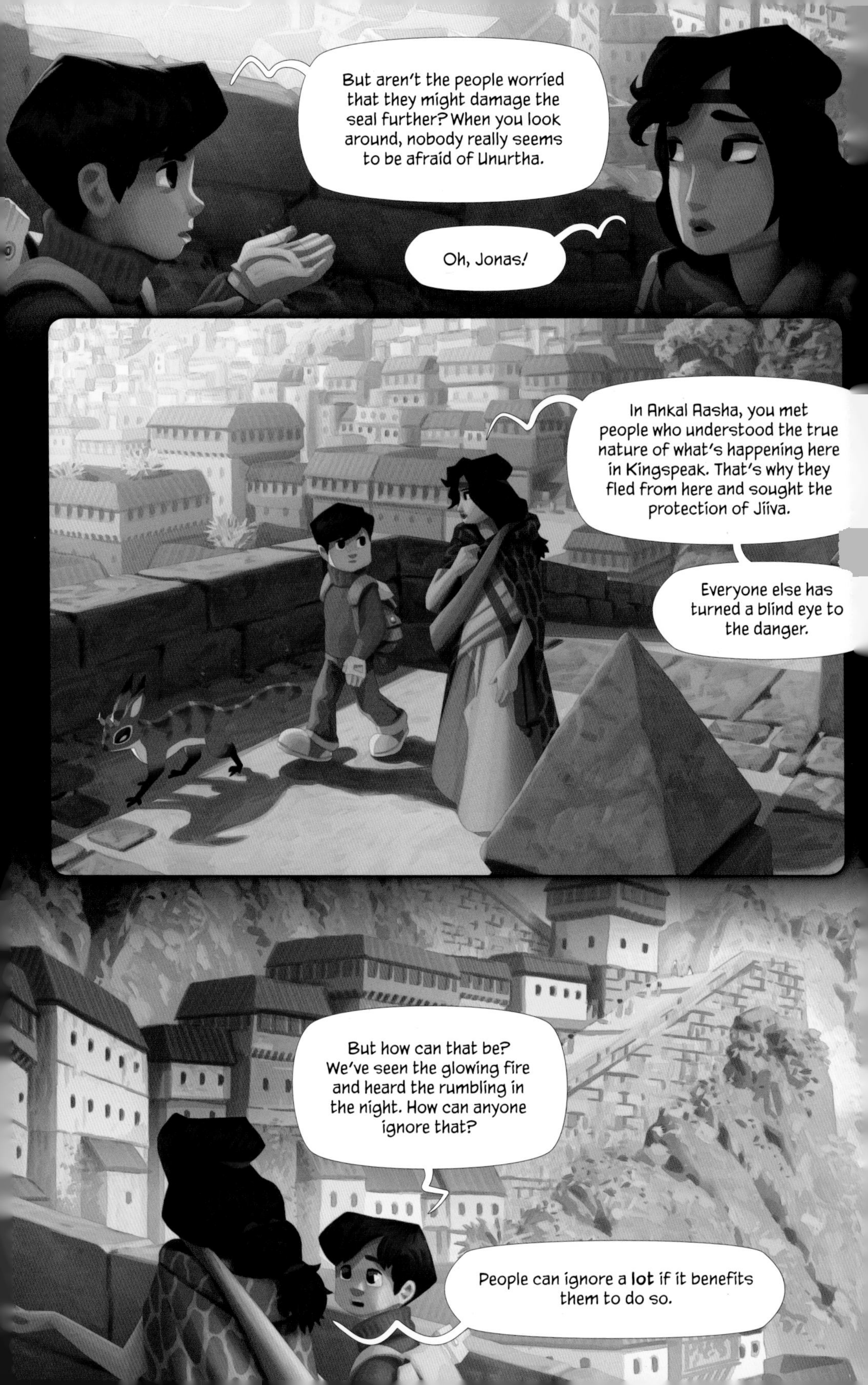
But aren't the people worried that they might damage the seal further? When you look around, nobody really seems to be afraid of Unurtha.
Oh, Jonas!
In Ankal Aasha, you met people who understood the true nature of what's happening here in Kingspeak. That's why they fled from here and sought the protection of Jiiva.
Everyone else has turned a blind eye to the danger.
But how can that be? We've seen the glowing fire and heard the rumbling in the night. How can anyone ignore that?
People can ignore a **lot** if it benefits them to do so.

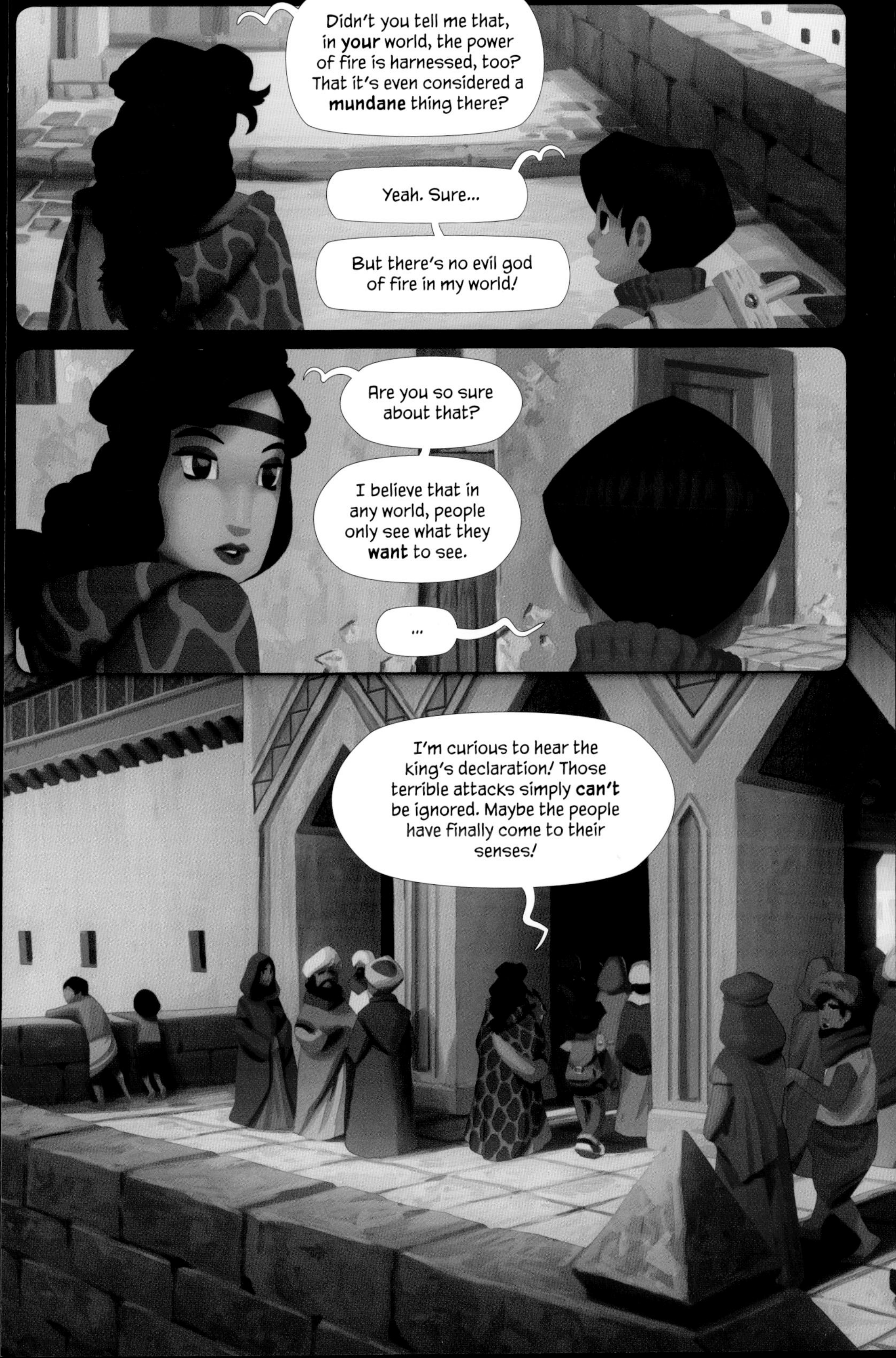
Didn't you tell me that, in **your** world, the power of fire is harnessed, too? That it's even considered a **mundane** thing there?
Yeah. Sure...
But there's no evil god of fire in my world!
Are you so sure about that?
I believe that in any world, people only see what they **want** to see.
...
I'm curious to hear the king's declaration! Those terrible attacks simply **can't** be ignored. Maybe the people have finally come to their senses!

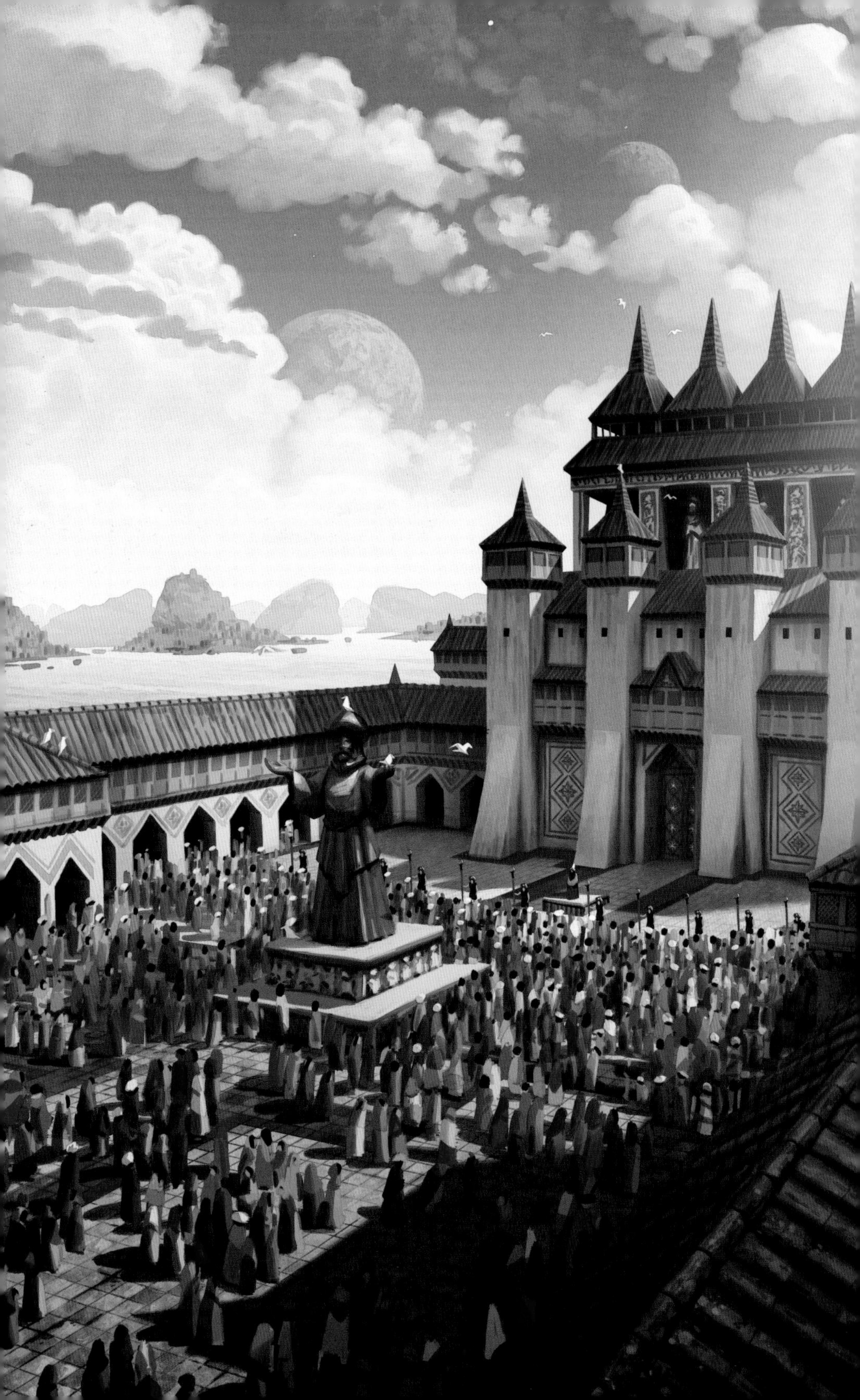

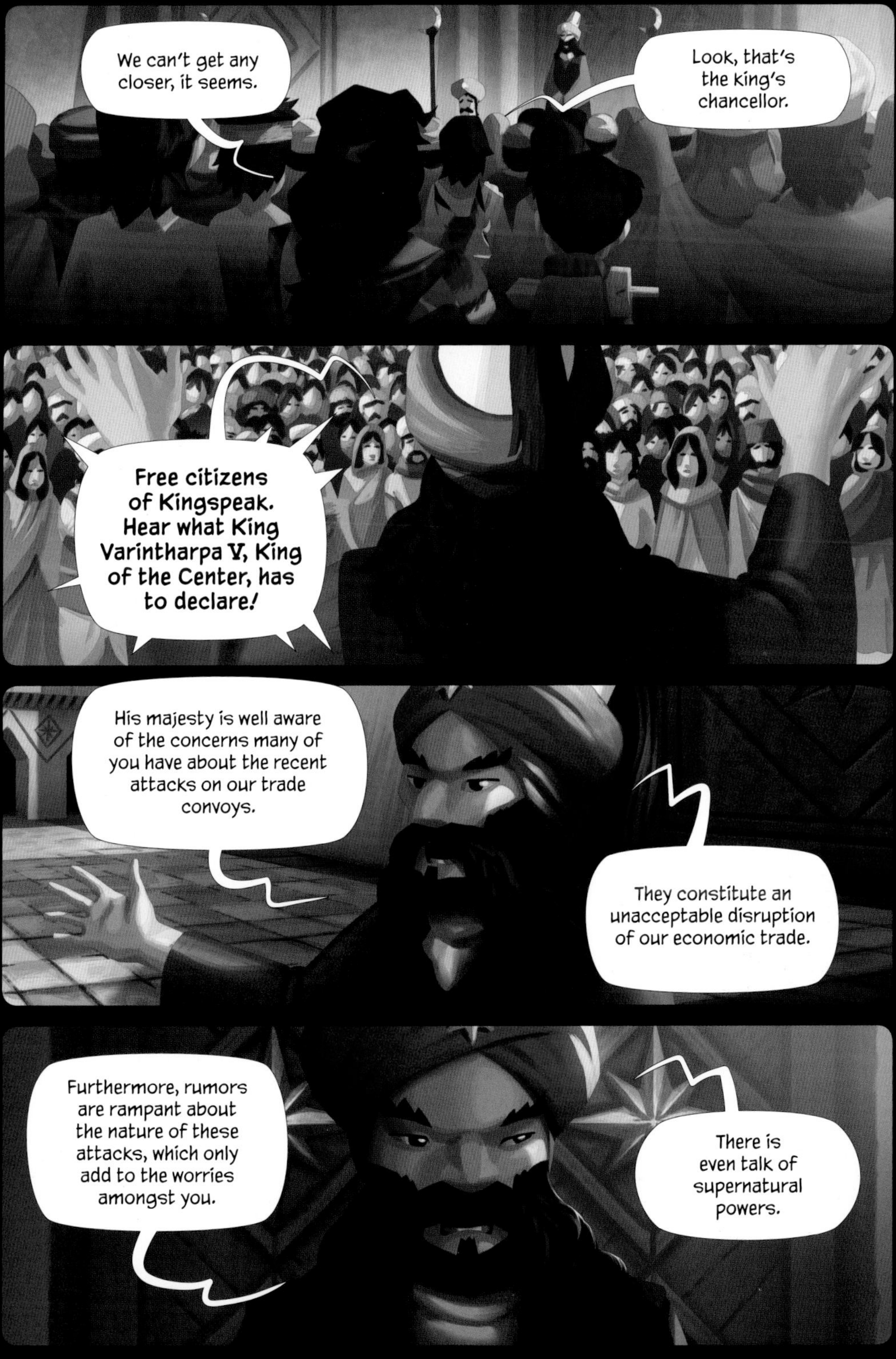
We can't get any closer, it seems.
Look, that's the king's chancellor.
Free citizens of Kingspeak. Hear what King Varintharpa V, King of the Center, has to declare!
His majesty is well aware of the concerns many of you have about the recent attacks on our trade convoys.
They constitute an unacceptable disruption of our economic trade.
Furthermore, rumors are rampant about the nature of these attacks, which only add to the worries amongst you.
There is even talk of supernatural powers.

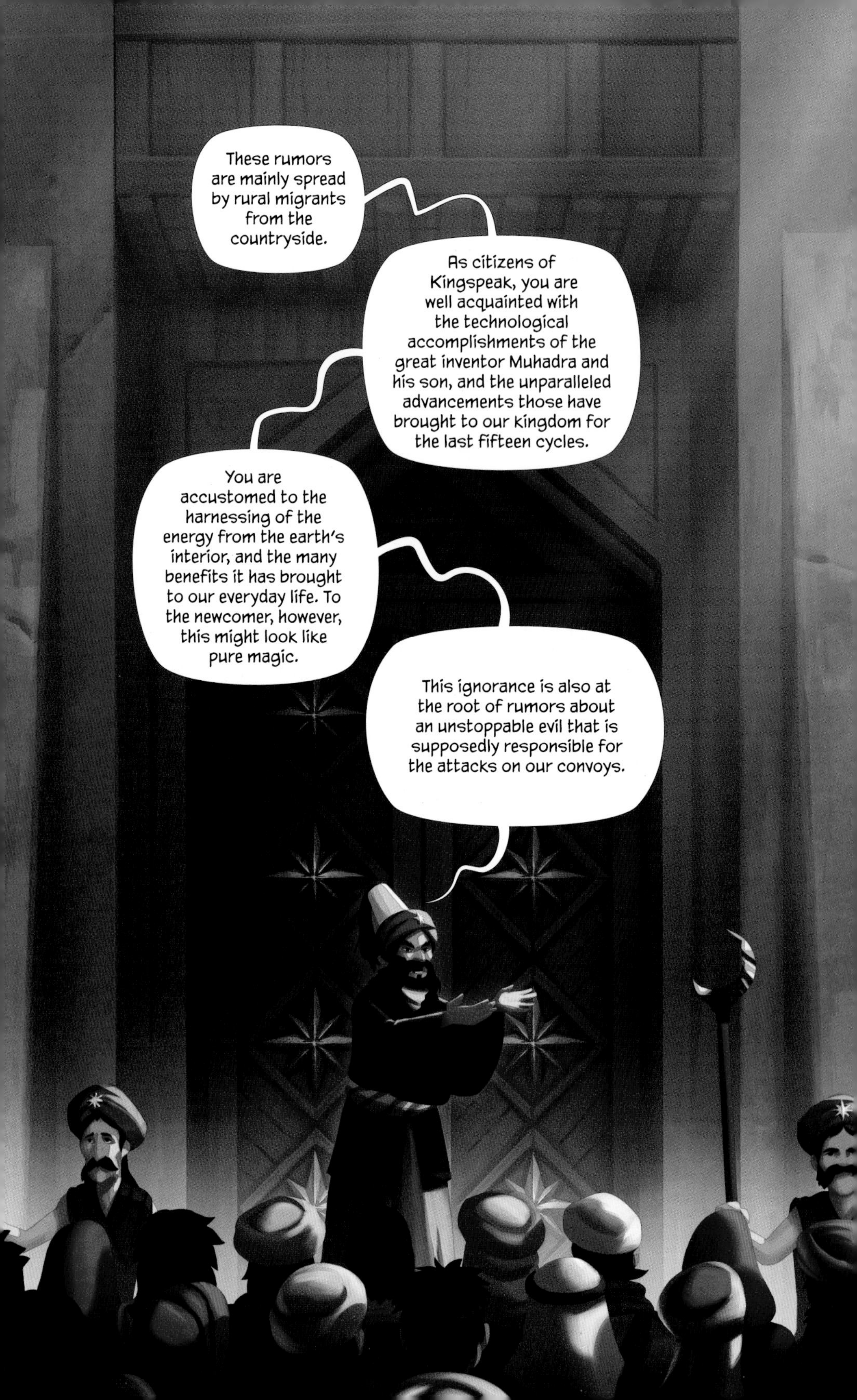
These rumors are mainly spread by rural migrants from the countryside.
As citizens of Kingspeak, you are well acquainted with the technological accomplishments of the great inventor Muhadra and his son, and the unparalleled advancements those have brought to our kingdom for the last fifteen cycles.
You are accustomed to the harnessing of the energy from the earth's interior, and the many benefits it has brought to our everyday life. To the newcomer, however, this might look like pure magic.
This ignorance is also at the root of rumors about an unstoppable evil that is supposedly responsible for the attacks on our convoys.

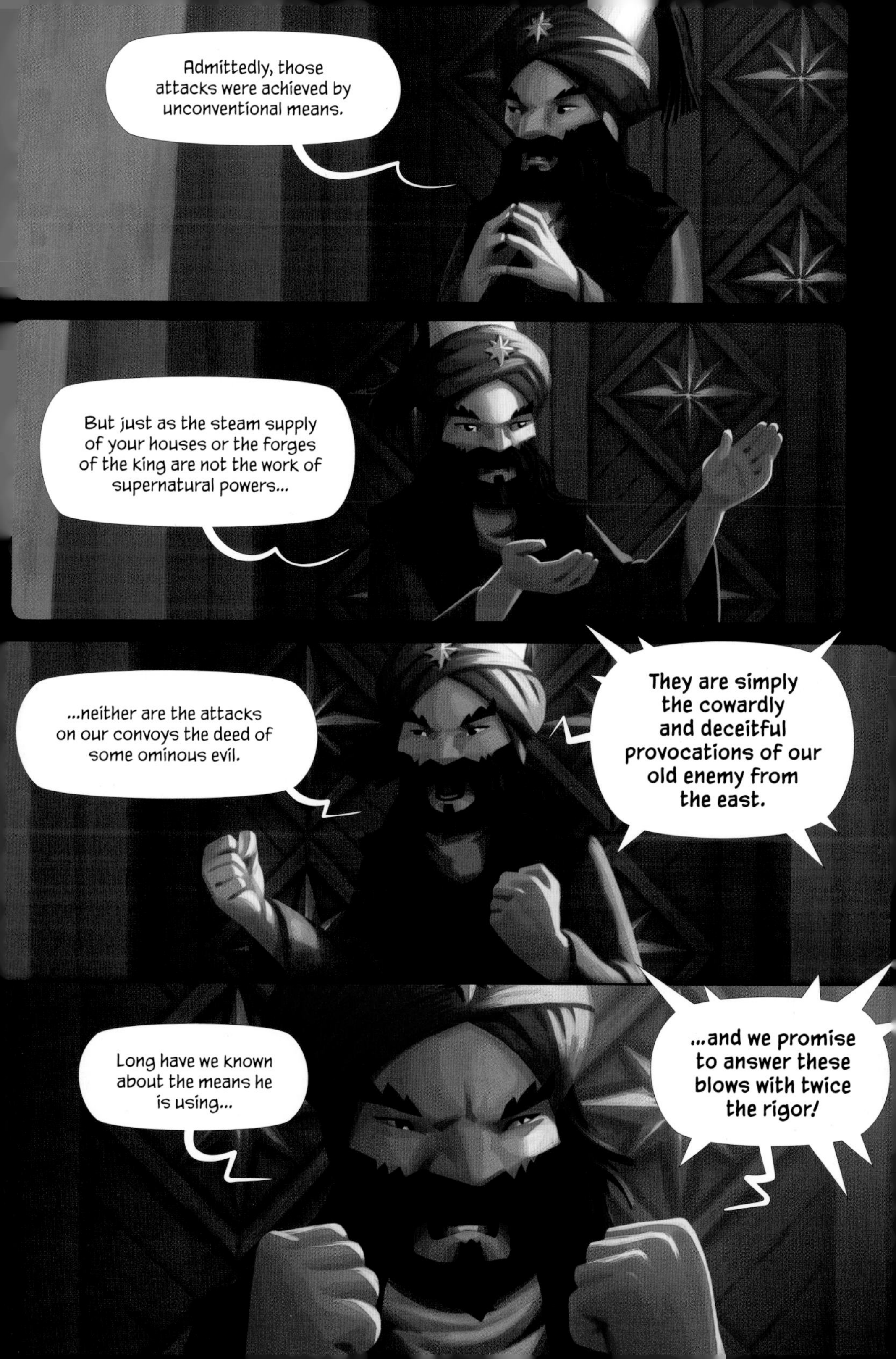
Admittedly, those attacks were achieved by unconventional means.
But just as the steam supply of your houses or the forges of the king are not the work of supernatural powers...
...neither are the attacks on our convoys the deed of some ominous evil.
They are simply the cowardly and deceitful provocations of our old enemy from the east.
Long have we known about the means he is using...
...and we promise to answer these blows with twice the rigor!

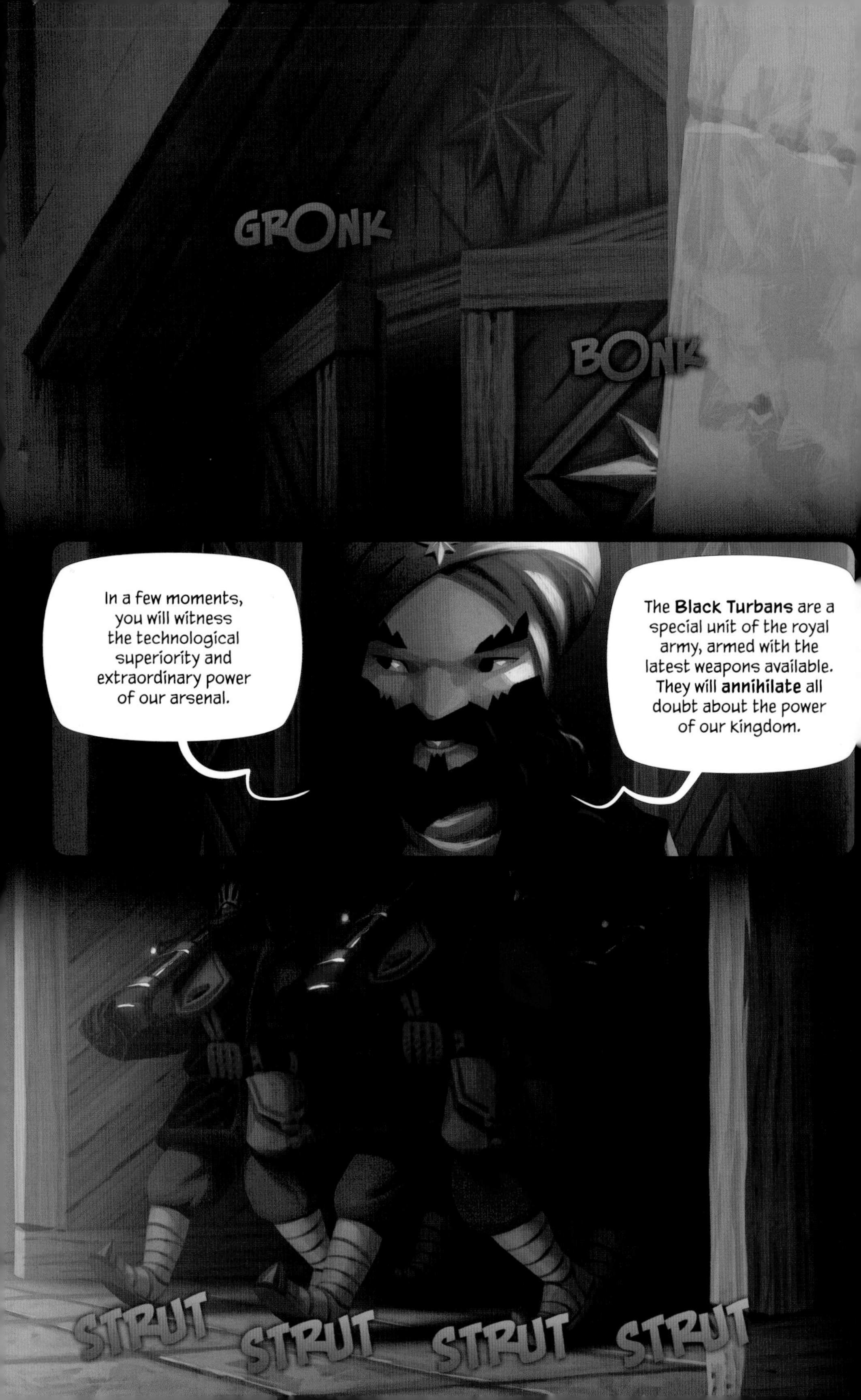
GRONK
BONK
In a few moments, you will witness the technological superiority and extraordinary power of our arsenal.
The **Black Turbans** are a special unit of the royal army, armed with the latest weapons available. They will **annihilate** all doubt about the power of our kingdom.
STRUT
STRUT
STRUT
STRUT

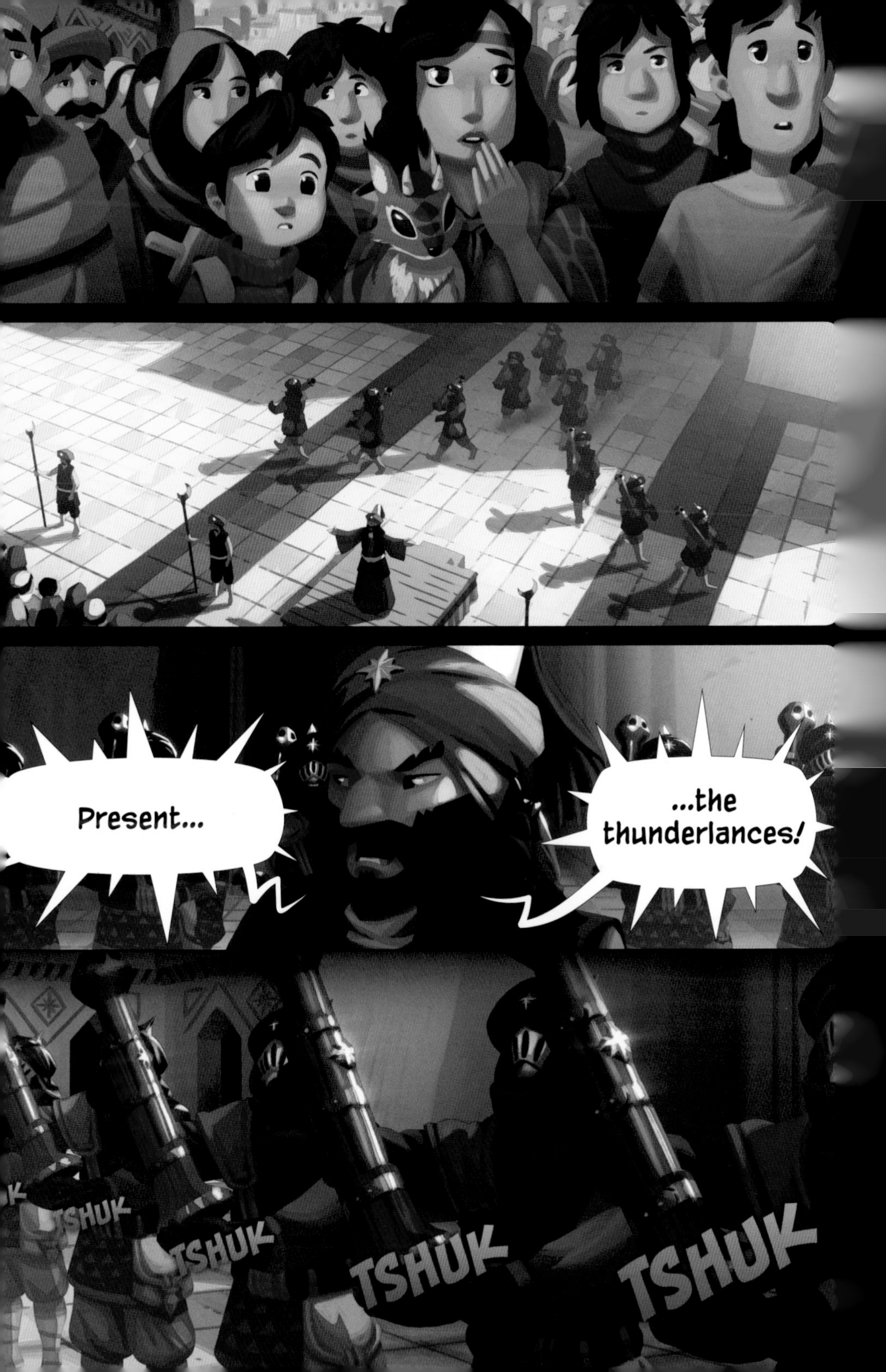
Present...
...the thunderlances!
TSHUK
TSHUK
TSHUK
TSHUK

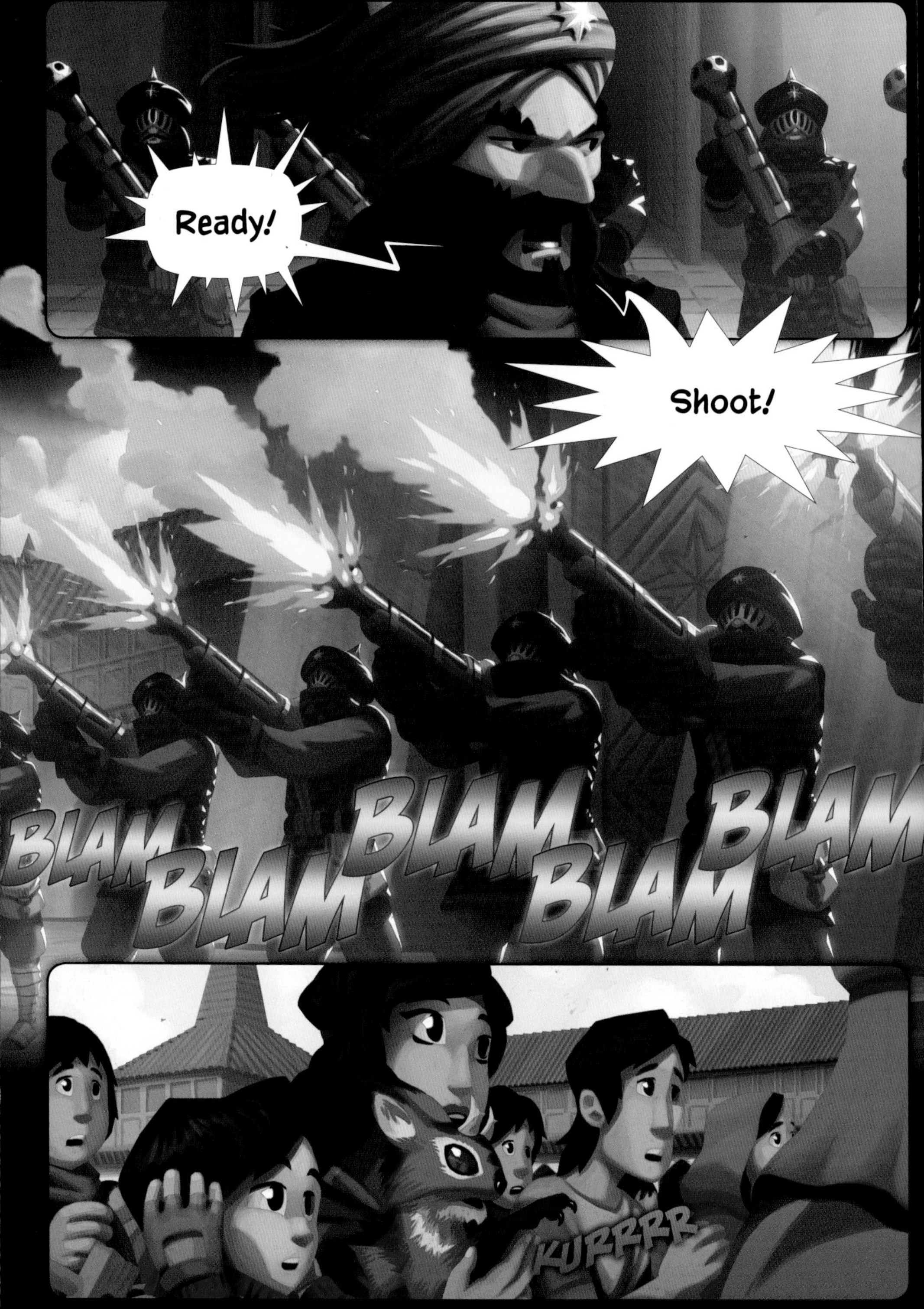
Ready!
Shoot!
BLAM
BLAM
BLAM
BLAM
BLAM
KURRRR

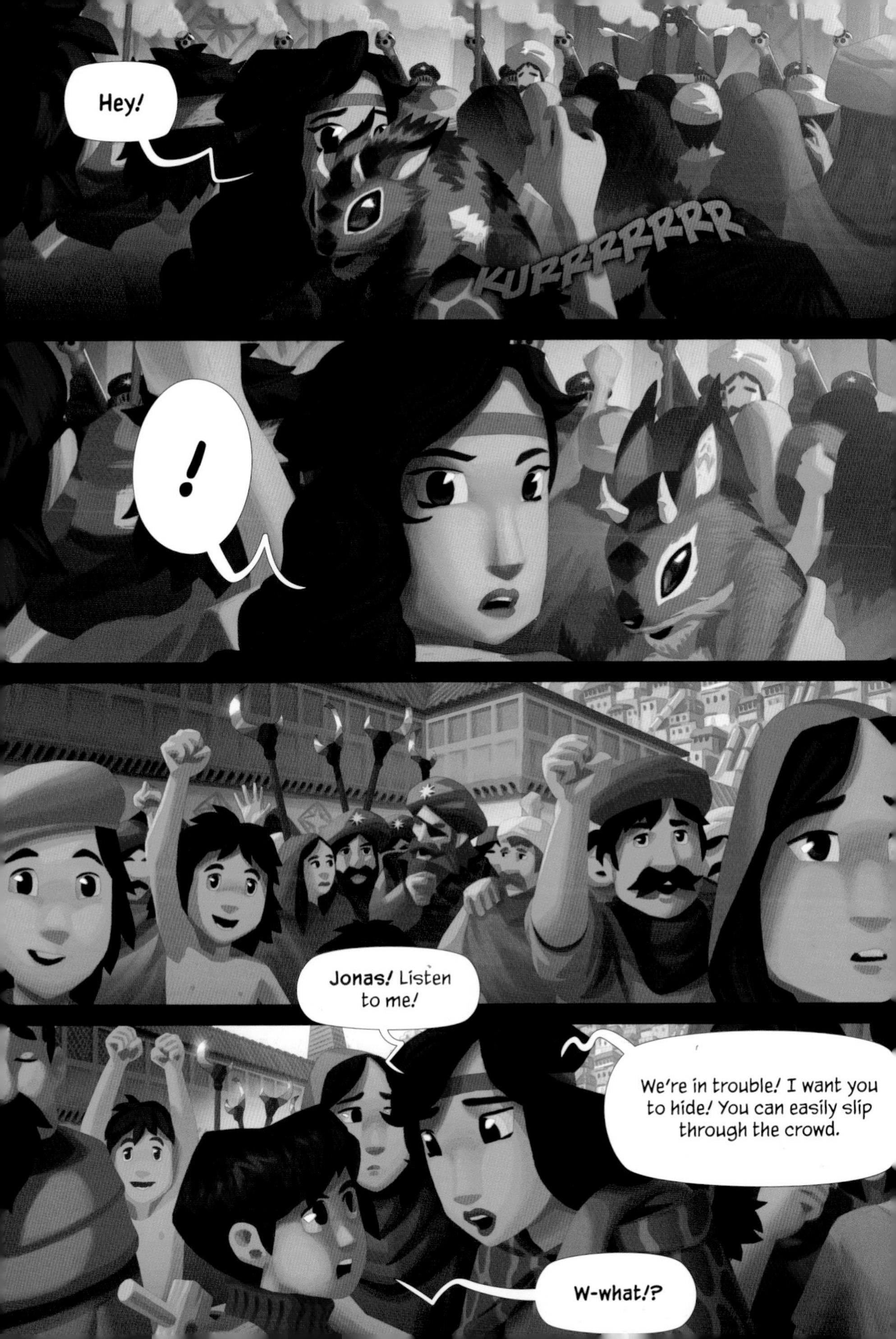
Hey!
KURRRRRRR
!
Jonas! Listen to me!
We're in trouble! I want you to hide! You can easily slip through the crowd.
W-what!?

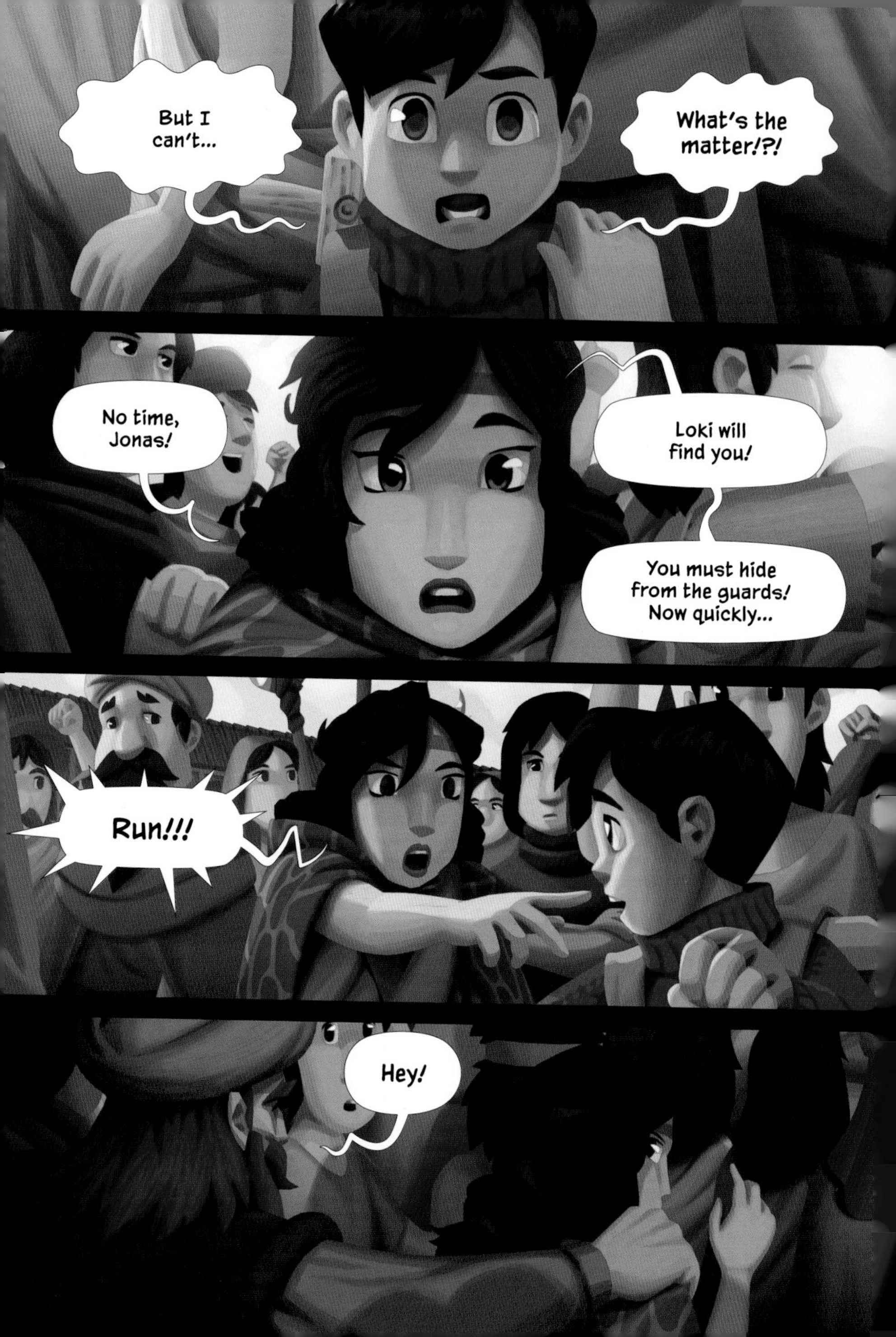
But I can't...
What's the matter!?!
No time, Jonas!
Loki will find you!
You must hide from the guards! Now quickly...
Run!!!
Hey!

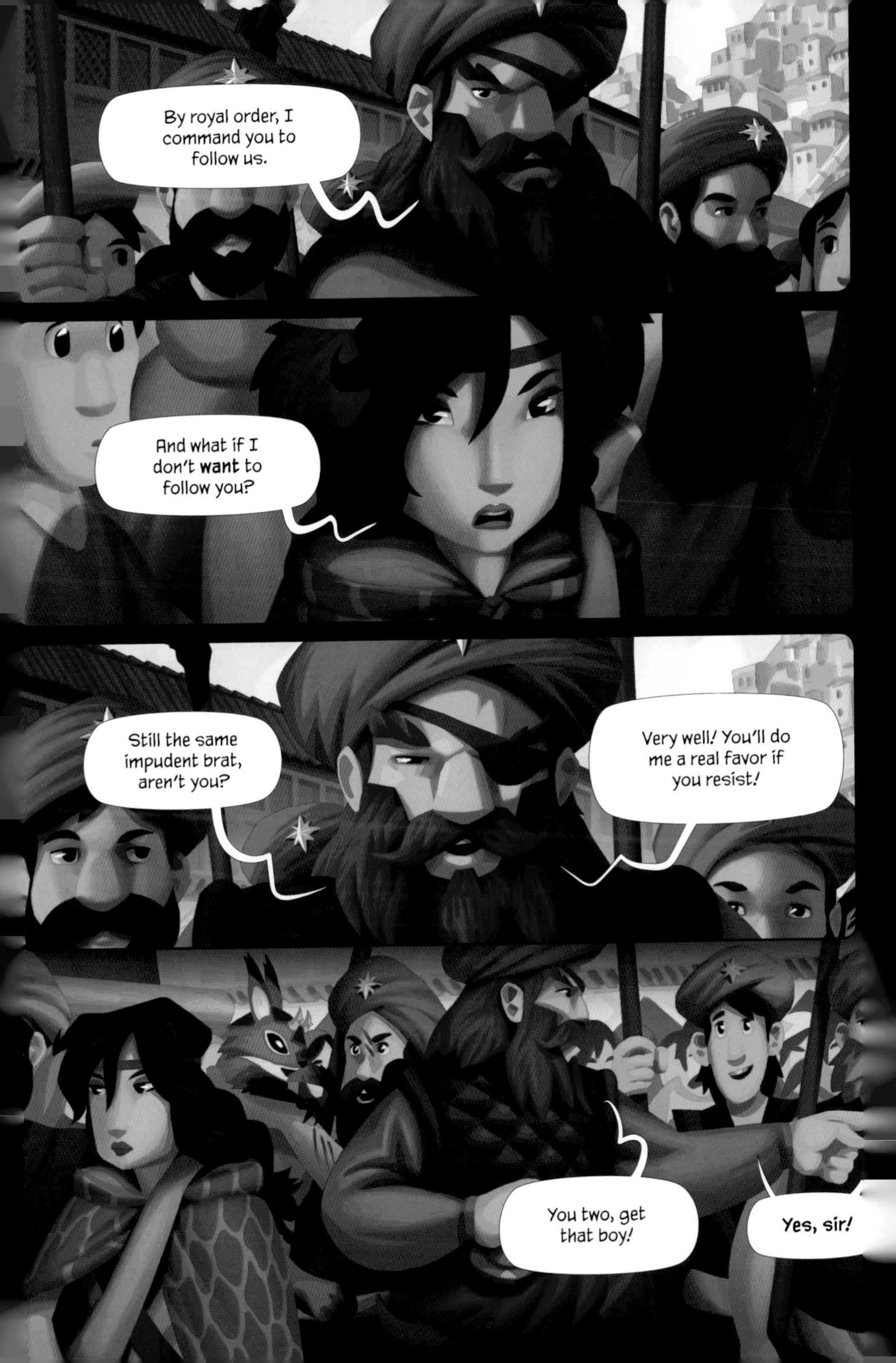

By royal order, I command you to follow us.
And what if I don't **want** to follow you?
Still the same impudent brat, aren't you?
Very well! You'll do me a real favor if you resist!
You two, get that boy!
Yes, sir!

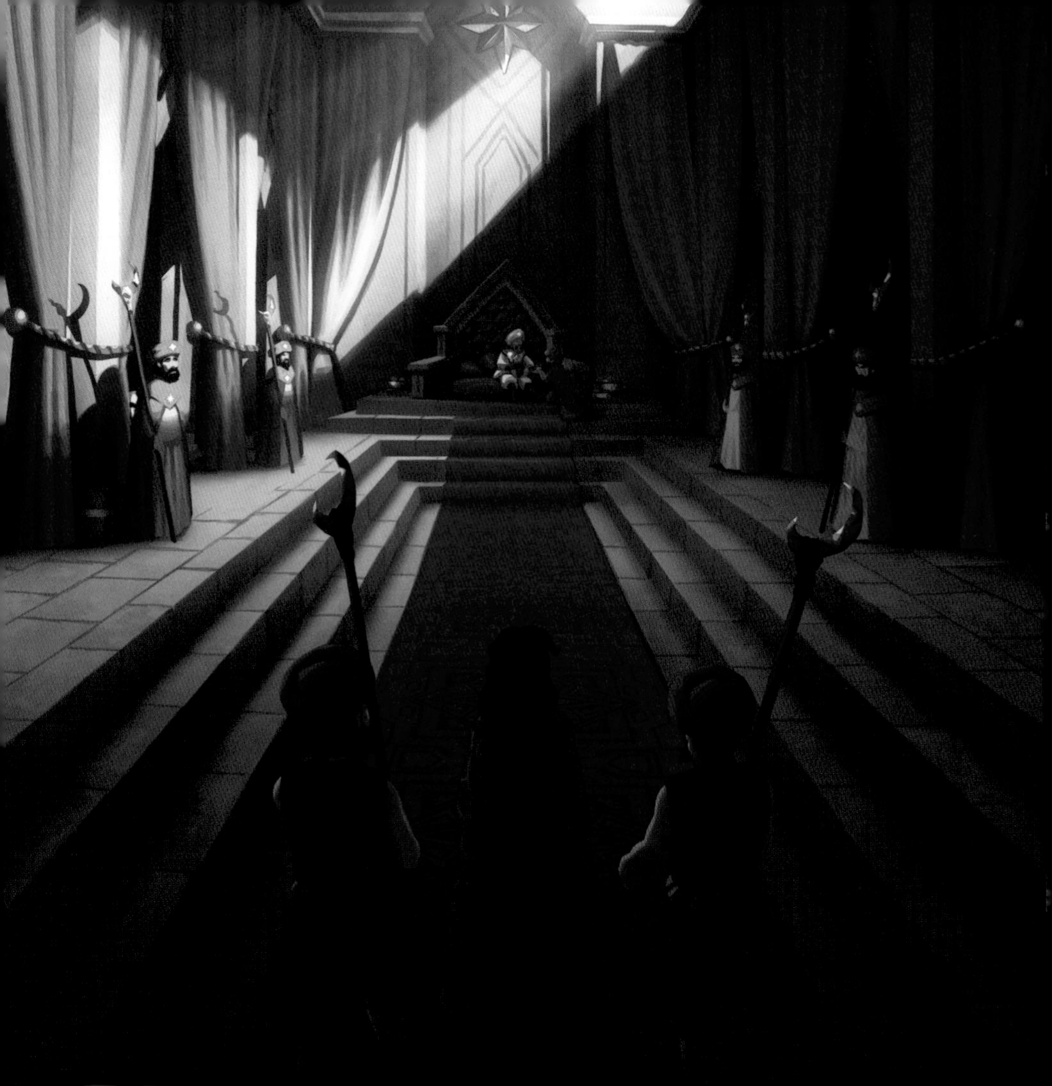

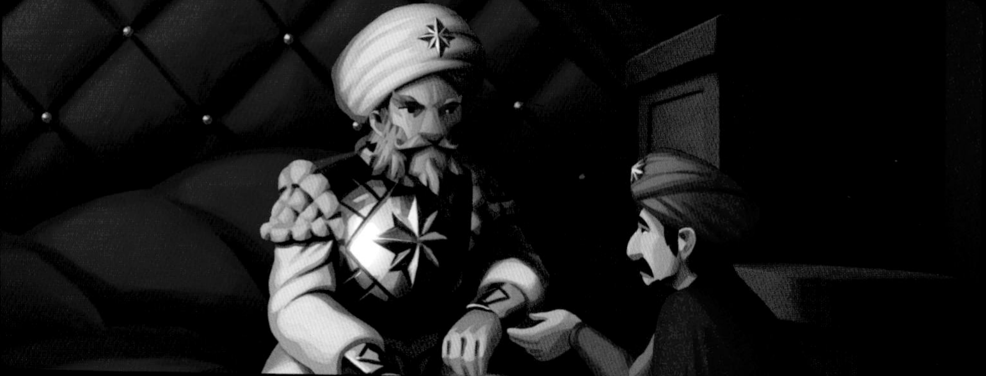

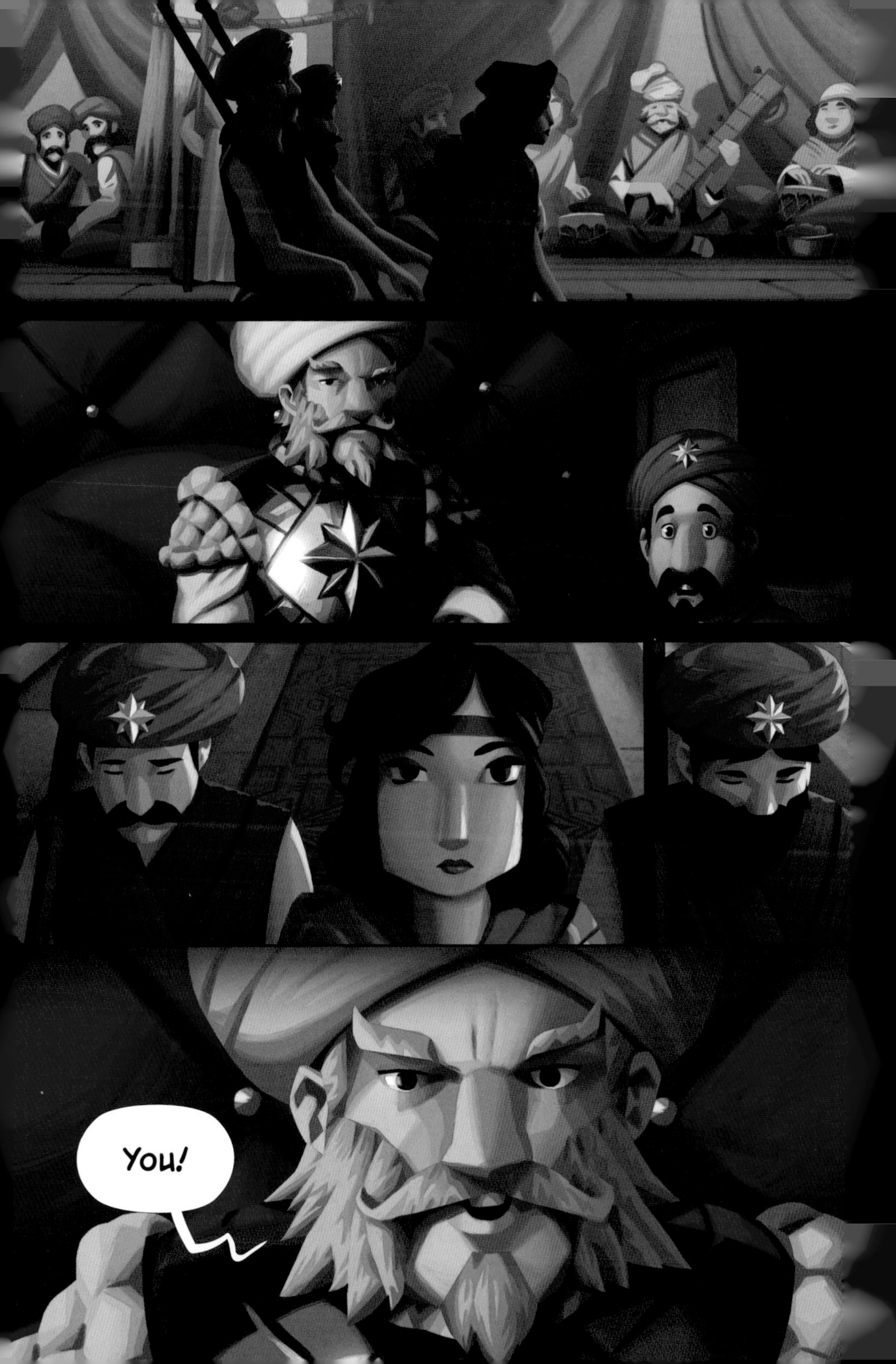
You!

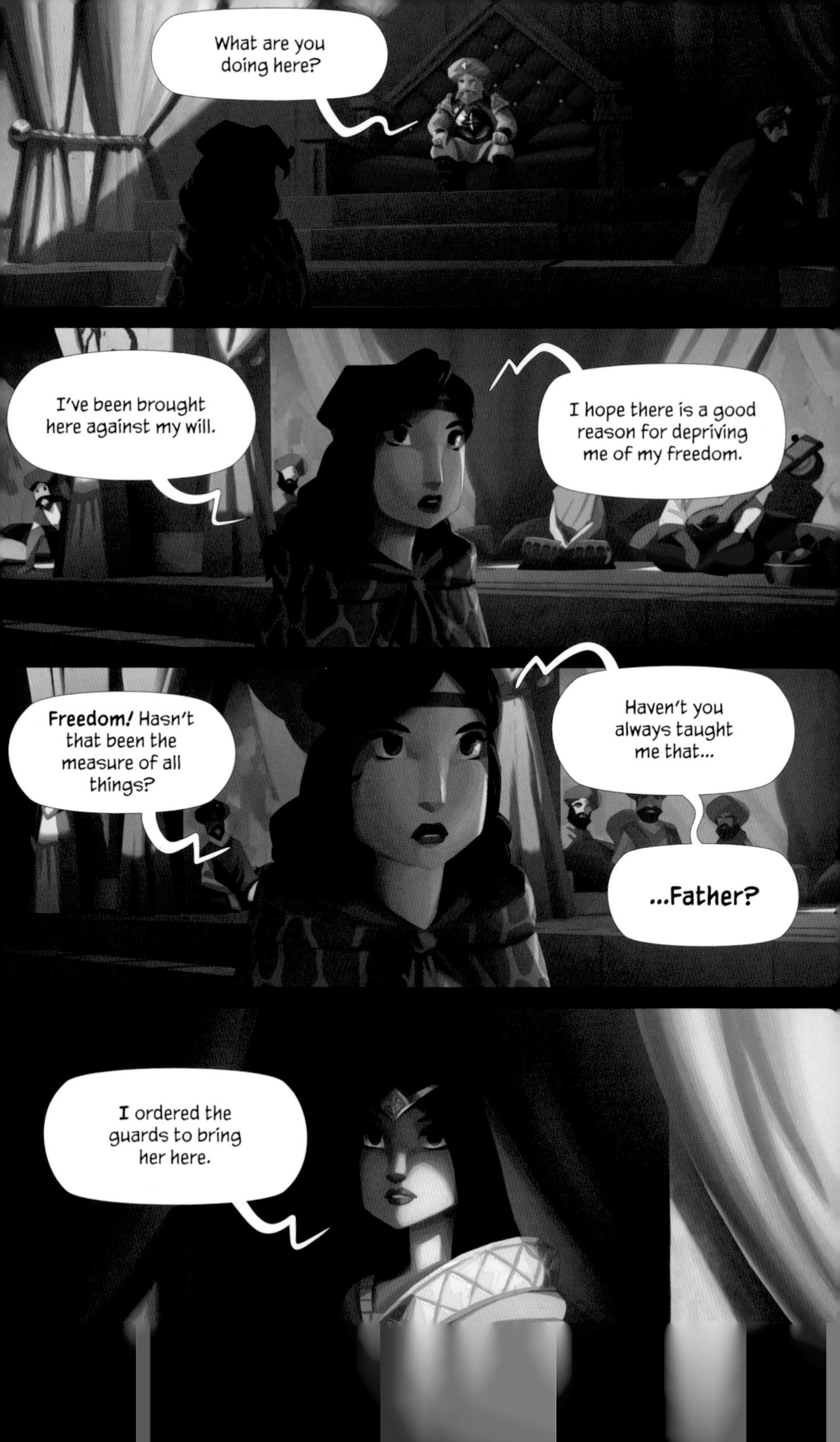
What are you doing here?
I've been brought here against my will.
I hope there is a good reason for depriving me of my freedom.
Freedom! Hasn't that been the measure of all things?
Haven't you always taught me that...
...Father?
I ordered the guards to bring her here.

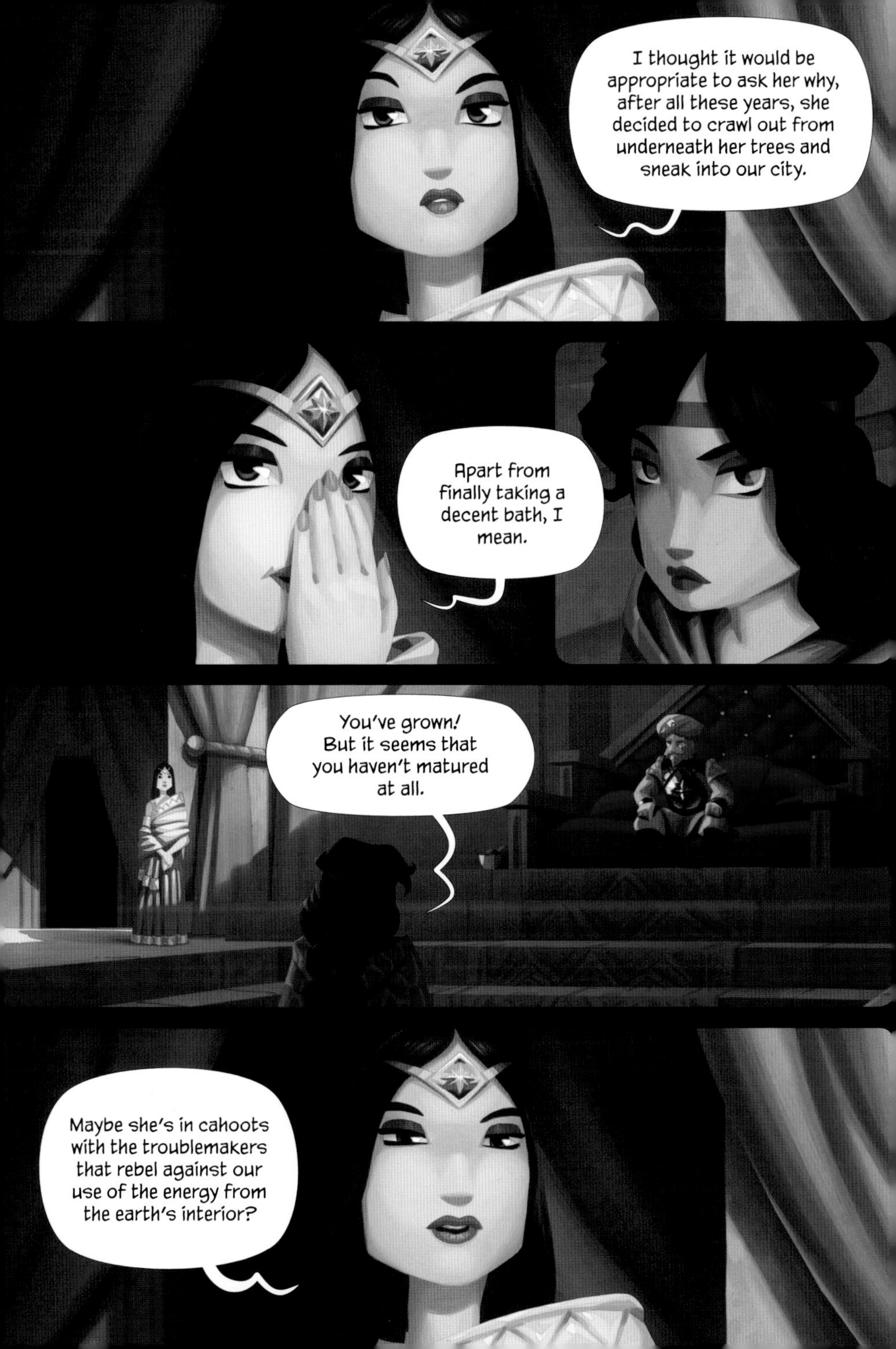
I thought it would be appropriate to ask her why, after all these years, she decided to crawl out from underneath her trees and sneak into our city.
Apart from finally taking a decent bath, I mean.
You've grown! But it seems that you haven't matured at all.
Maybe she's in cahoots with the troublemakers that rebel against our use of the energy from the earth's interior?

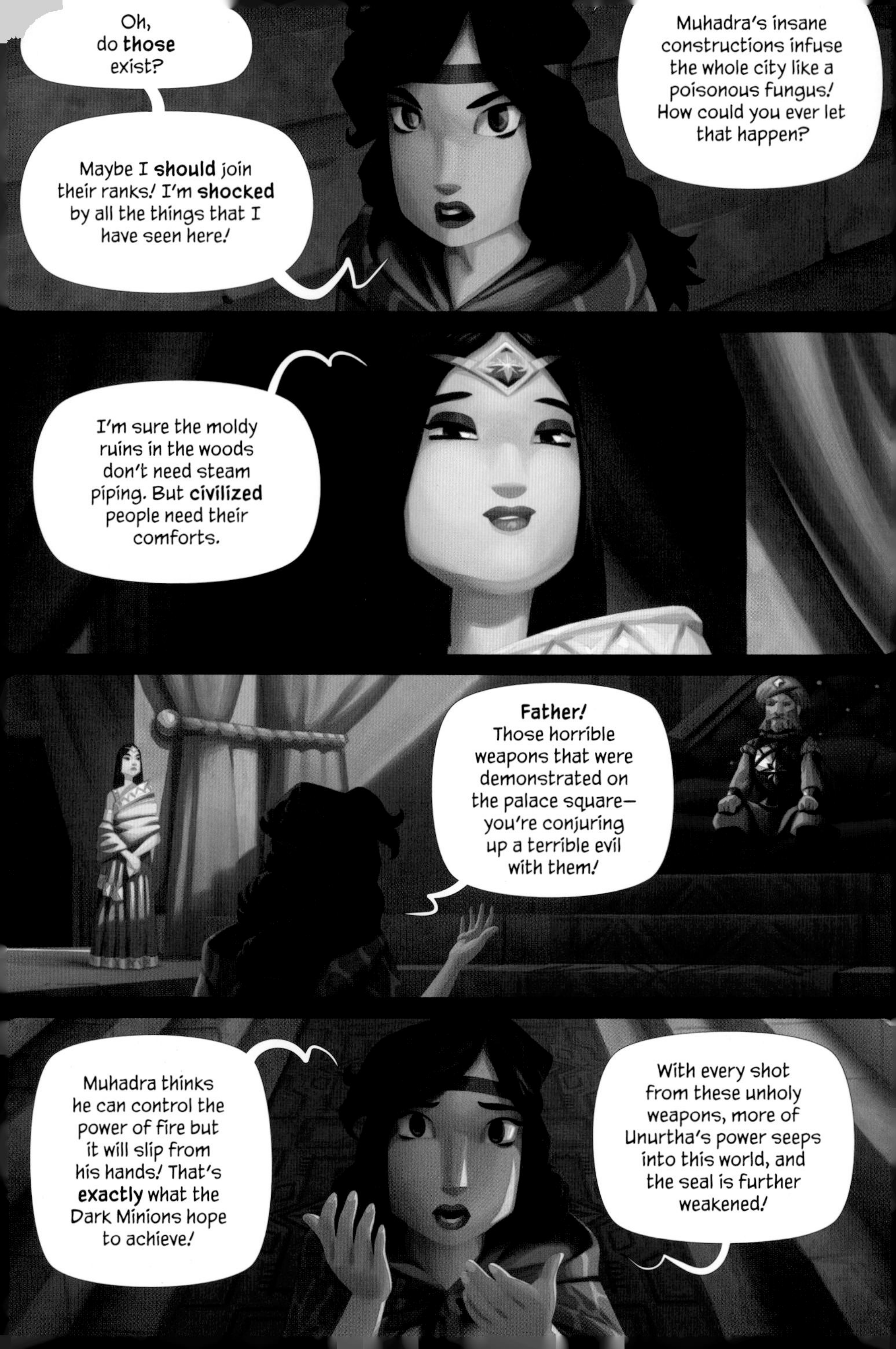
Oh, do **those** exist?
Maybe I **should** join their ranks! I'm **shocked** by all the things that I have seen here!
Muhadra's insane constructions infuse the whole city like a poisonous fungus! How could you ever let that happen?
I'm sure the moldy ruins in the woods don't need steam piping. But **civilized** people need their comforts.
Father! Those horrible weapons that were demonstrated on the palace square— you're conjuring up a terrible evil with them!
Muhadra thinks he can control the power of fire but it will slip from his hands! That's **exactly** what the Dark Minions hope to achieve!
With every shot from these unholy weapons, more of Unurtha's power seeps into this world, and the seal is further weakened!

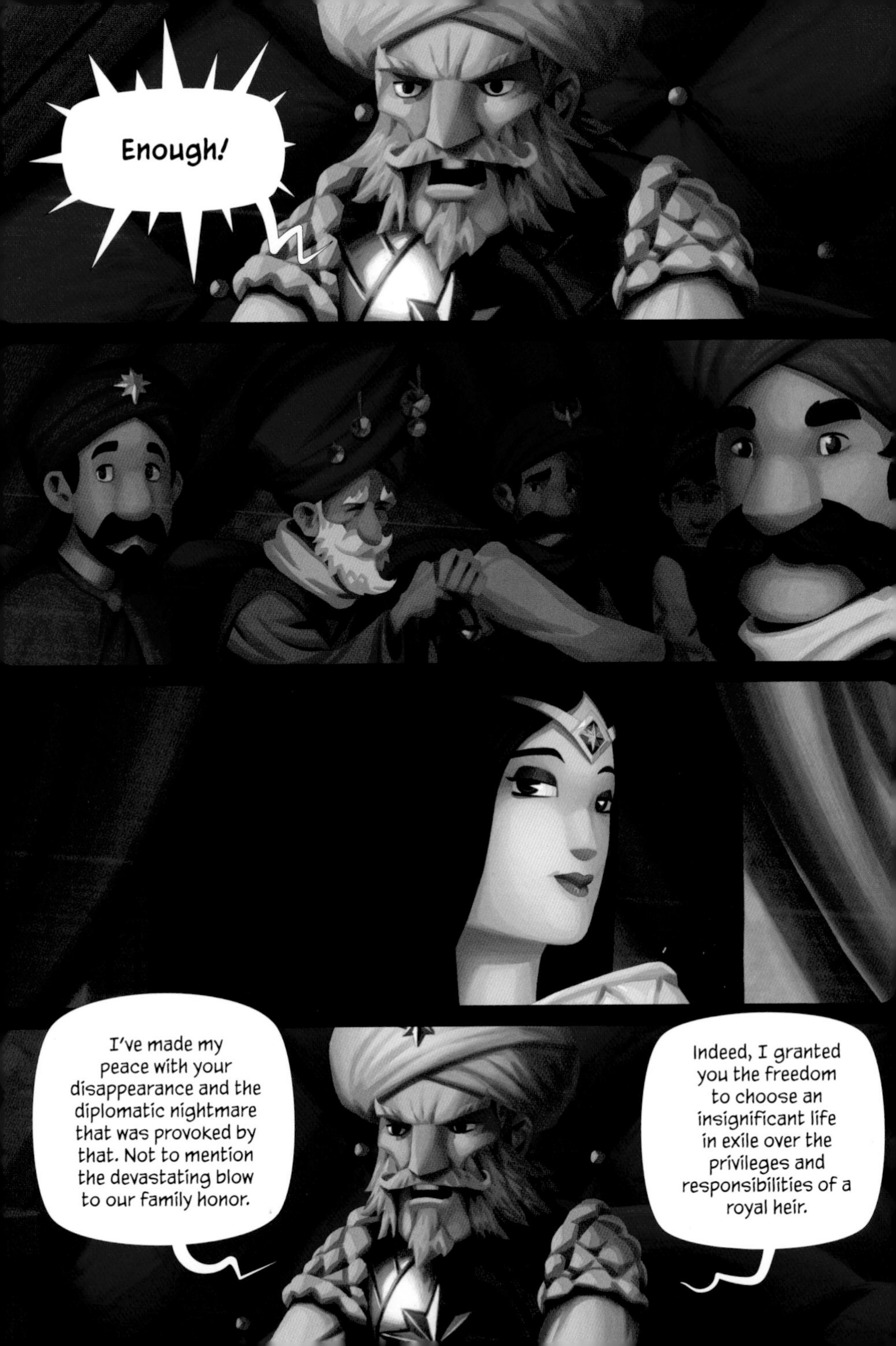
Enough!
I've made my peace with your disappearance and the diplomatic nightmare that was provoked by that. Not to mention the devastating blow to our family honor.
Indeed, I granted you the freedom to choose an insignificant life in exile over the privileges and responsibilities of a royal heir.

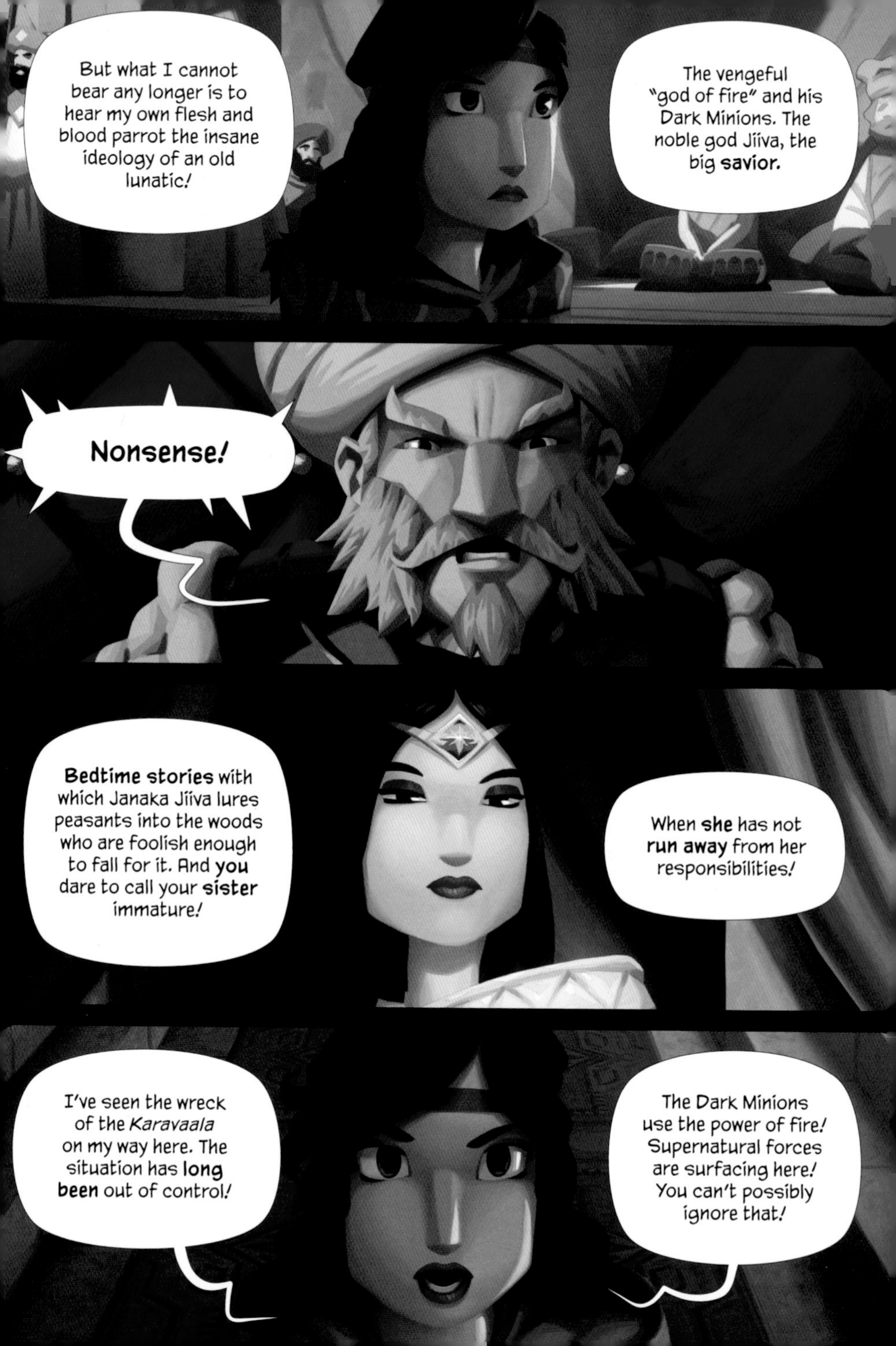
But what I cannot bear any longer is to hear my own flesh and blood parrot the insane ideology of an old lunatic!
The vengeful "god of fire" and his Dark Minions. The noble god Jiíva, the big **savior.**
Nonsense!
Bedtime stories with which Janaka Jiíva lures peasants into the woods who are foolish enough to fall for it. And **you** dare to call your **sister** immature!
When **she** has not **run away** from her responsibilities!
I've seen the wreck of the *Karavaala* on my way here. The situation has **long been** out of control!
The Dark Minions use the power of fire! Supernatural forces are surfacing here! You can't possibly ignore that!

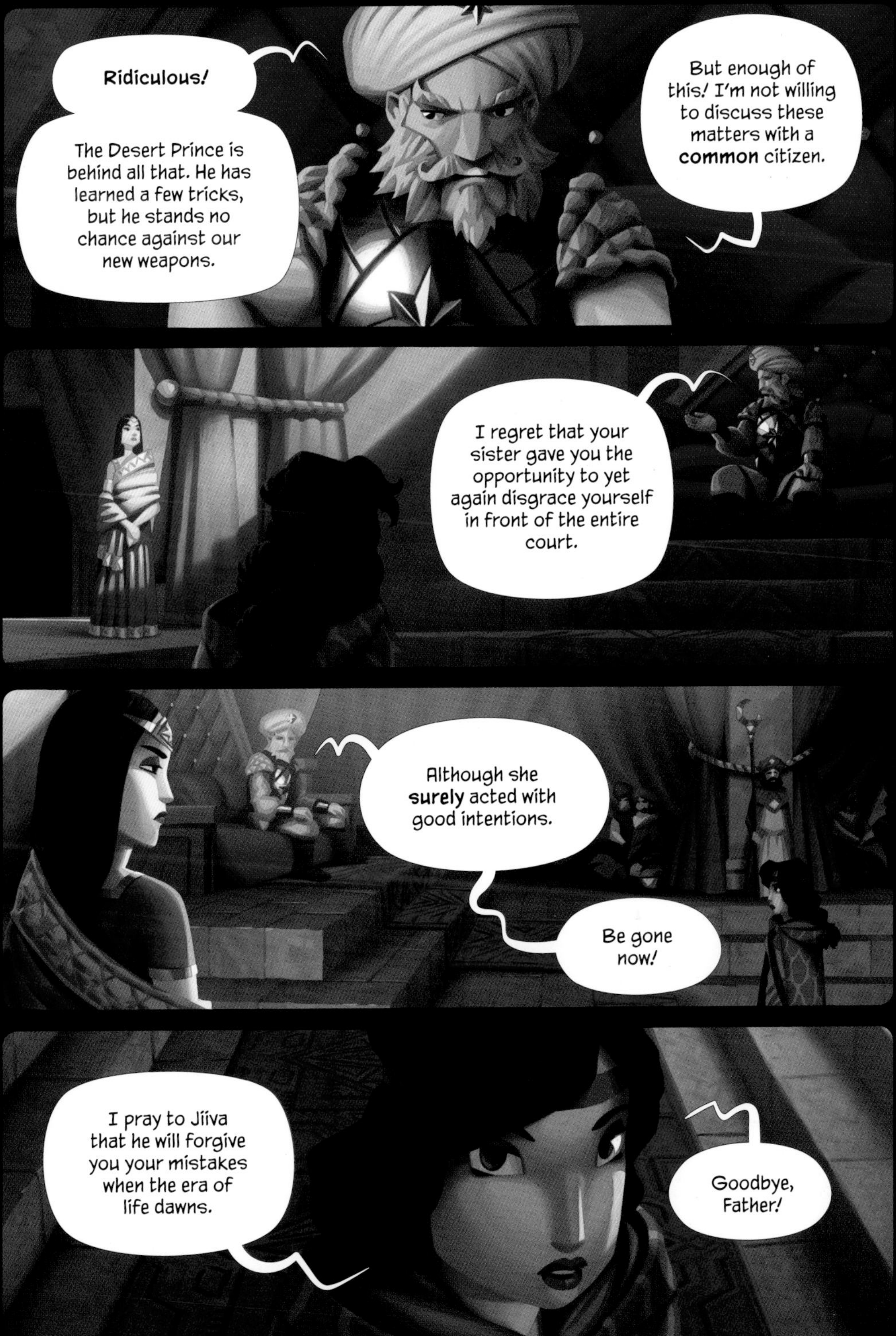
Ridiculous!
The Desert Prince is behind all that. He has learned a few tricks, but he stands no chance against our new weapons.
But enough of this! I'm not willing to discuss these matters with a **common** citizen.
I regret that your sister gave you the opportunity to yet again disgrace yourself in front of the entire court.
Although she **surely** acted with good intentions.
Be gone now!
I pray to Jiíva that he will forgive you your mistakes when the era of life dawns.
Goodbye, Father!

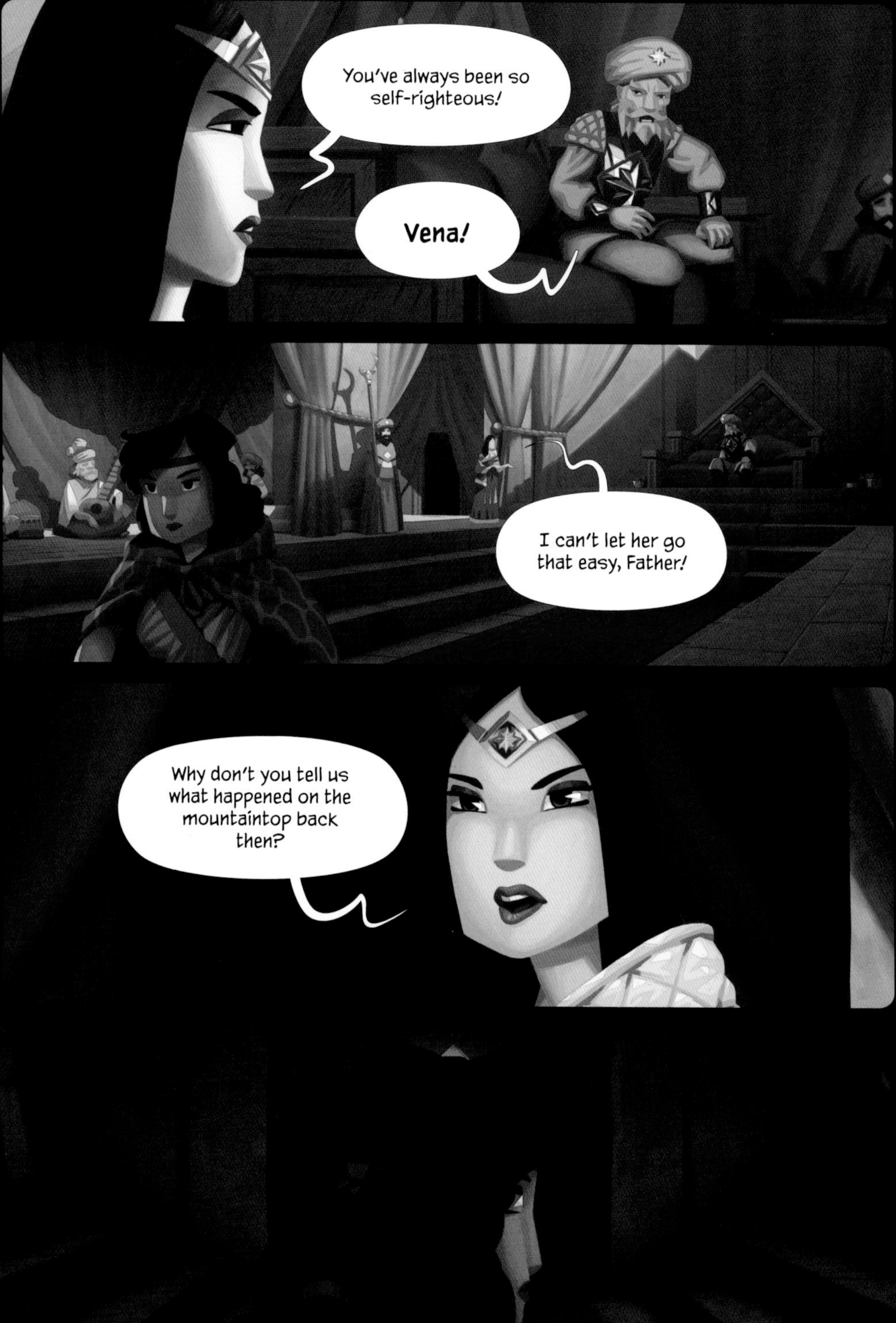
You've always been so self-righteous!
Vena!
I can't let her go that easy, Father!
Why don't you tell us what happened on the mountaintop back then?

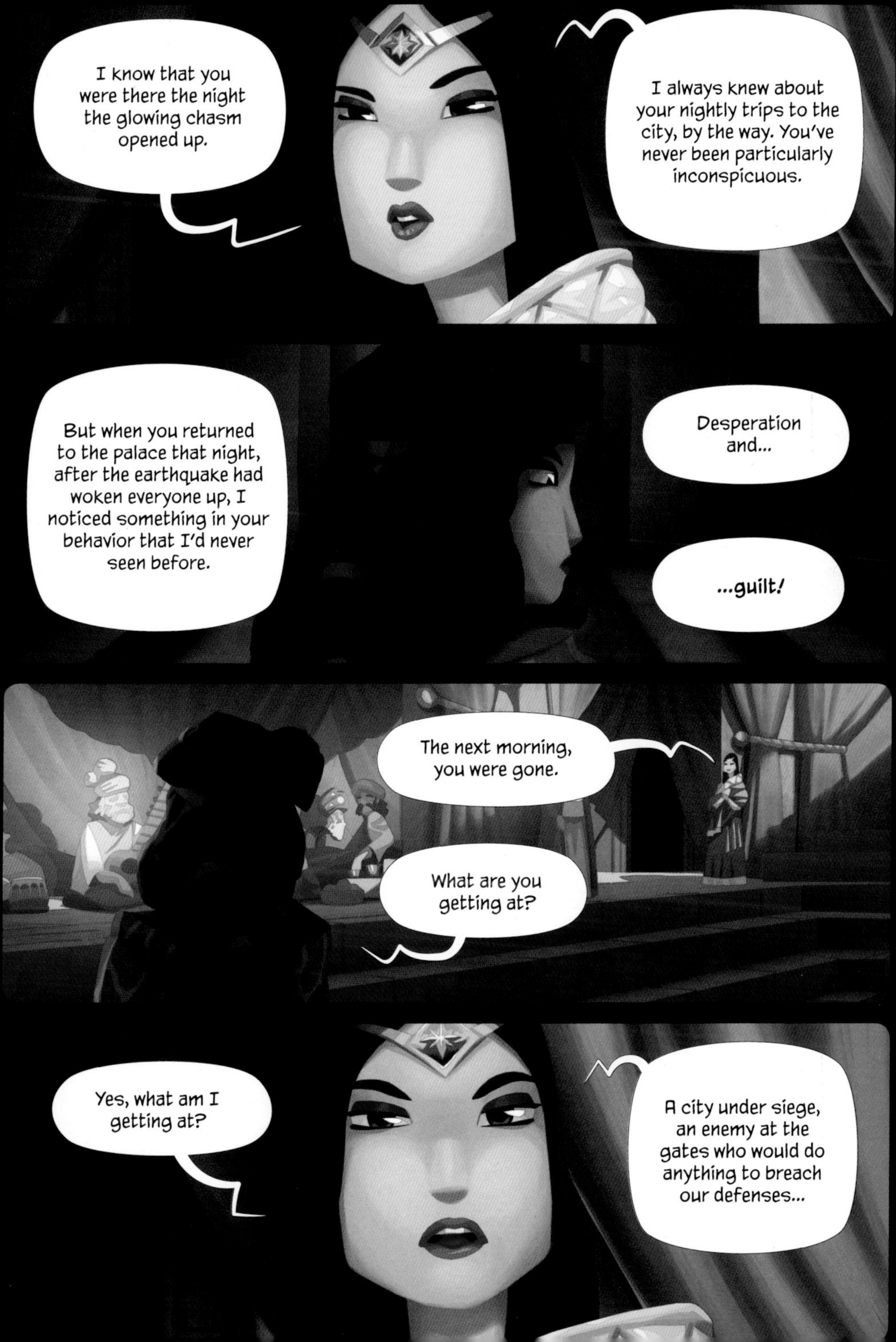
I know that you were there the night the glowing chasm opened up.
I always knew about your nightly trips to the city, by the way. You've never been particularly inconspicuous.
But when you returned to the palace that night, after the earthquake had woken everyone up, I noticed something in your behavior that I'd never seen before.
Desperation and...
...guilt!
The next morning, you were gone.
What are you getting at?
Yes, what am I getting at?
A city under siege, an enemy at the gates who would do anything to breach our defenses...

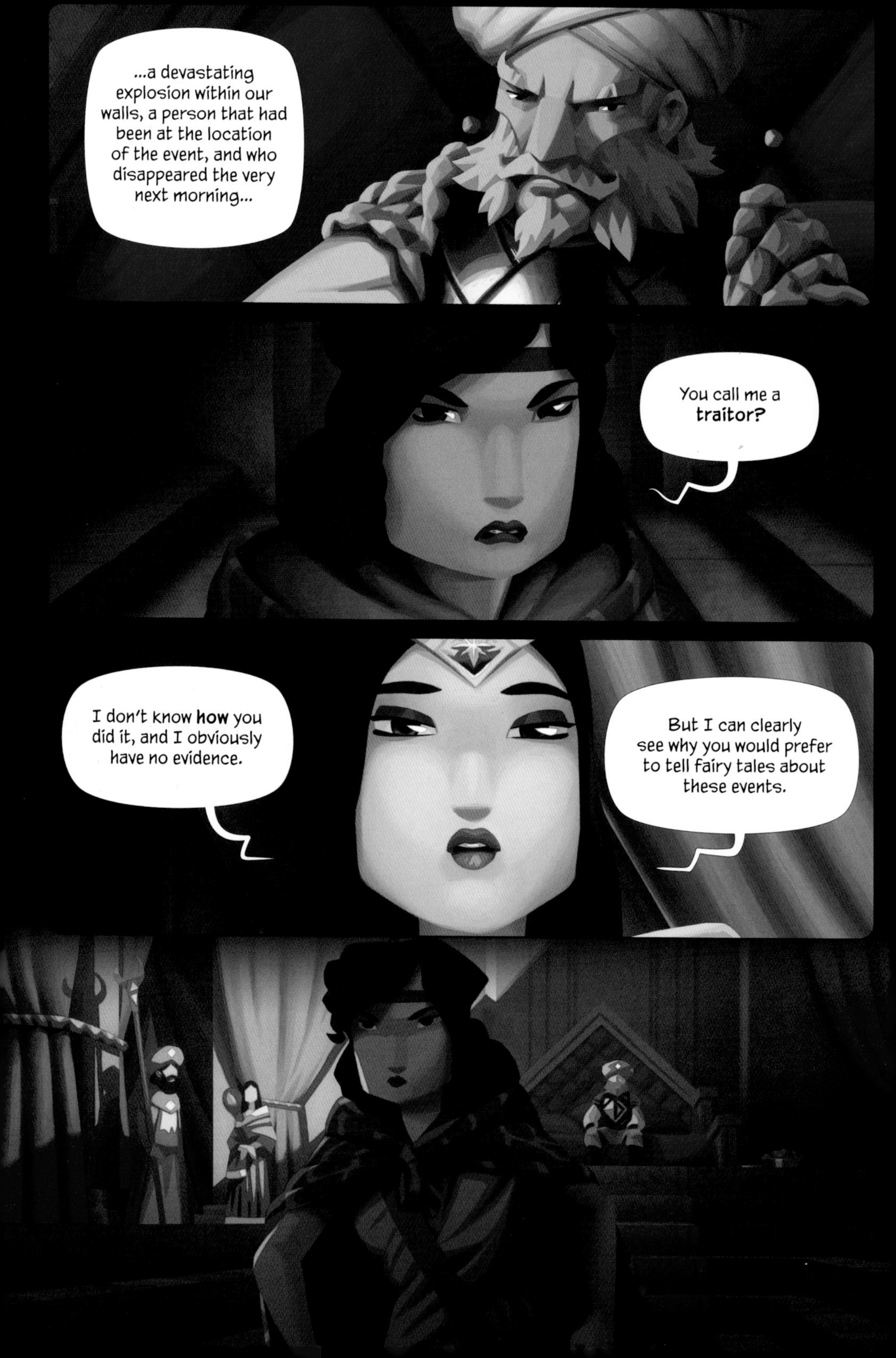
...a devastating explosion within our walls, a person that had been at the location of the event, and who disappeared the very next morning...
You call me a traitor?
I don't know how you did it, and I obviously have no evidence.
But I can clearly see why you would prefer to tell fairy tales about these events.

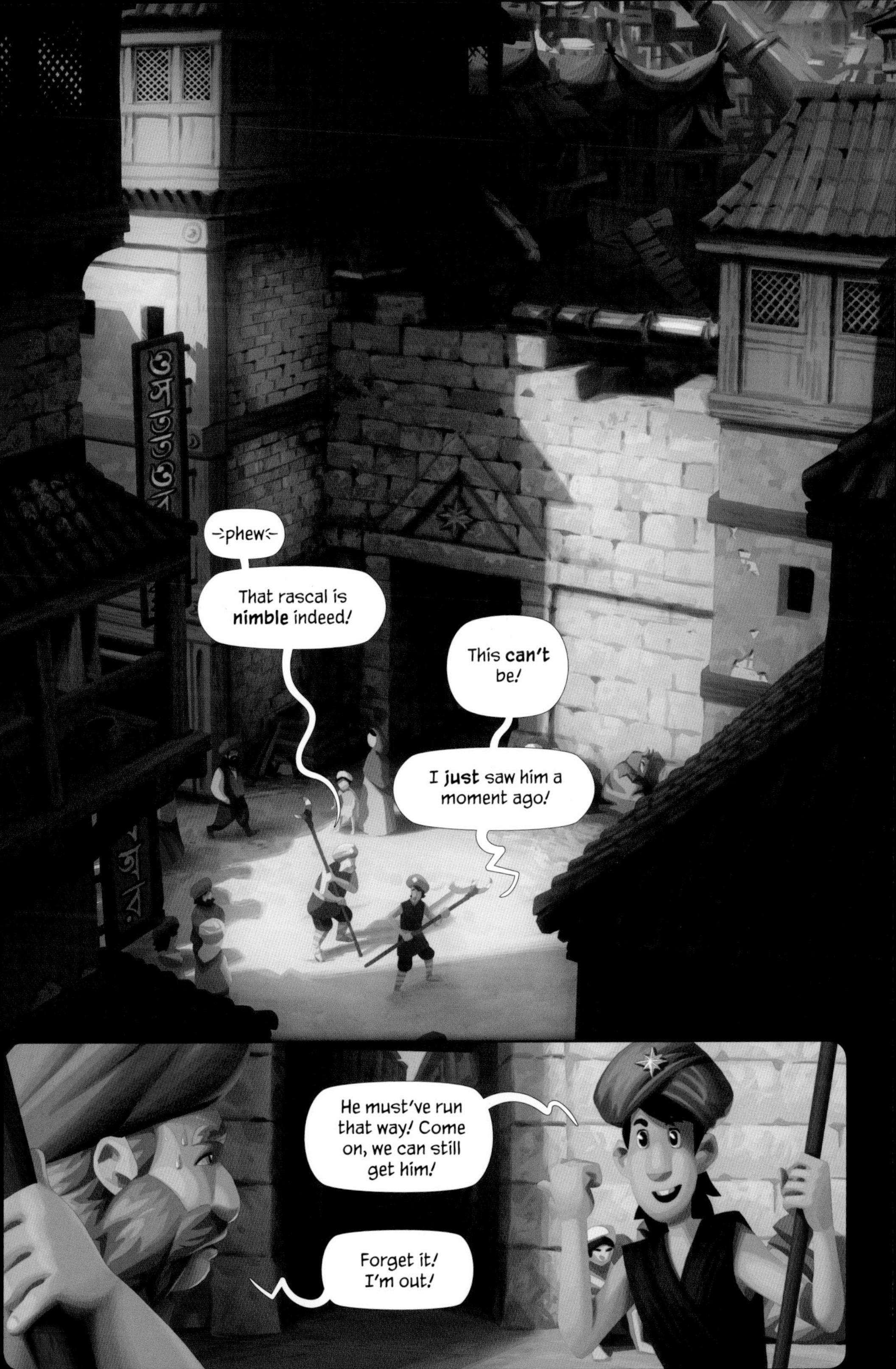
phew
That rascal is **nimble** indeed!
This **can't** be!
I **just** saw him a moment ago!
He must've run that way! Come on, we can still get him!
Forget it! I'm out!

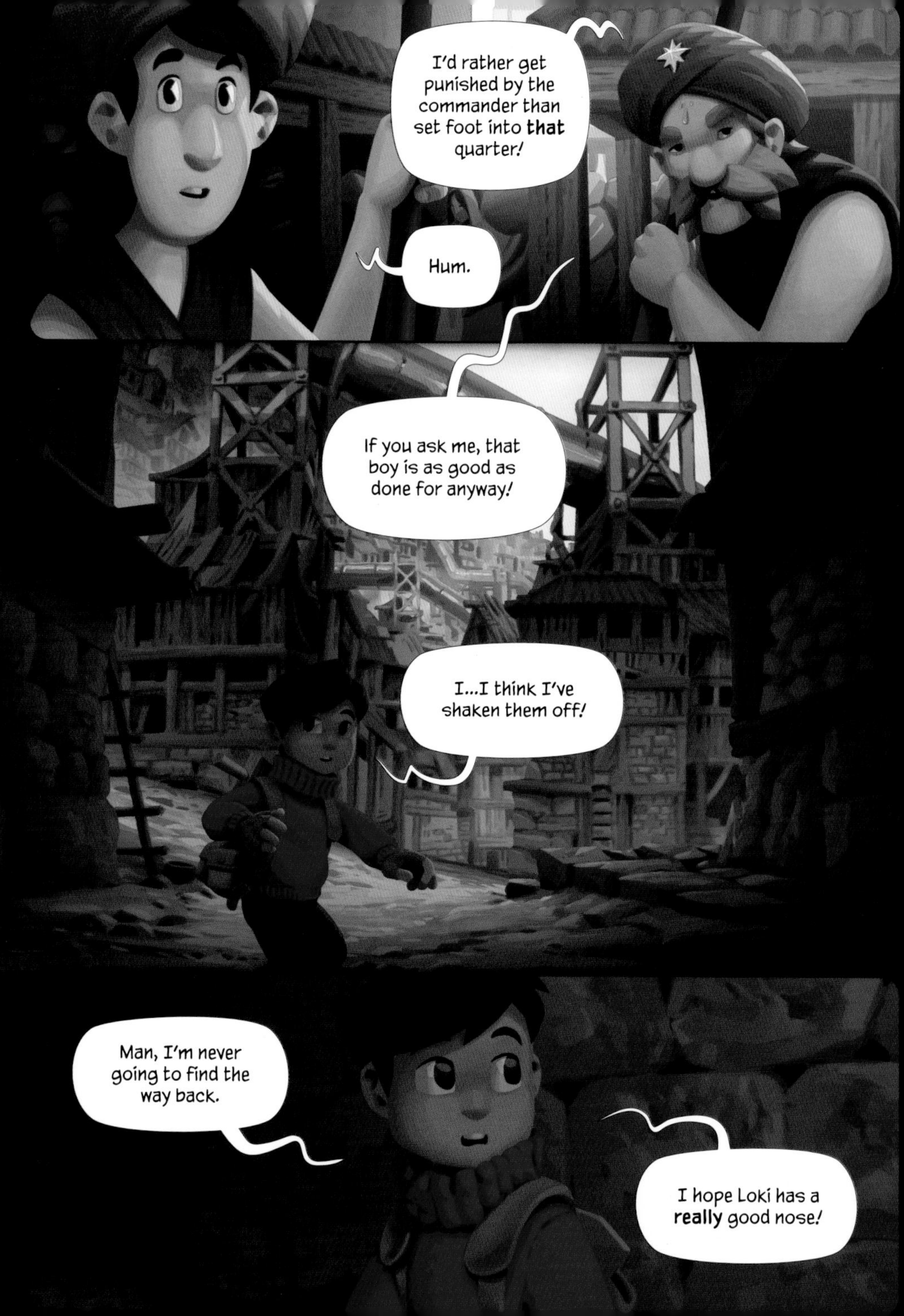
I'd rather get punished by the commander than set foot into **that** quarter!
Hum.
If you ask me, that boy is as good as done for anyway!
I...I think I've shaken them off!
Man, I'm never going to find the way back.
I hope Loki has a **really** good nose!

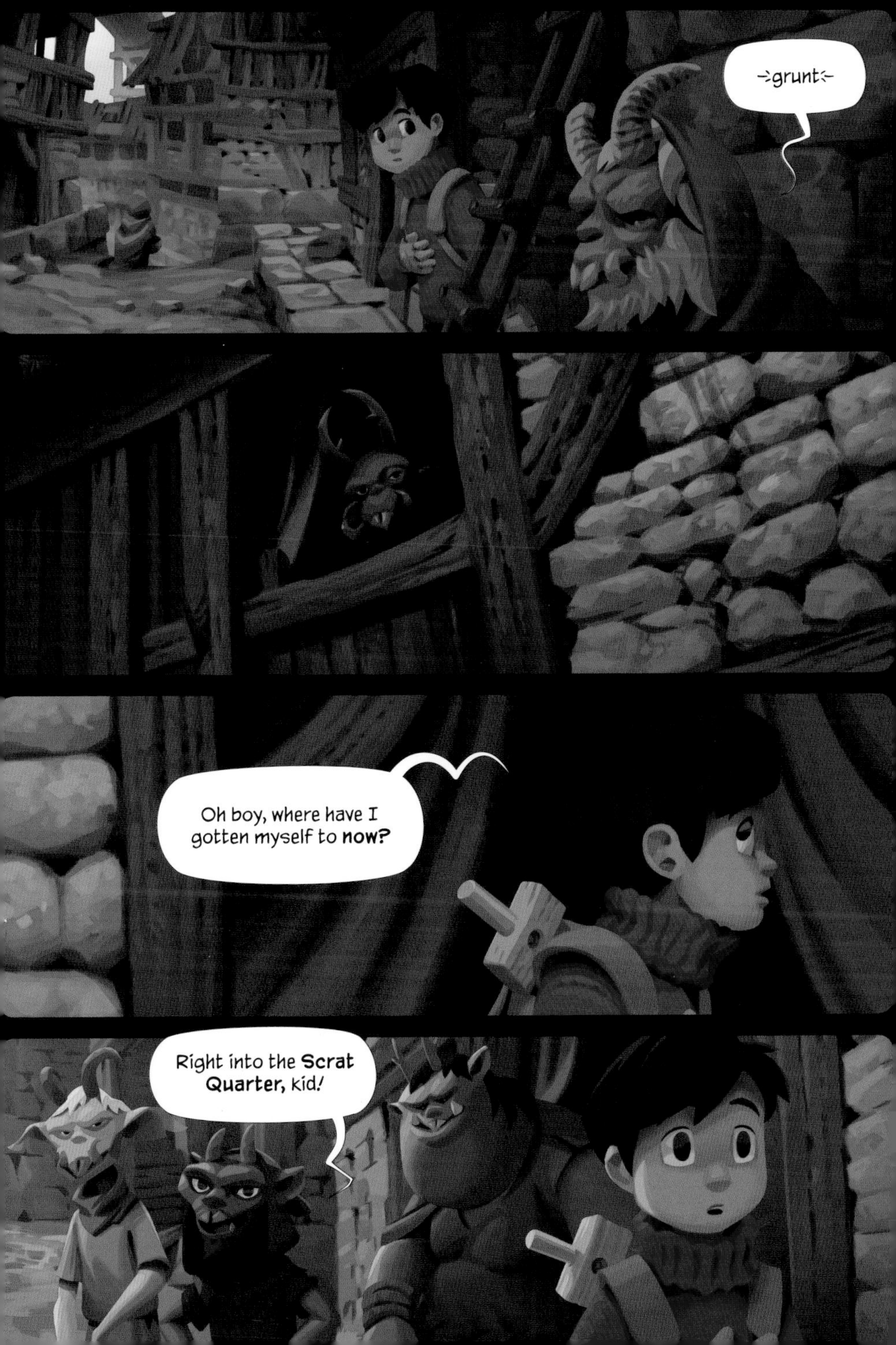
grunt
Oh boy, where have I gotten myself to **now?**
Right into the **Scrat Quarter,** kid!

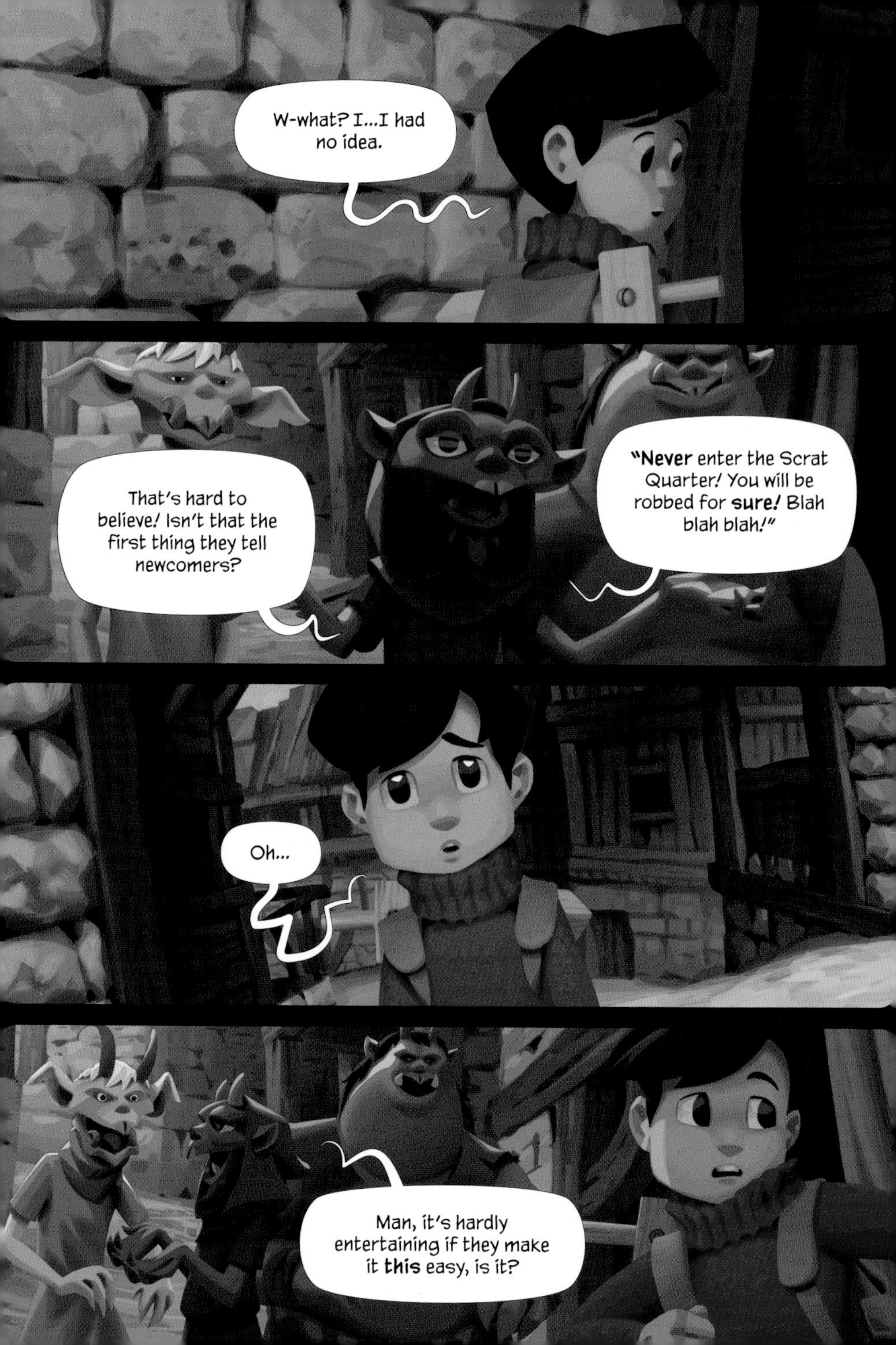
W-what? I...I had no idea.
That's hard to believe! Isn't that the first thing they tell newcomers?
"Never enter the Scrat Quarter! You will be robbed for sure! Blah blah blah!"
Oh...
Man, it's hardly entertaining if they make it this easy, is it?

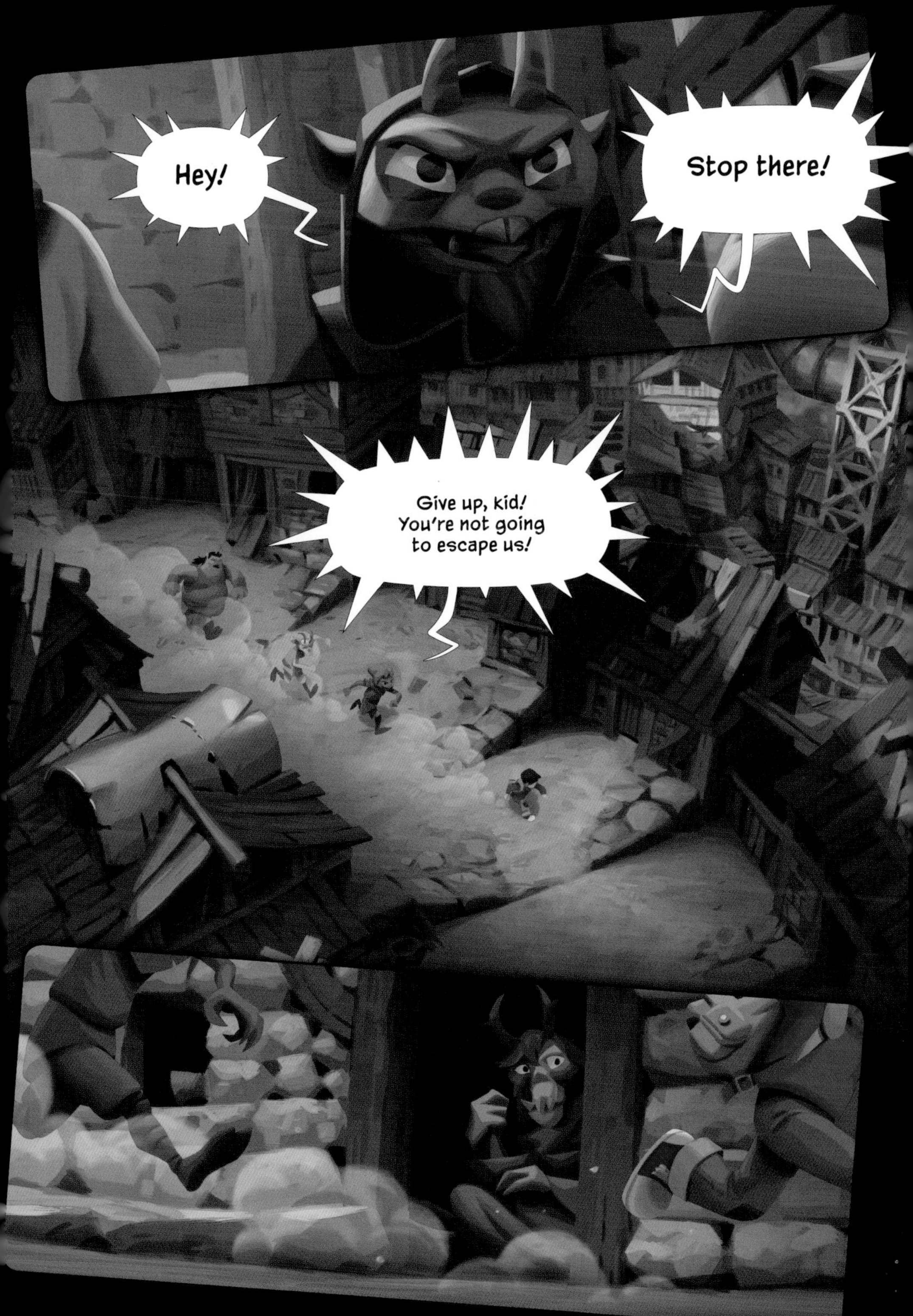
Hey!
Stop there!
Give up, kid! You're not going to escape us!

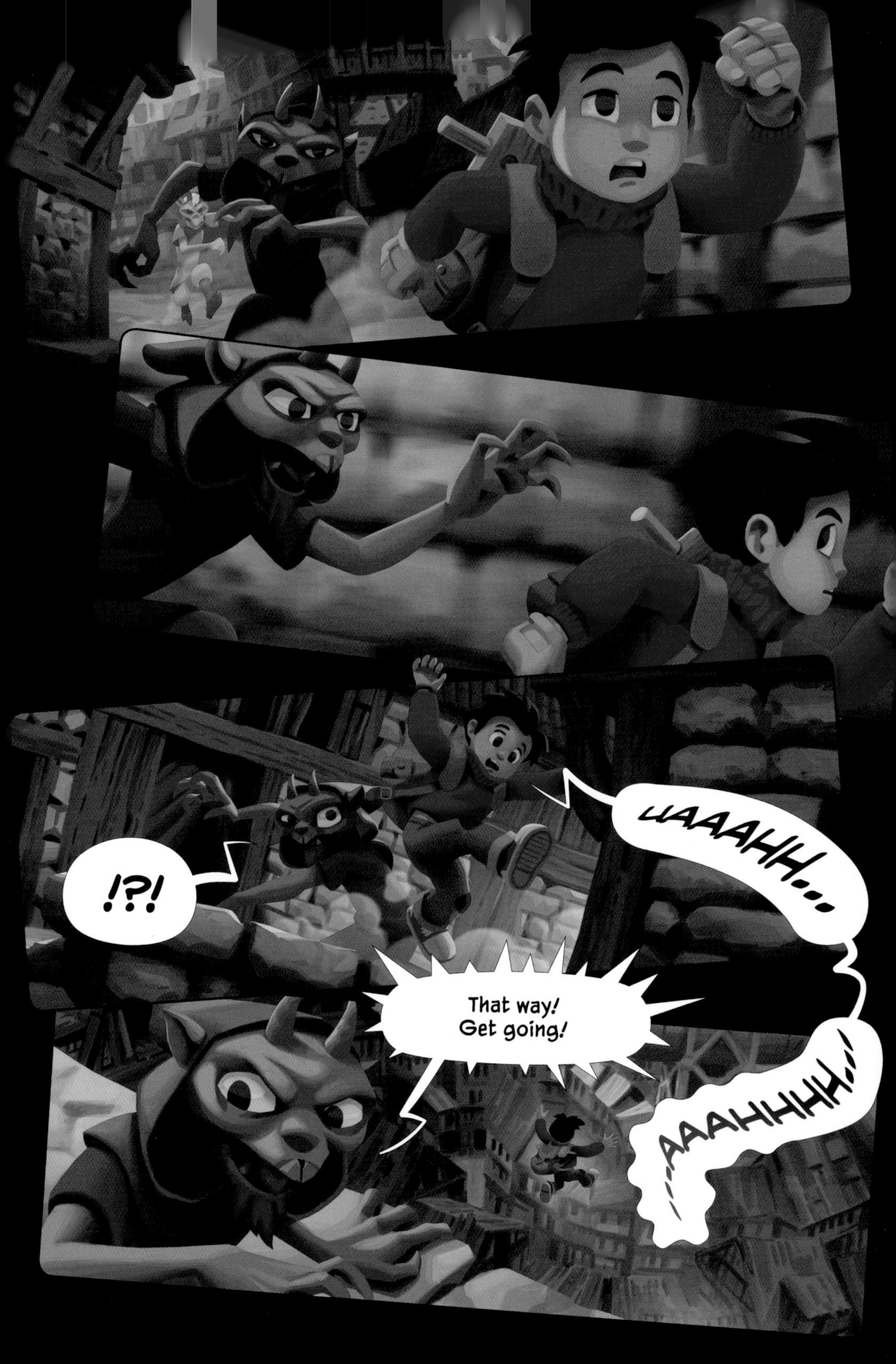
UAAAHH...
!?!
That way! Get going!
...AAAHHH...!

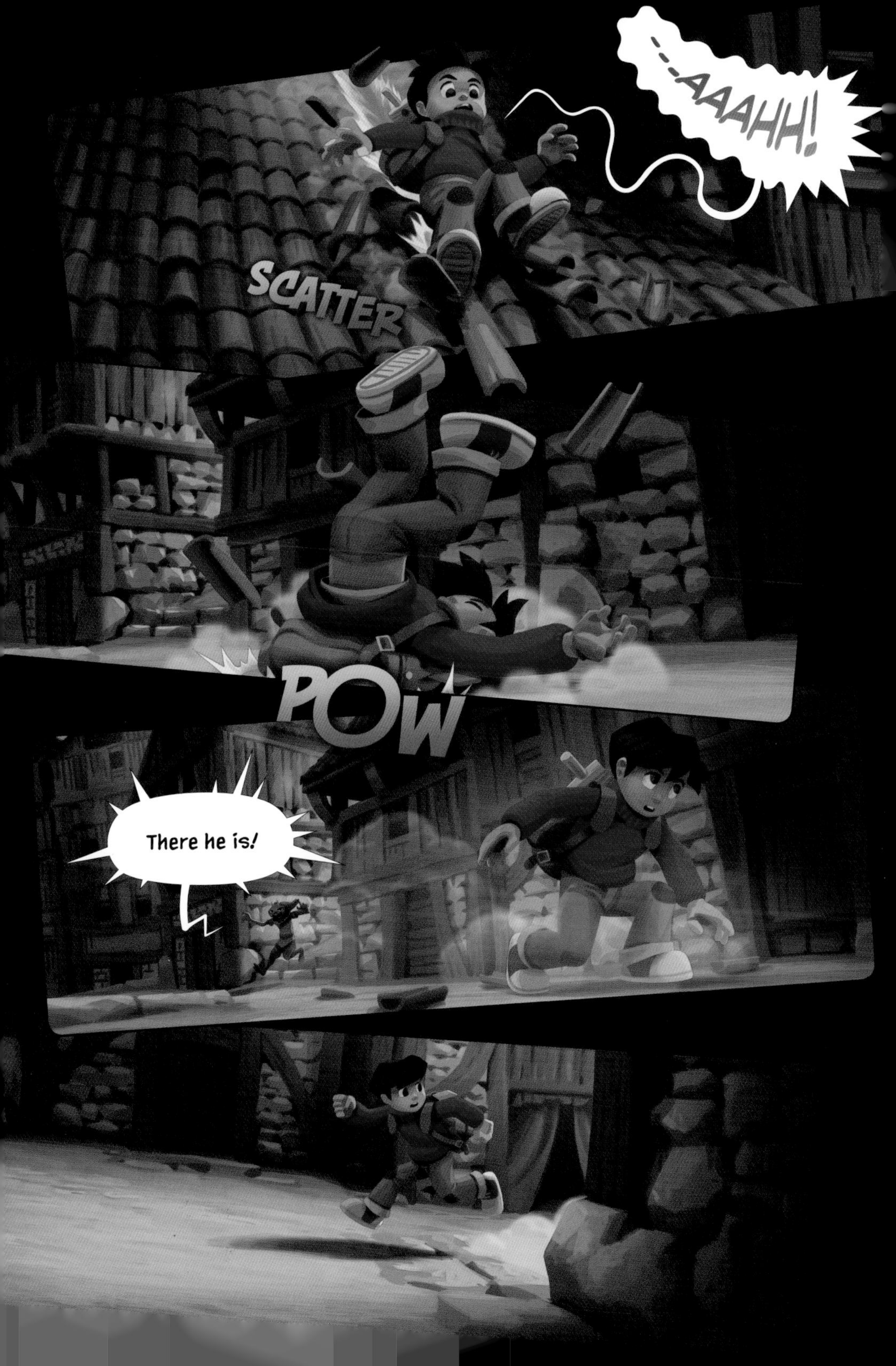

...AAAHH!
SCATTER
POW
There he is!

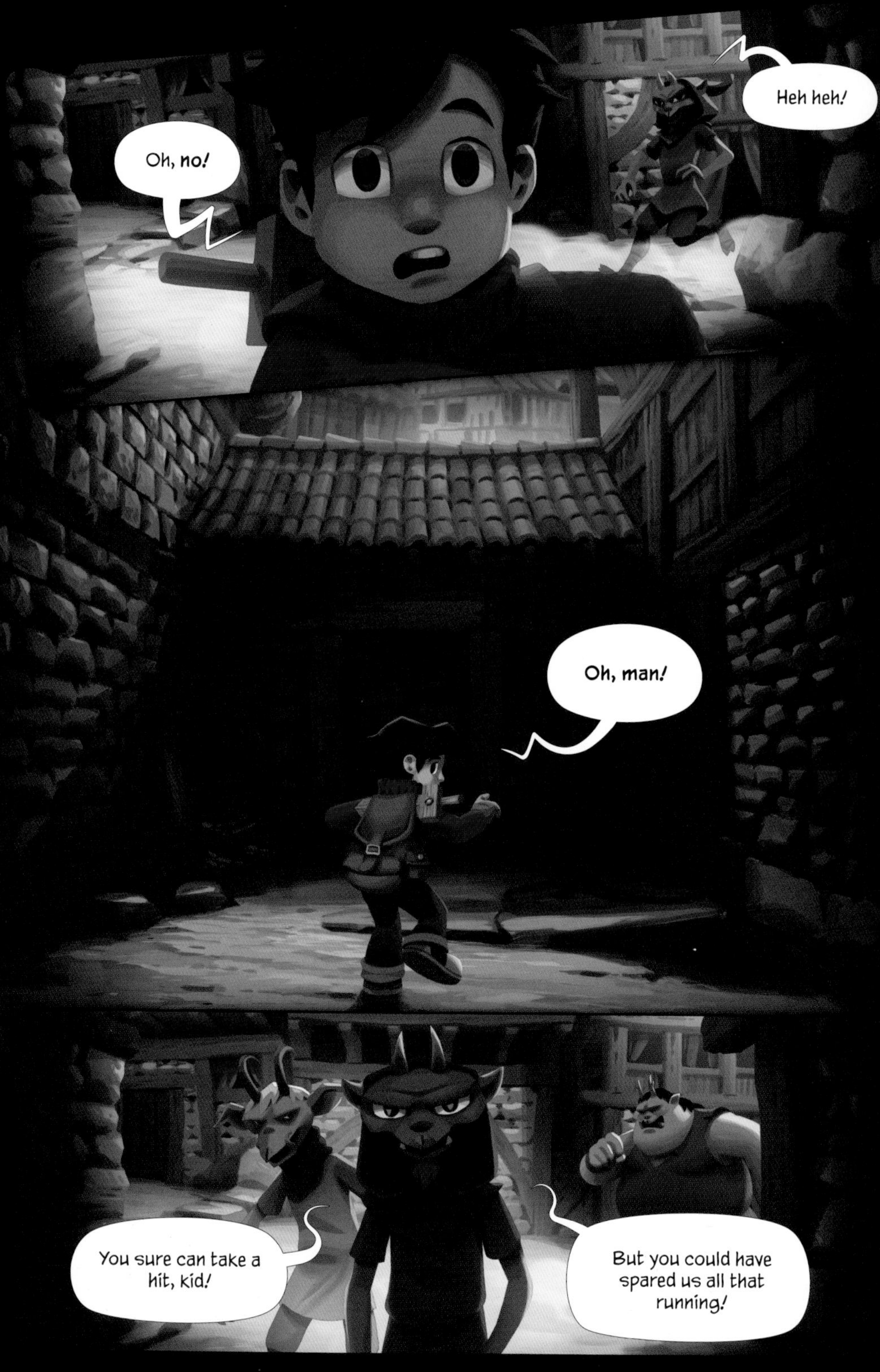
Oh, no!
Heh heh!
Oh, man!
You sure can take a hit, kid!
But you could have spared us all that running!

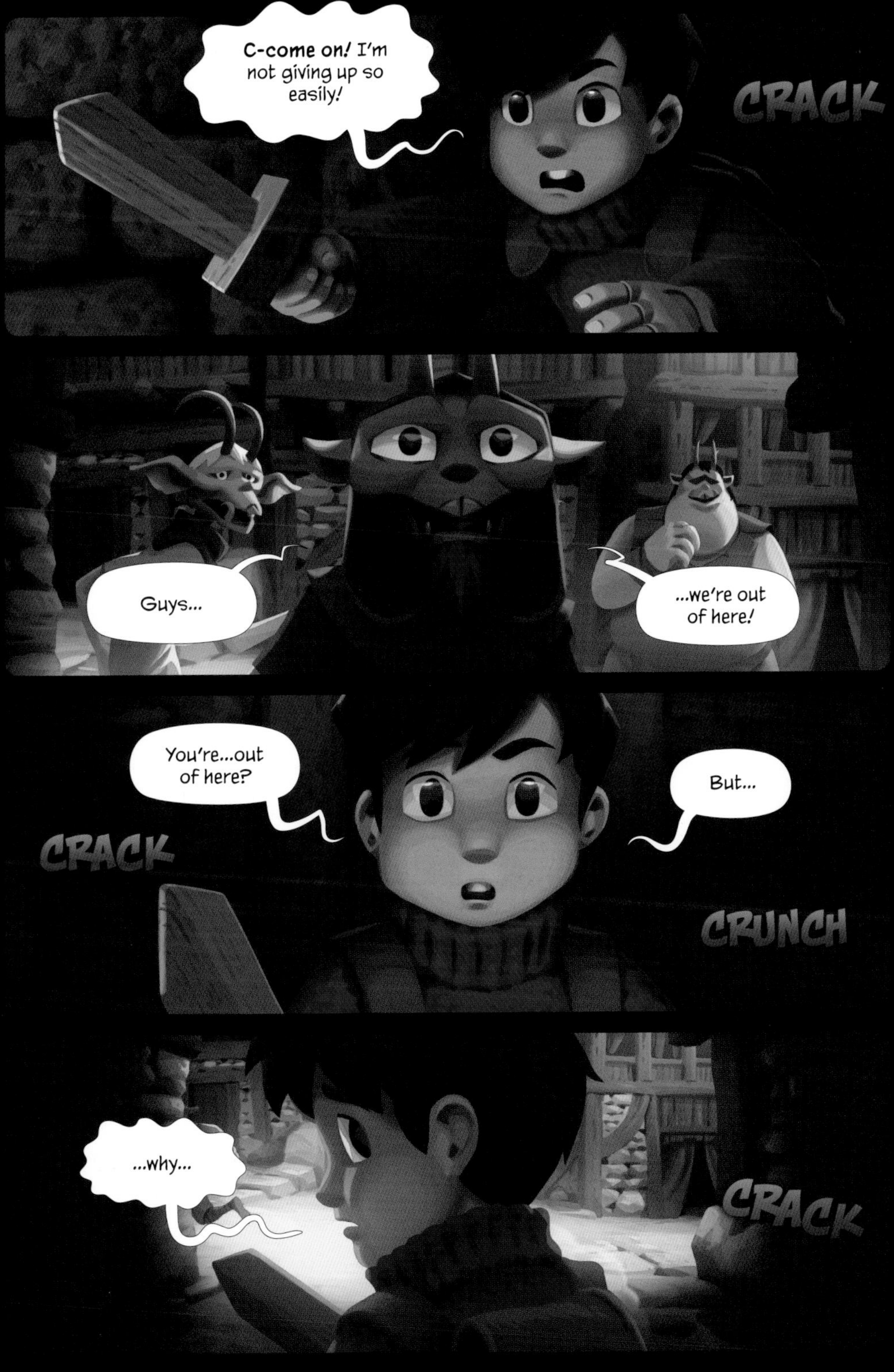
C-come on! I'm not giving up so easily!
CRACK
Guys...
...we're out of here!
You're...out of here?
But...
CRACK
CRUNCH
...why...
CRACK

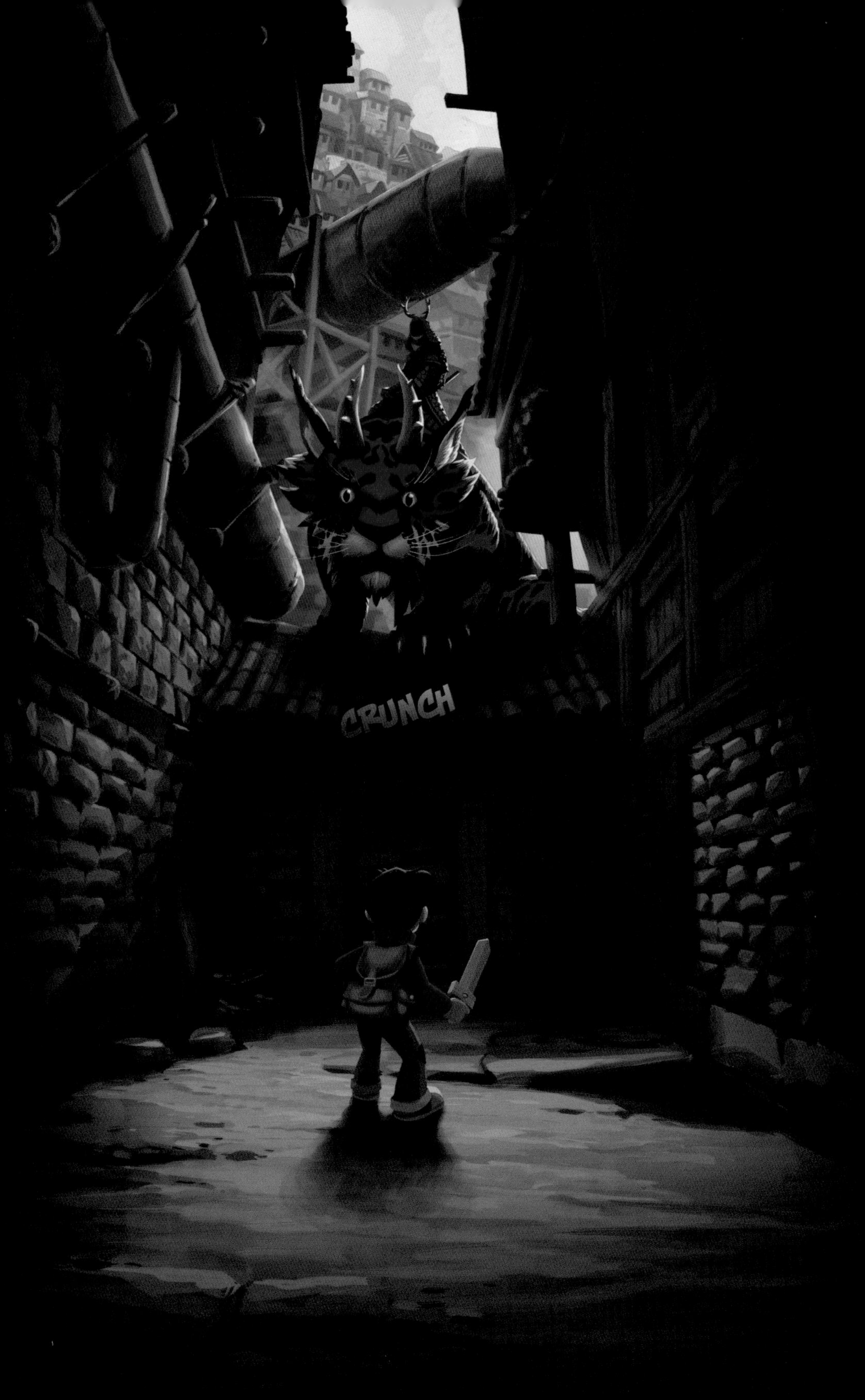
CRUNCH

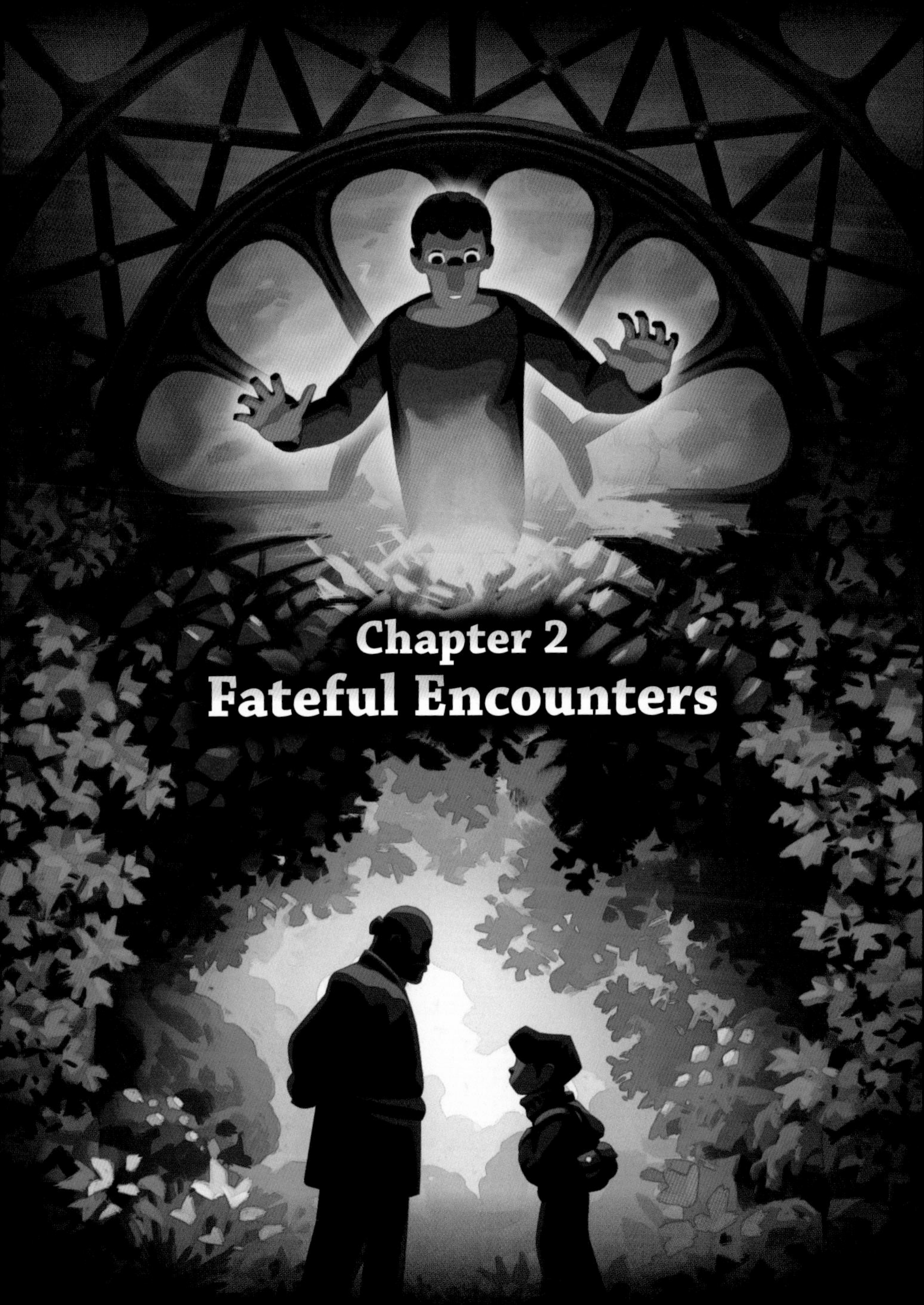

Chapter 2
Fateful Encounters

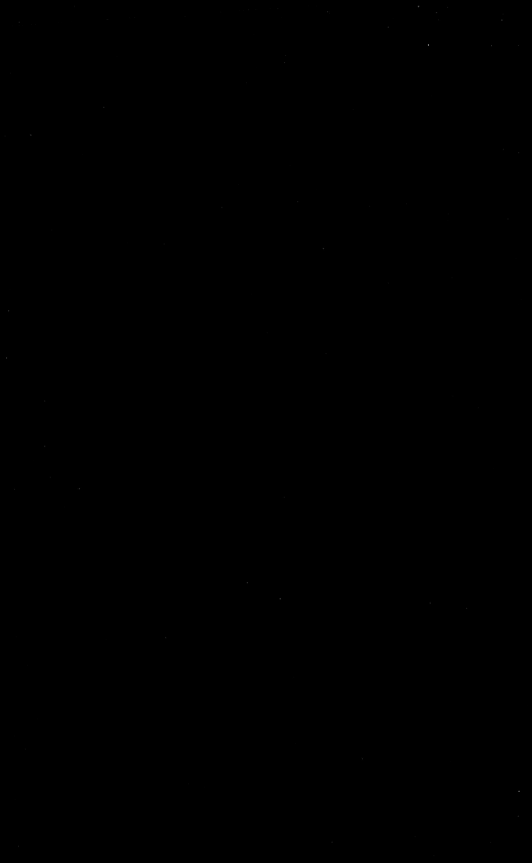

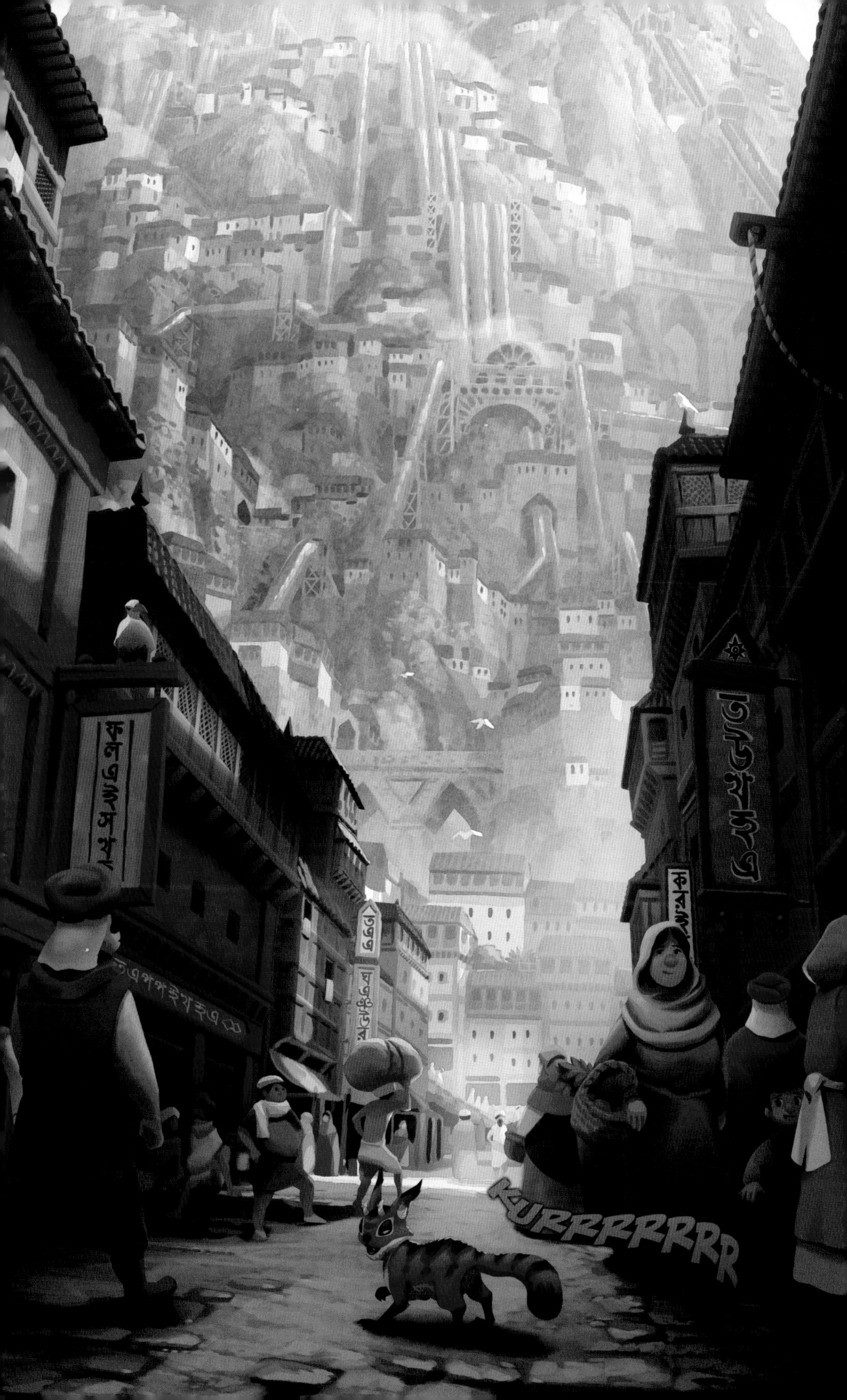
KURRRRRRR

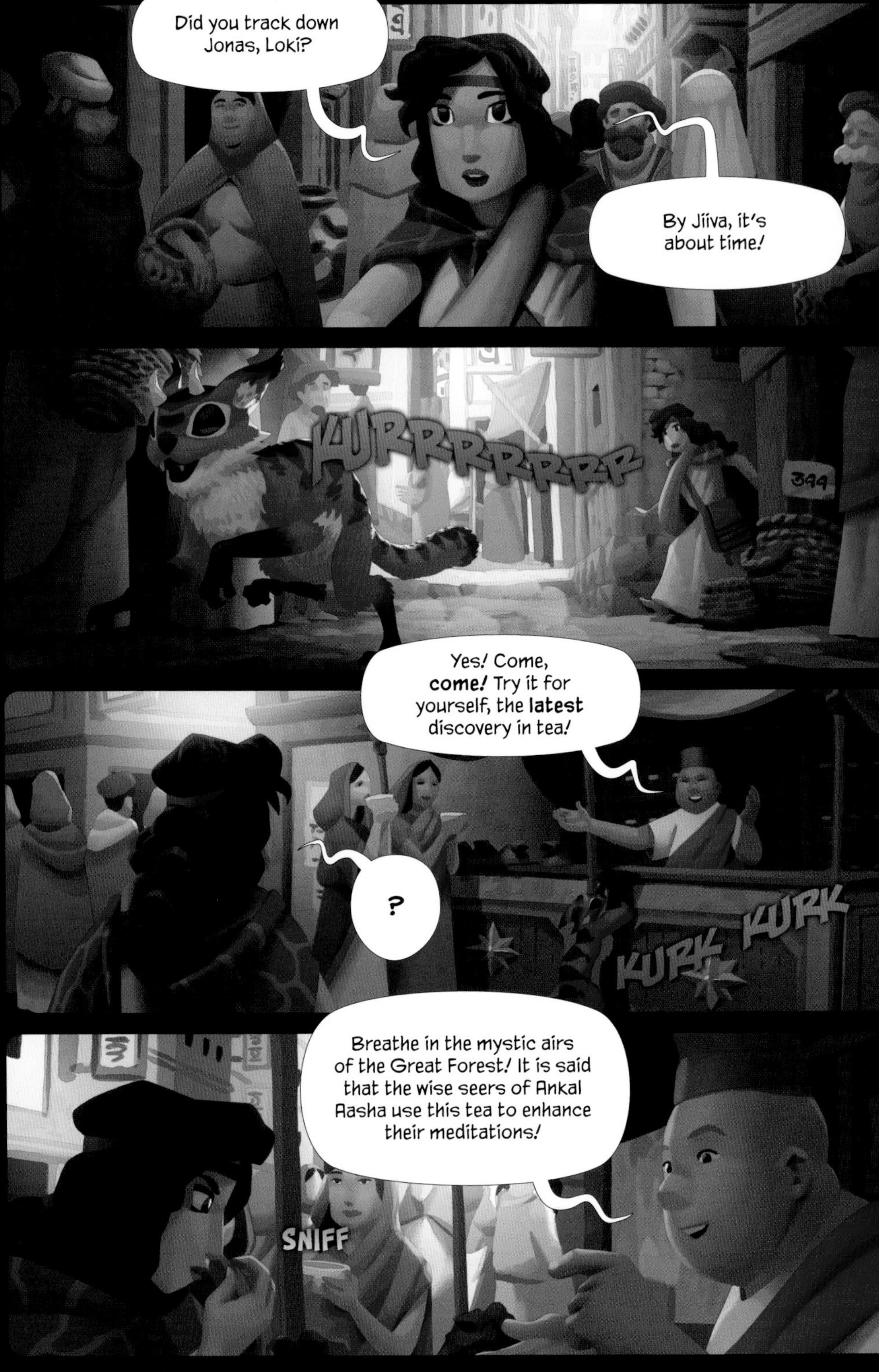
Did you track down Jonas, Loki?
By Jiiva, it's about time!
KURRRRRRRR
344
Yes! Come, **come!** Try it for yourself, the **latest** discovery in tea!
?
KURK KURK
Breathe in the mystic airs of the Great Forest! It is said that the wise seers of Ankal Aasha use this tea to enhance their meditations!
SNIFF

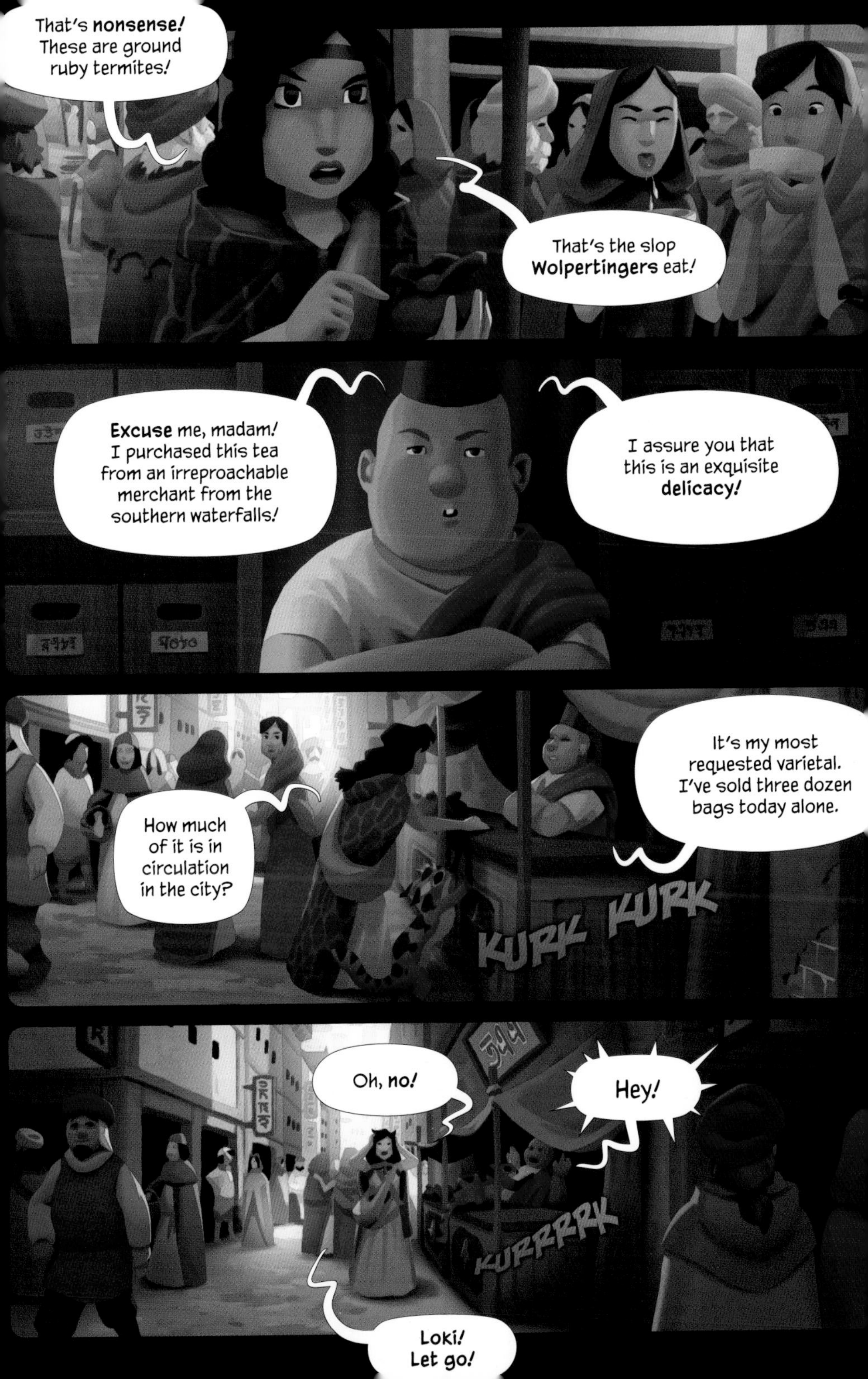
That's **nonsense!** These are ground ruby termites!
That's the slop **Wolpertingers** eat!
Excuse me, madam! I purchased this tea from an irreproachable merchant from the southern waterfalls!
I assure you that this is an exquisite **delicacy!**
How much of it is in circulation in the city?
It's my most requested varietal. I've sold three dozen bags today alone.
KURK KURK
Oh, **no!**
Hey!
KURRRRK
Loki! Let go!

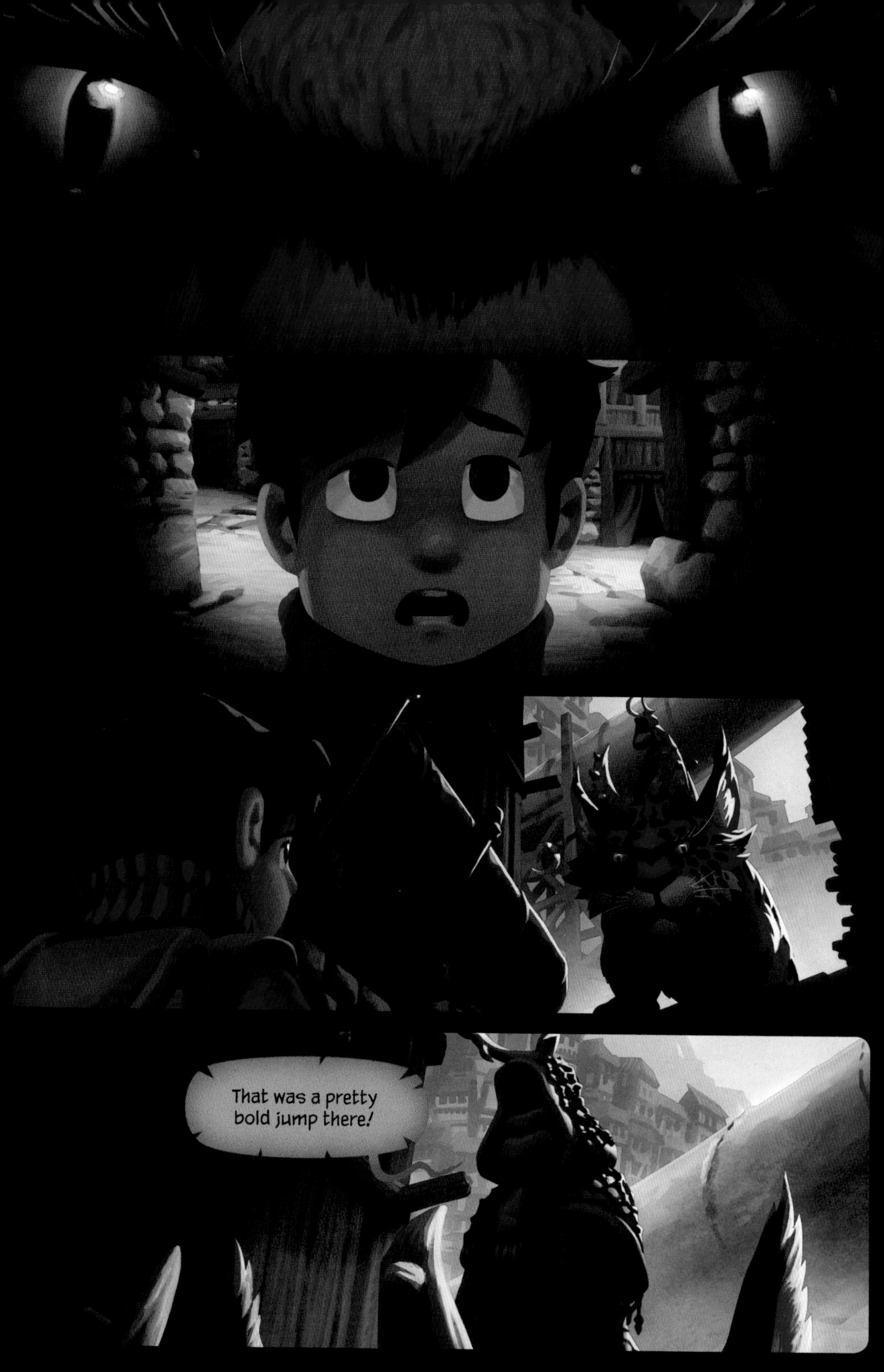
That was a pretty bold jump there!

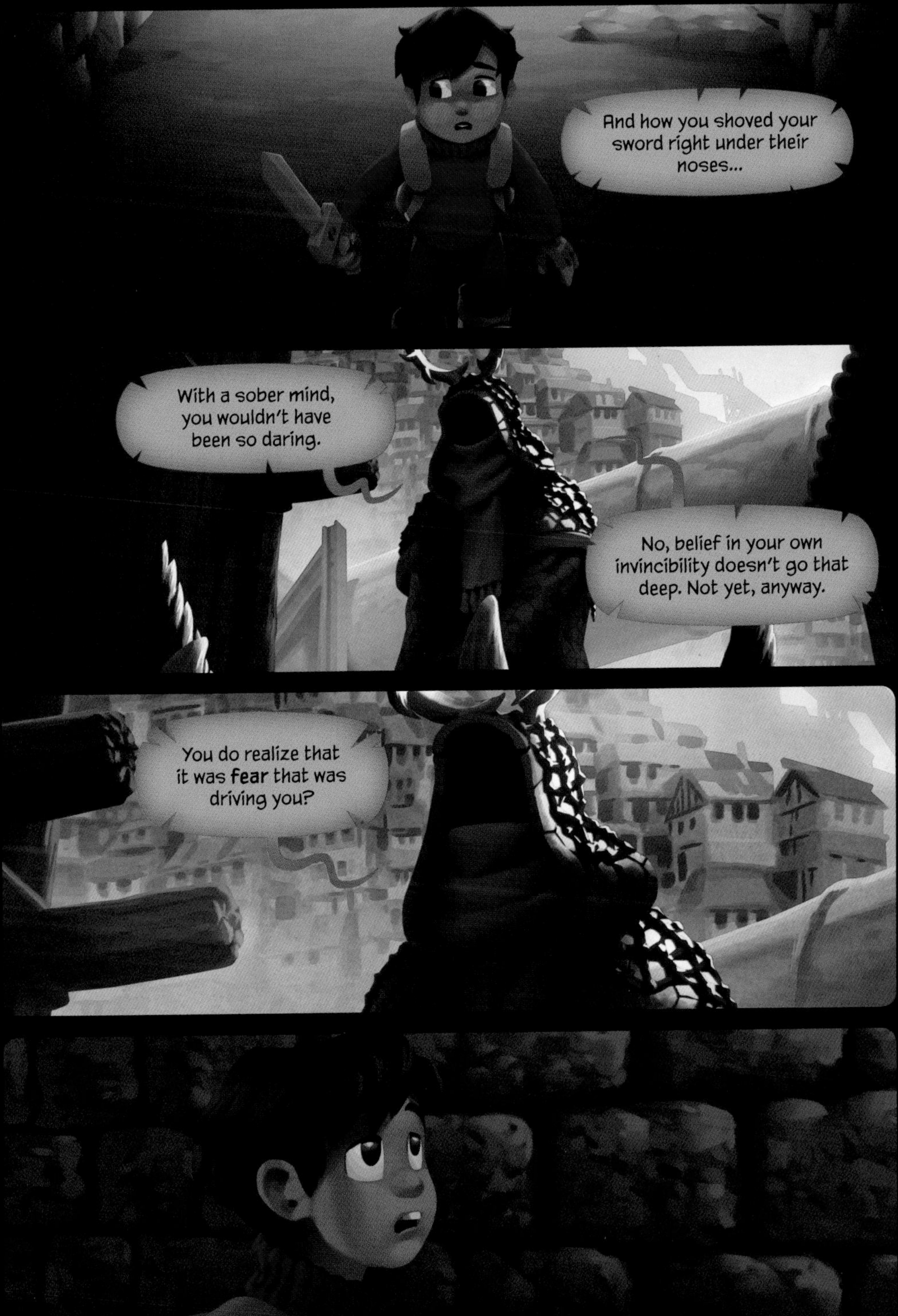
And how you shoved your sword right under their noses...
With a sober mind, you wouldn't have been so daring.
No, belief in your own invincibility doesn't go that deep. Not yet, anyway.
You do realize that it was **fear** that was driving you?

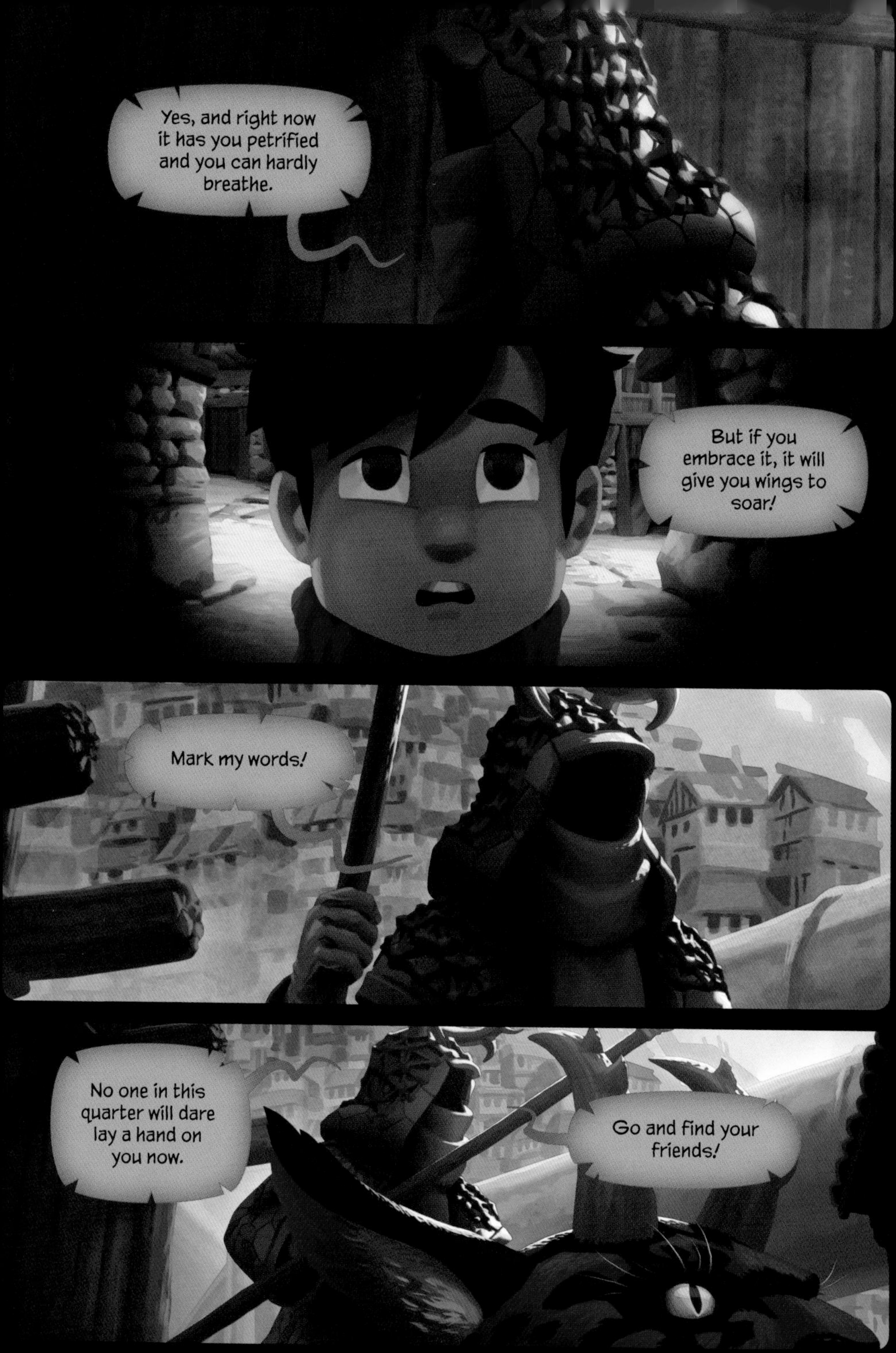
Yes, and right now it has you petrified and you can hardly breathe.
But if you embrace it, it will give you wings to soar!
Mark my words!
No one in this quarter will dare lay a hand on you now.
Go and find your friends!

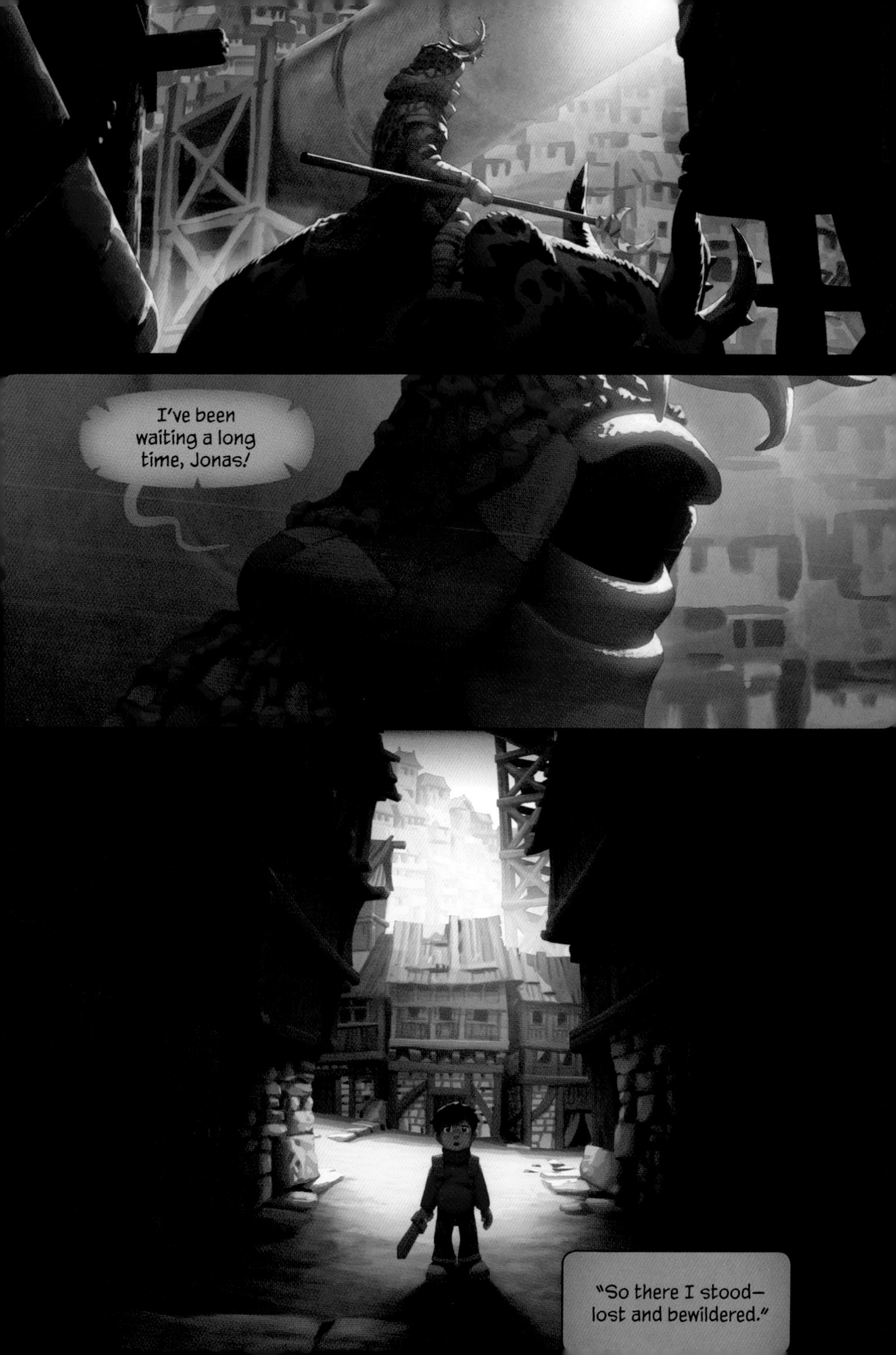
I've been waiting a long time, Jonas!
"So there I stood—lost and bewildered."

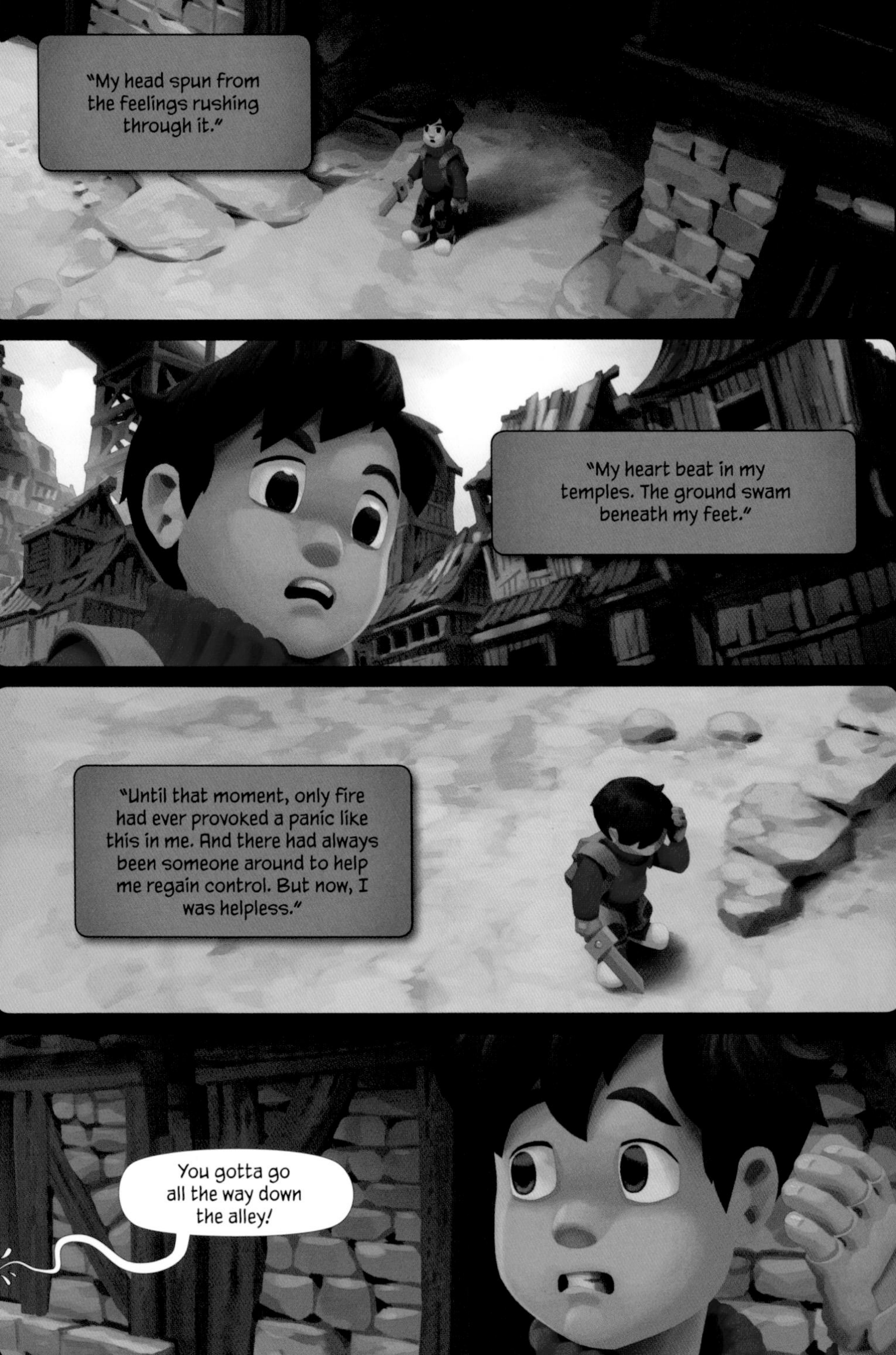
"My head spun from the feelings rushing through it."
"My heart beat in my temples. The ground swam beneath my feet."
"Until that moment, only fire had ever provoked a panic like this in me. And there had always been someone around to help me regain control. But now, I was helpless."
You gotta go all the way down the alley!

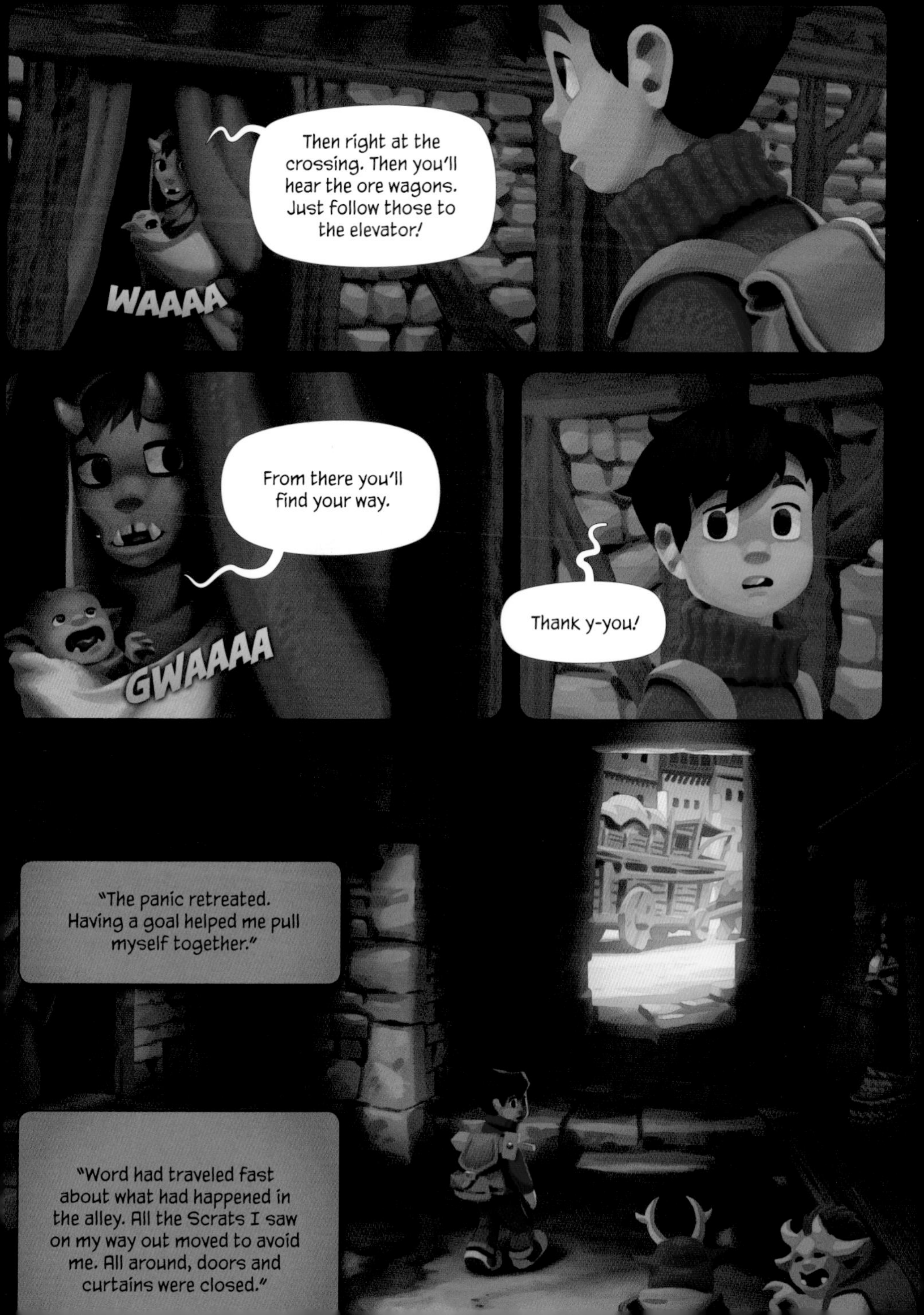
Then right at the crossing. Then you'll hear the ore wagons. Just follow those to the elevator!
WAAAA
From there you'll find your way.
GWAAAA
Thank y-you!
"The panic retreated. Having a goal helped me pull myself together."
"Word had traveled fast about what had happened in the alley. All the Scrats I saw on my way out moved to avoid me. All around, doors and curtains were closed."

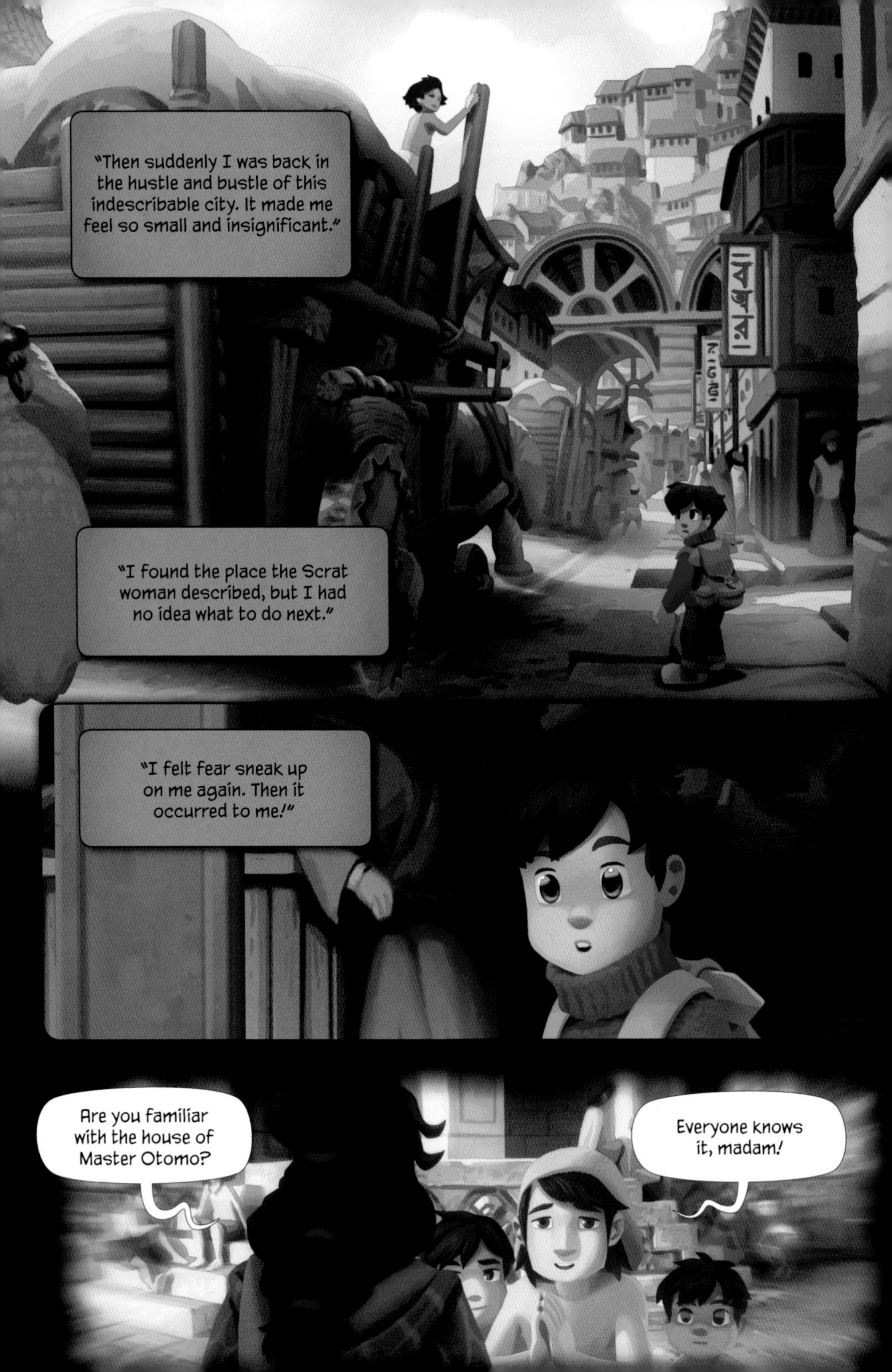
"Then suddenly I was back in the hustle and bustle of this indescribable city. It made me feel so small and insignificant."
"I found the place the Scrat woman described, but I had no idea what to do next."
"I felt fear sneak up on me again. Then it occurred to me!"
Are you familiar with the house of Master Otomo?
Everyone knows it, madam!

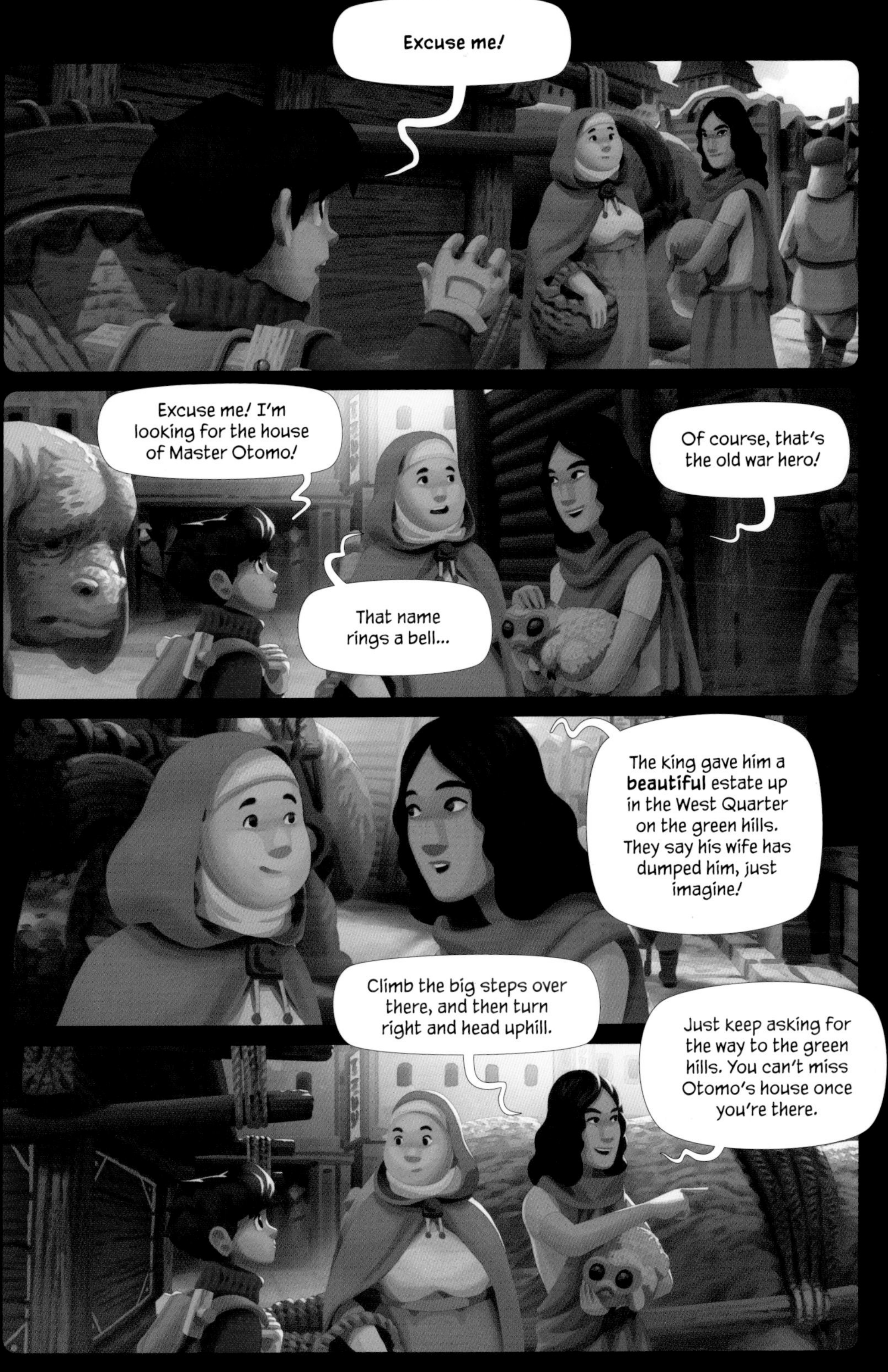
Excuse me!
Excuse me! I'm looking for the house of Master Otomo!
That name rings a bell...
Of course, that's the old war hero!
The king gave him a **beautiful** estate up in the West Quarter on the green hills. They say his wife has dumped him, just imagine!
Climb the big steps over there, and then turn right and head uphill.
Just keep asking for the way to the green hills. You can't miss Otomo's house once you're there.

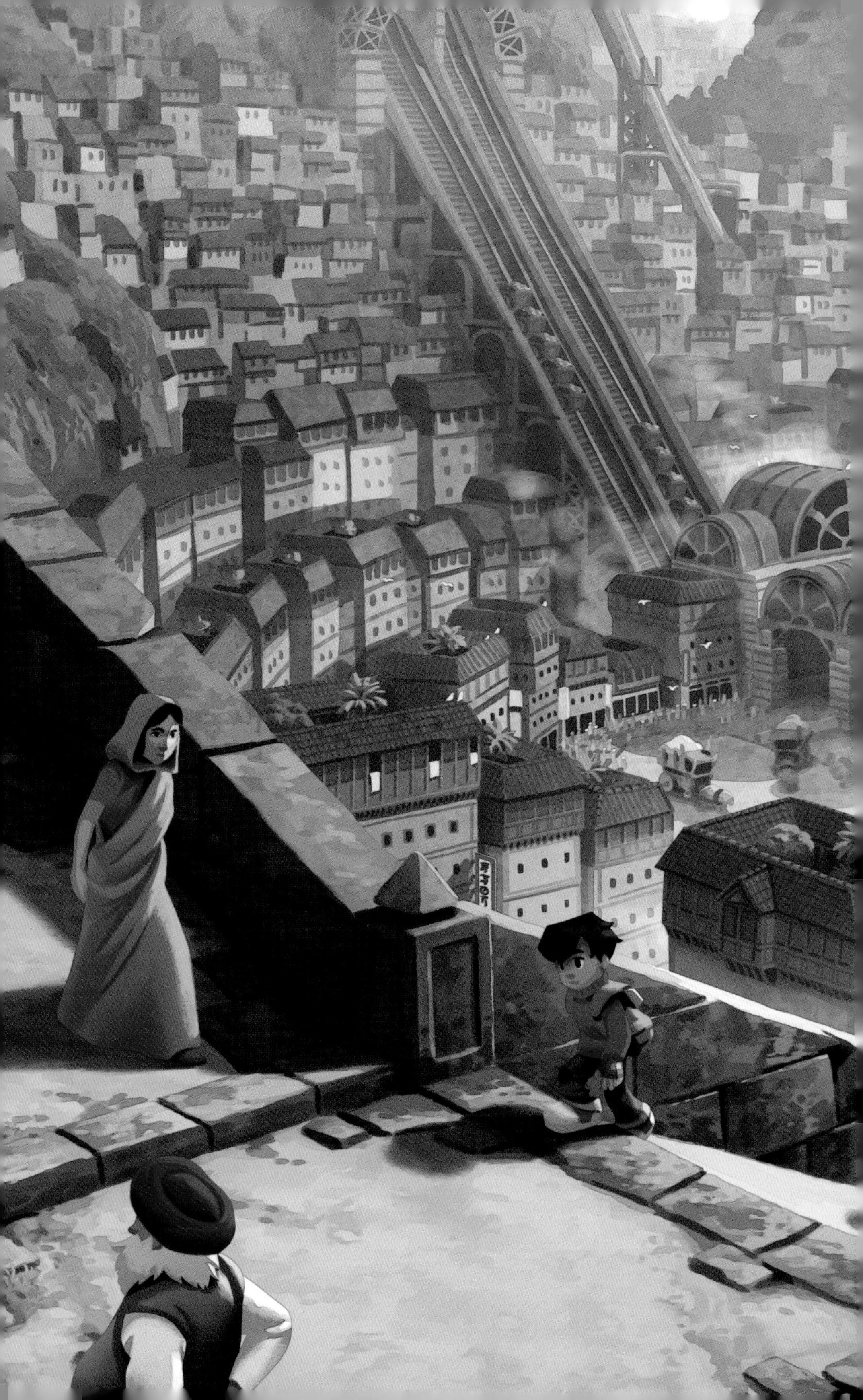

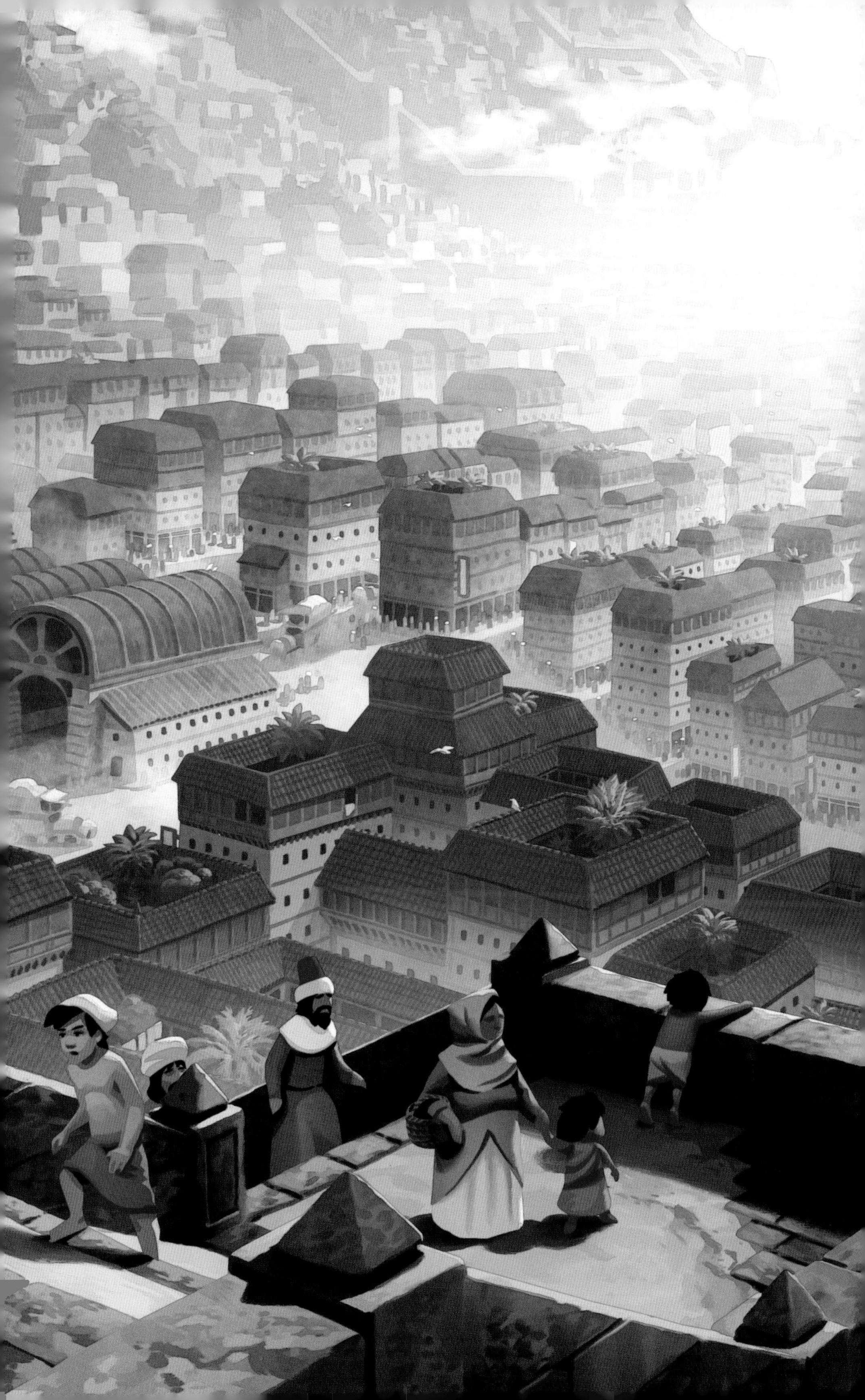

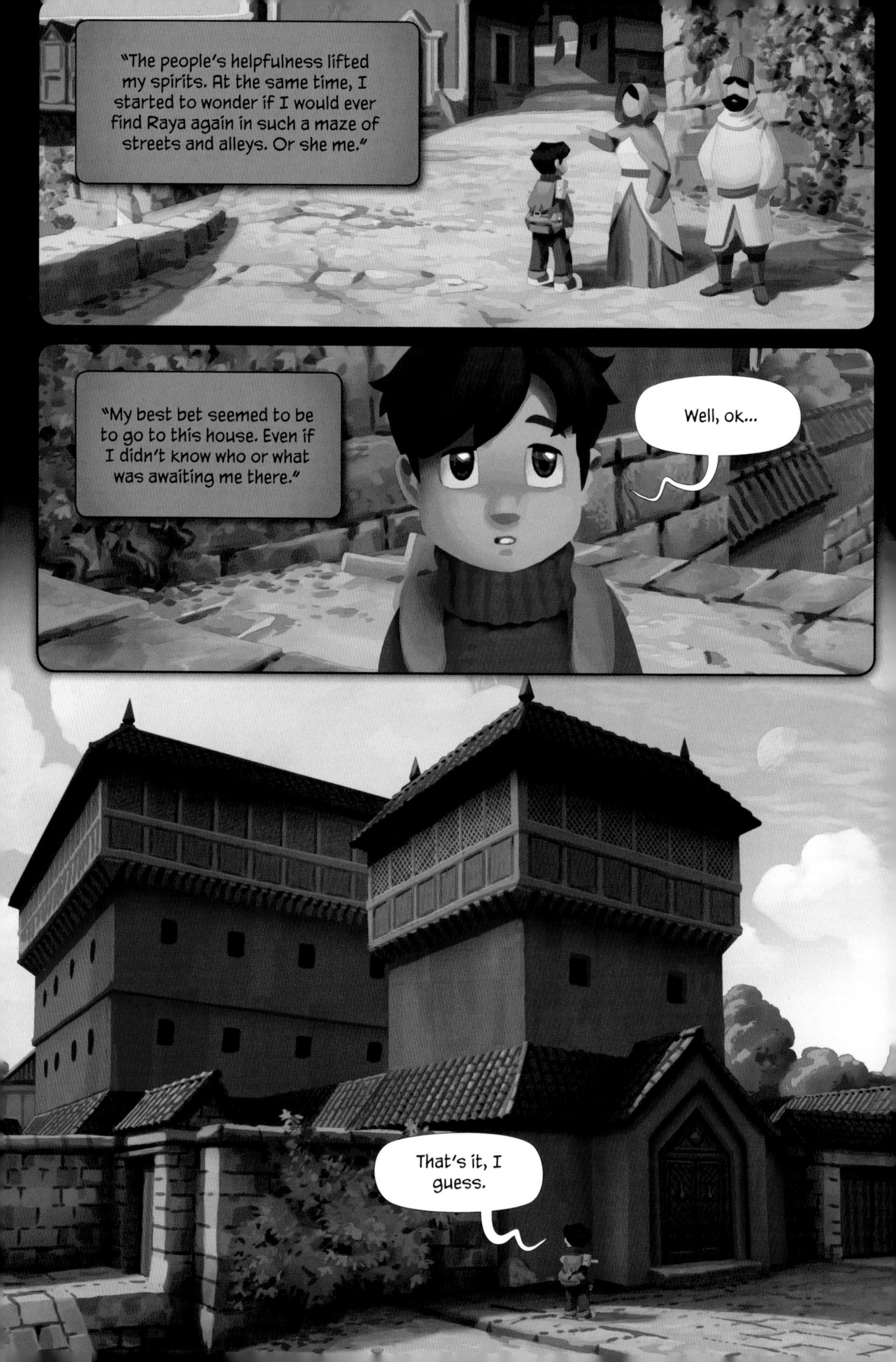
"The people's helpfulness lifted my spirits. At the same time, I started to wonder if I would ever find Raya again in such a maze of streets and alleys. Or she me."
"My best bet seemed to be to go to this house. Even if I didn't know who or what was awaiting me there."
Well, ok...
That's it, I guess.

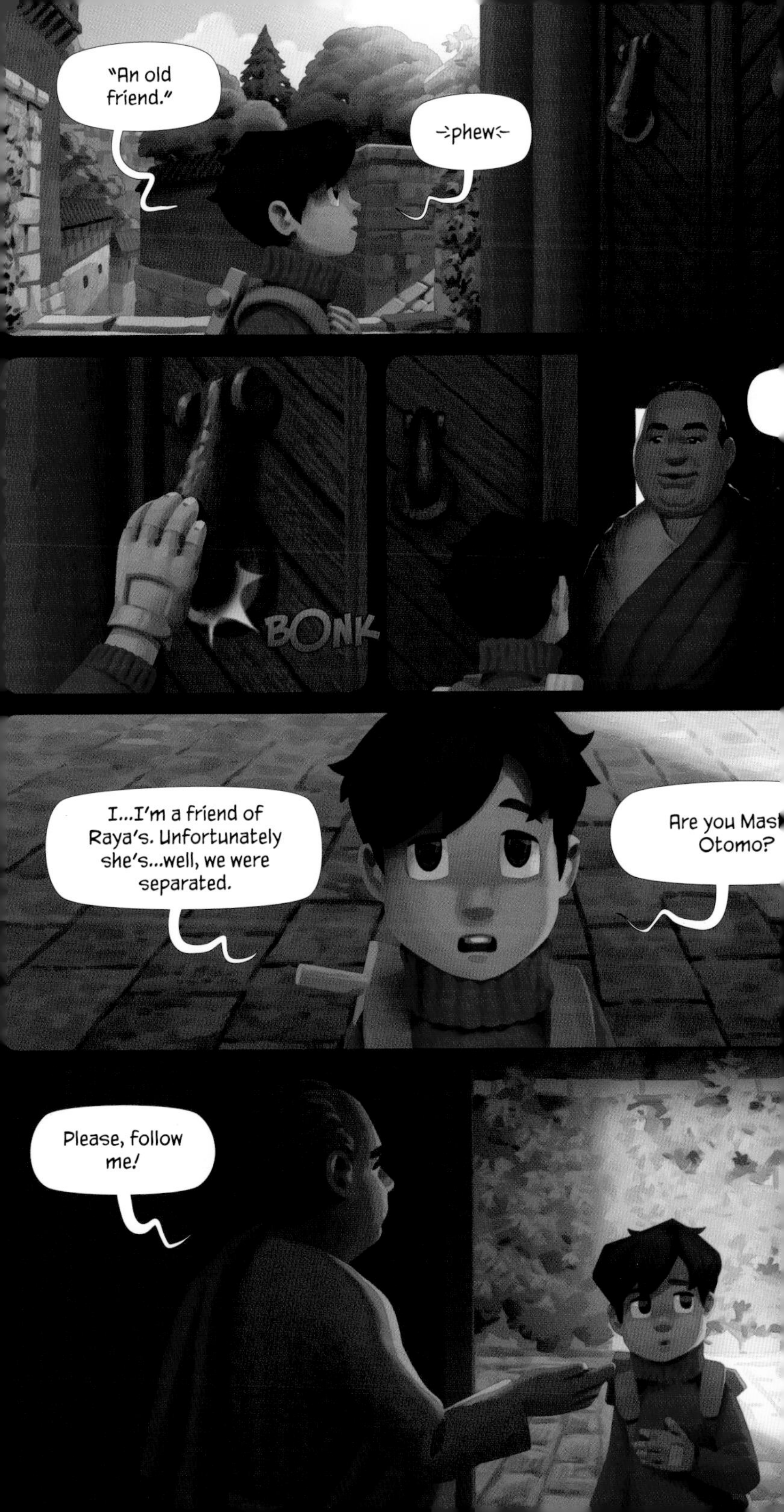
"An old friend."
phew
BONK
I...I'm a friend of Raya's. Unfortunately she's...well, we were separated.
Are you Mas
Otomo?
Please, follow me!

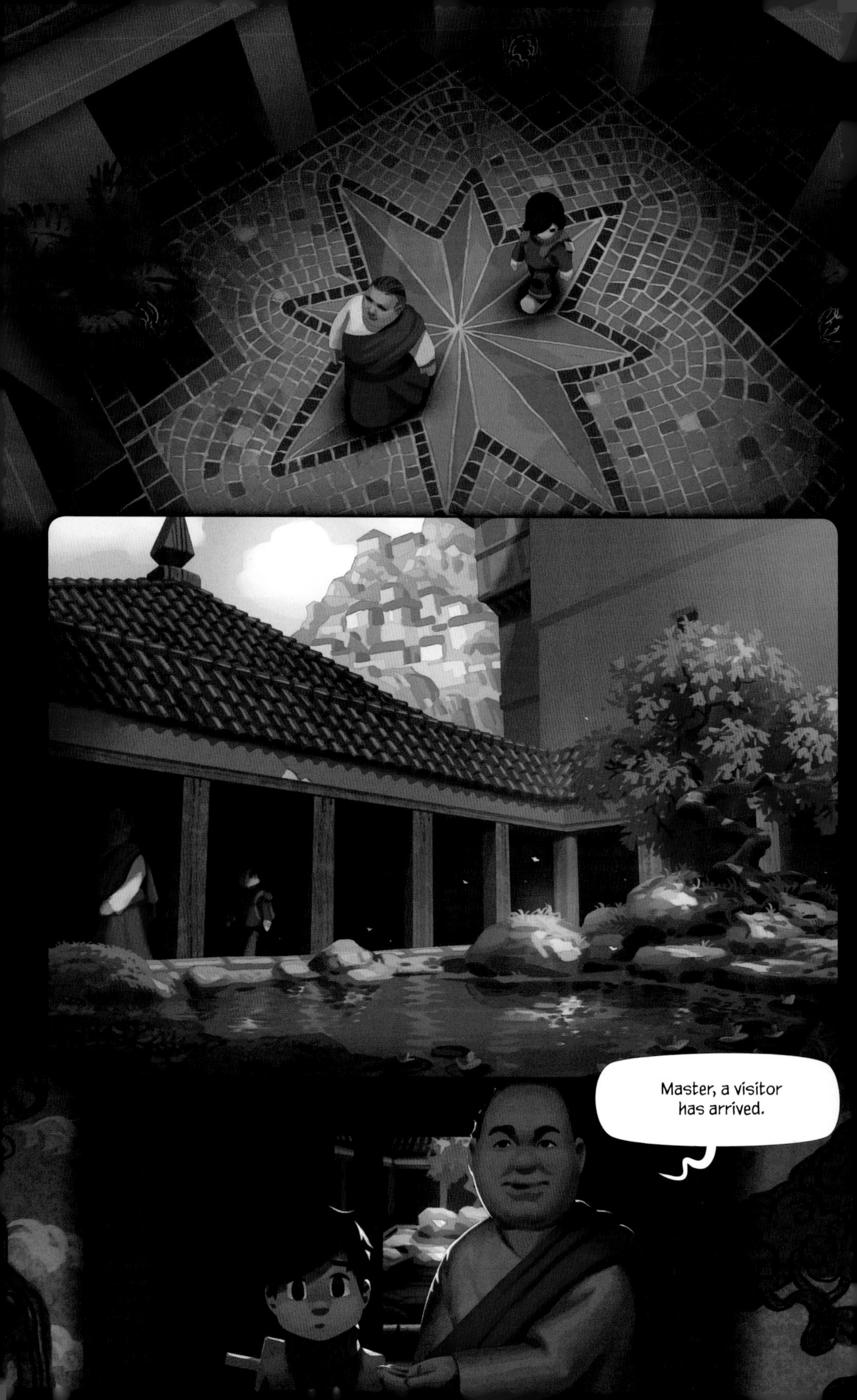
Master, a visitor has arrived.

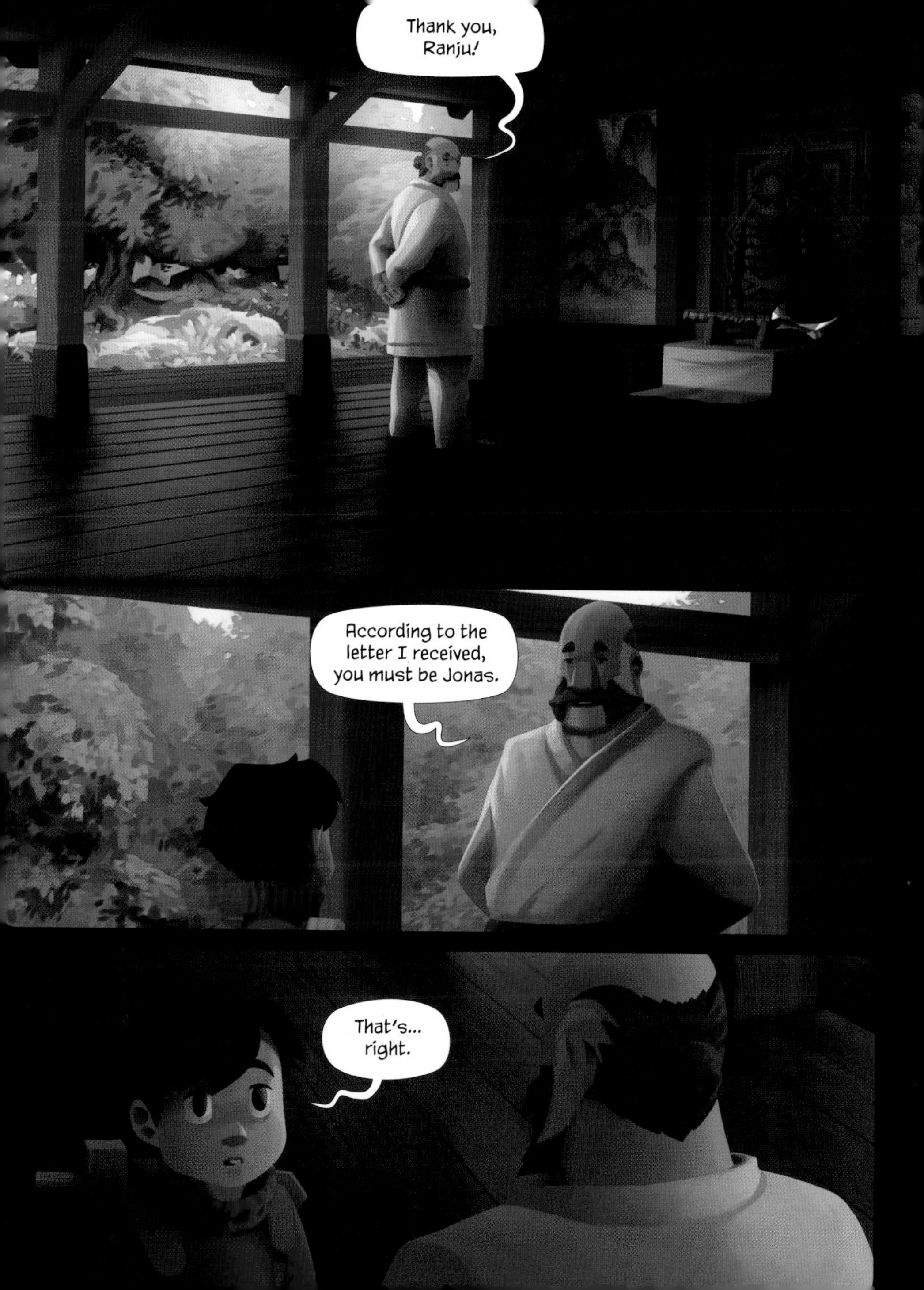
Thank you, Ranju!
According to the letter I received, you must be Jonas.
That's... right.

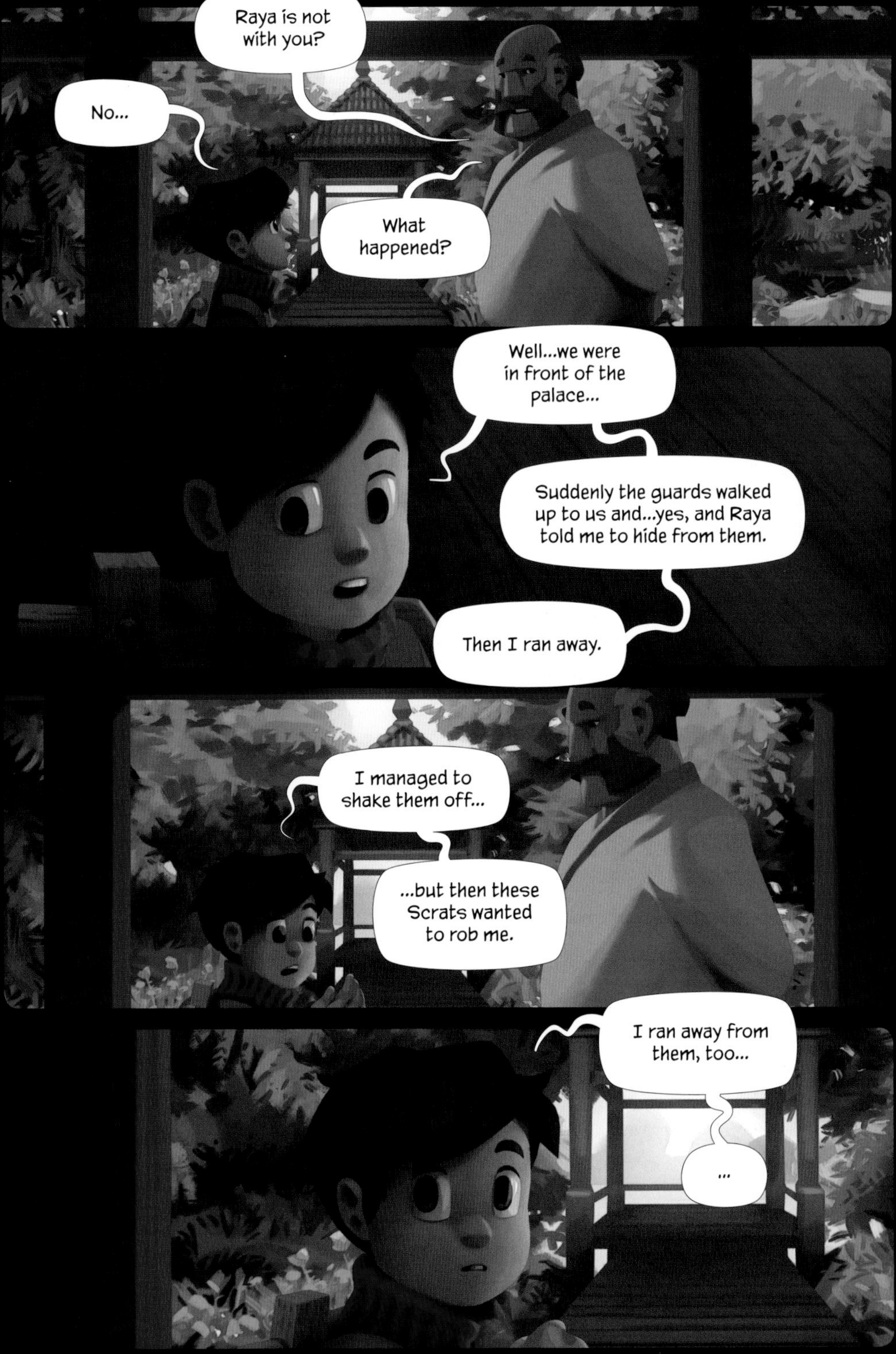
Raya is not with you?
No...
What happened?
Well...we were in front of the palace...
Suddenly the guards walked up to us and...yes, and Raya told me to hide from them.
Then I ran away.
I managed to shake them off...
...but then these Scrats wanted to rob me.
I ran away from them, too...
...

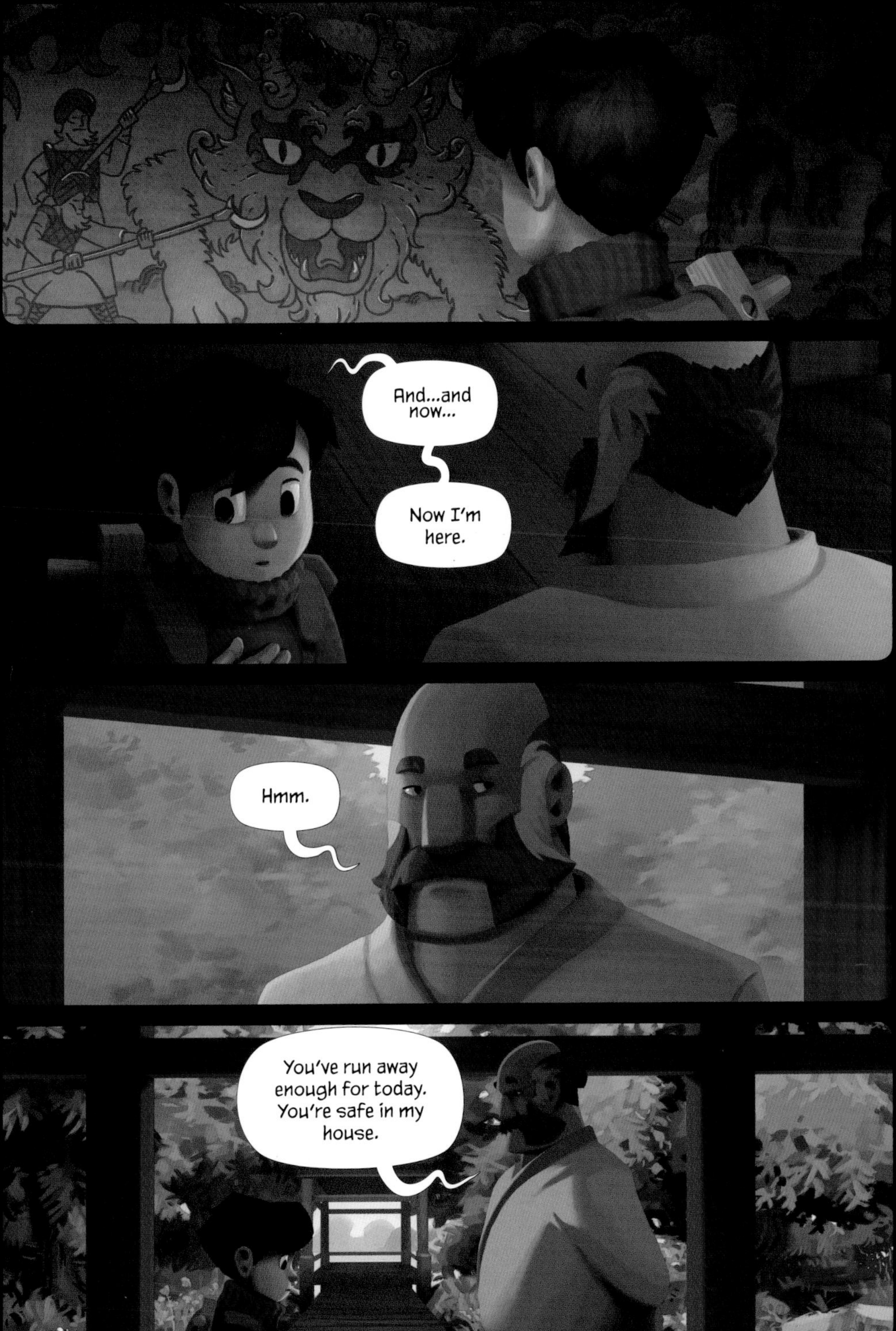
And...and now...
Now I'm here.
Hmm.
You've run away enough for today. You're safe in my house.

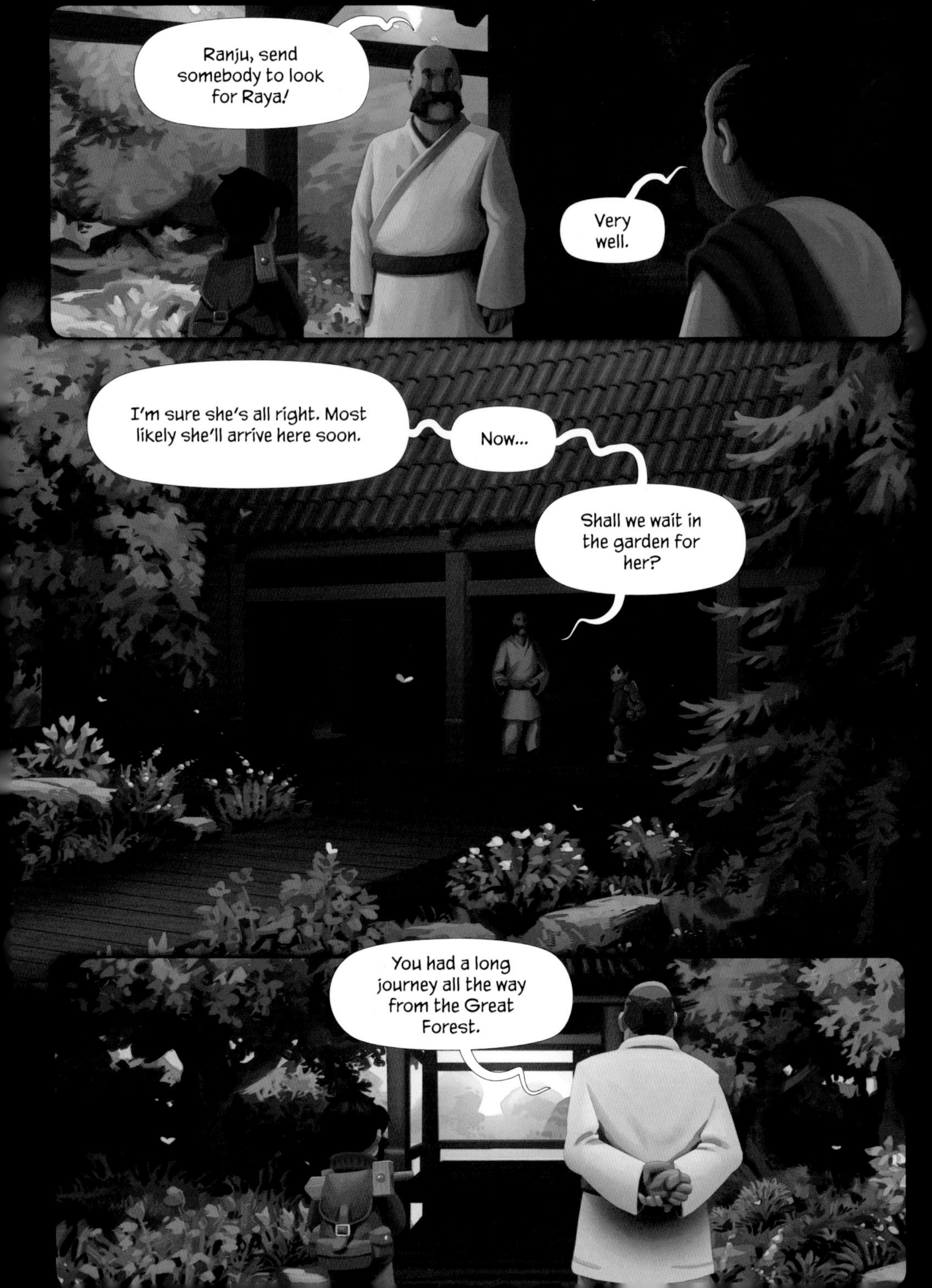
Ranju, send somebody to look for Raya!
Very well.
I'm sure she's all right. Most likely she'll arrive here soon.
Now...
Shall we wait in the garden for her?
You had a long journey all the way from the Great Forest.

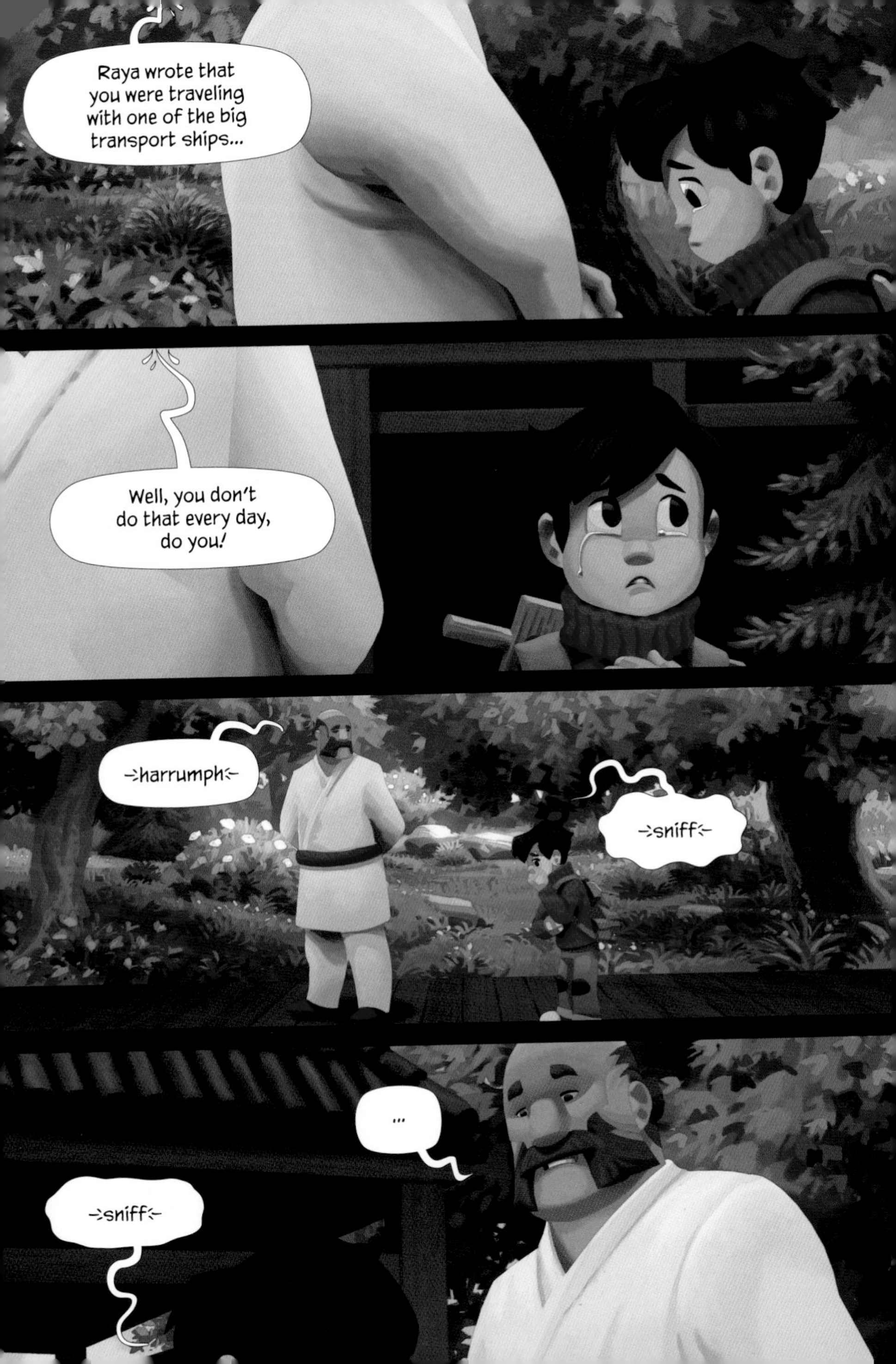
Raya wrote that you were traveling with one of the big transport ships...
Well, you don't do that every day, do you!
harrumph
sniff
...
sniff

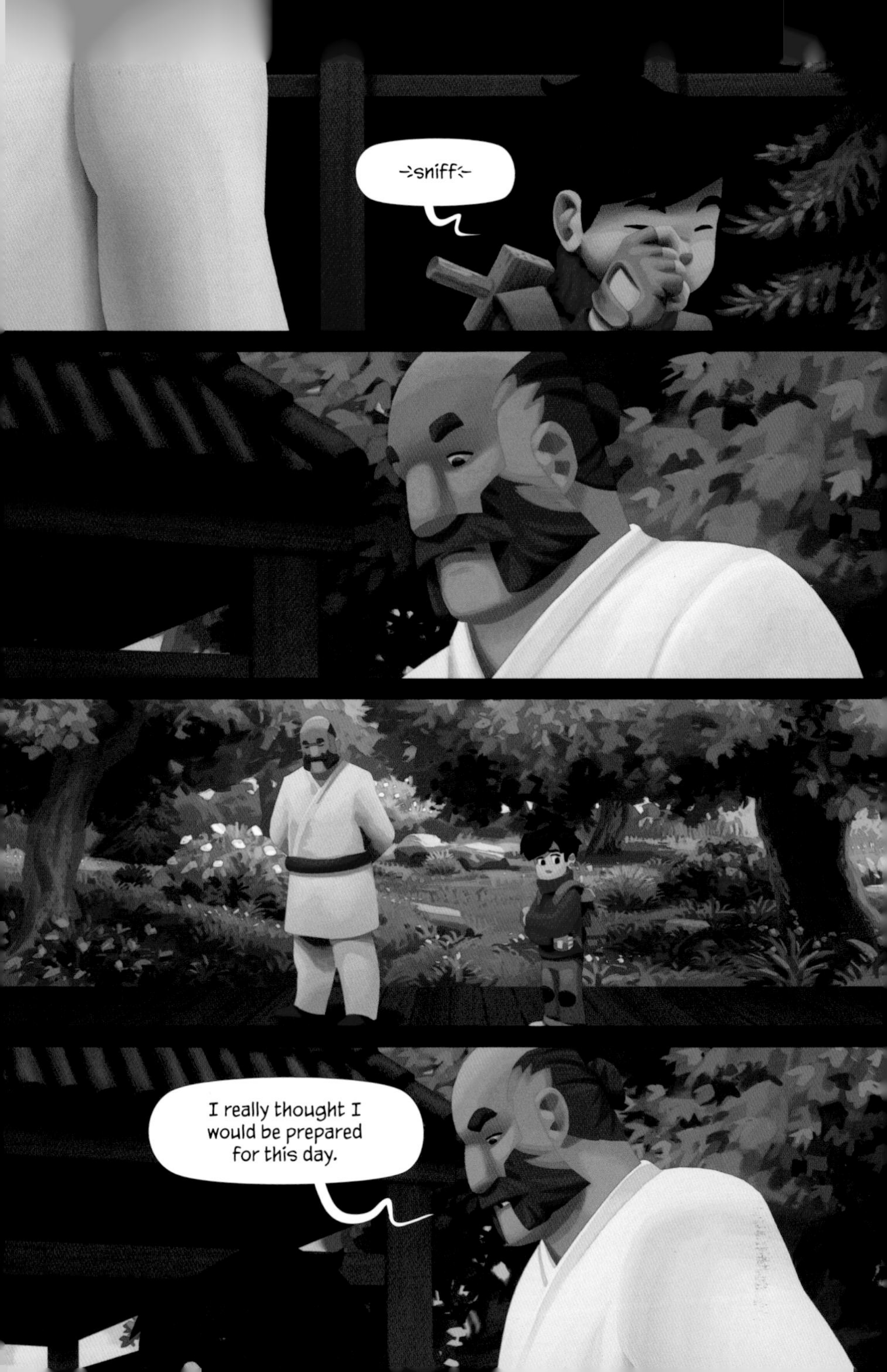
-sniff-
I really thought I would be prepared for this day.

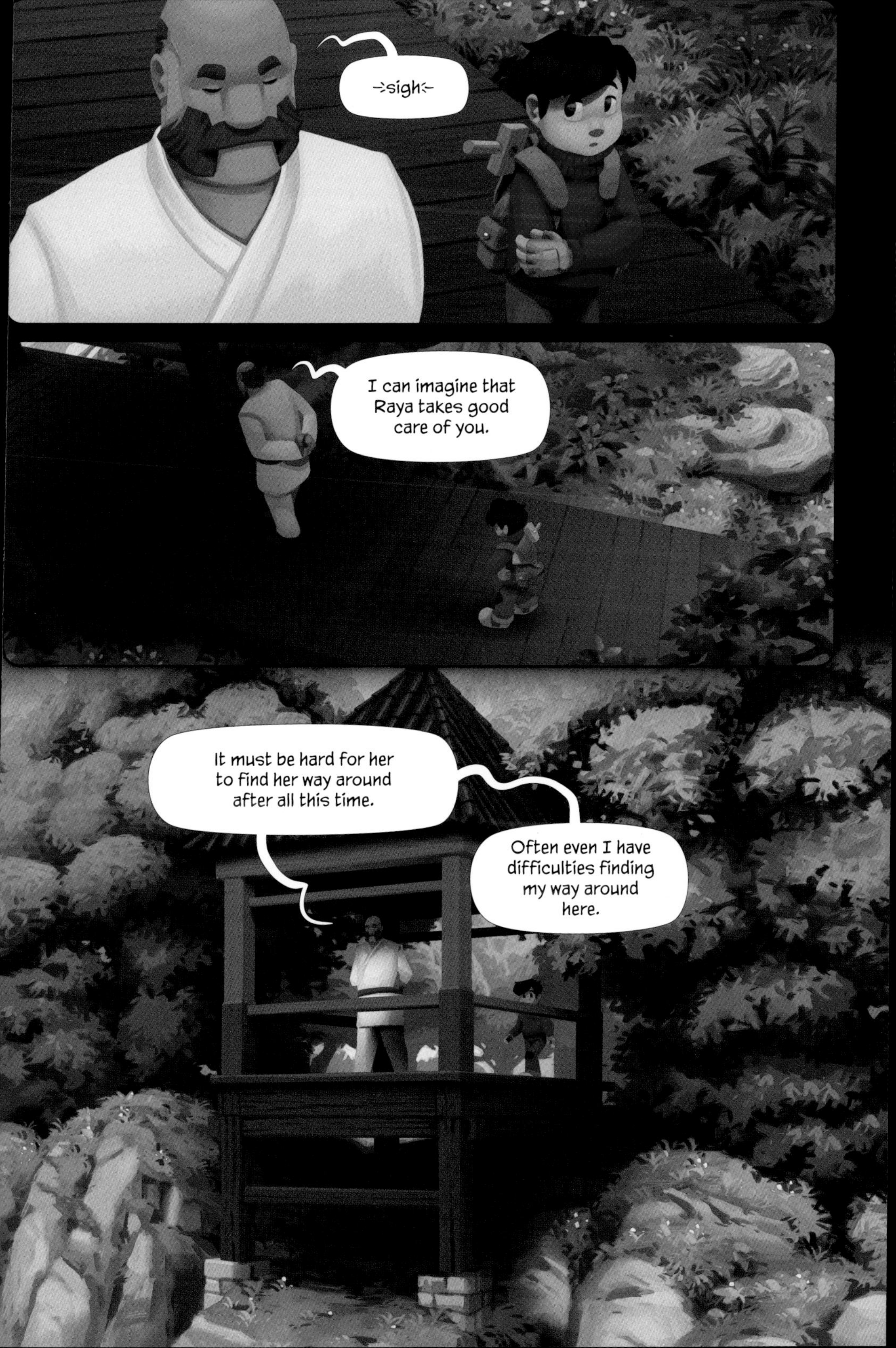
-sigh-
I can imagine that Raya takes good care of you.
It must be hard for her to find her way around after all this time.
Often even I have difficulties finding my way around here.

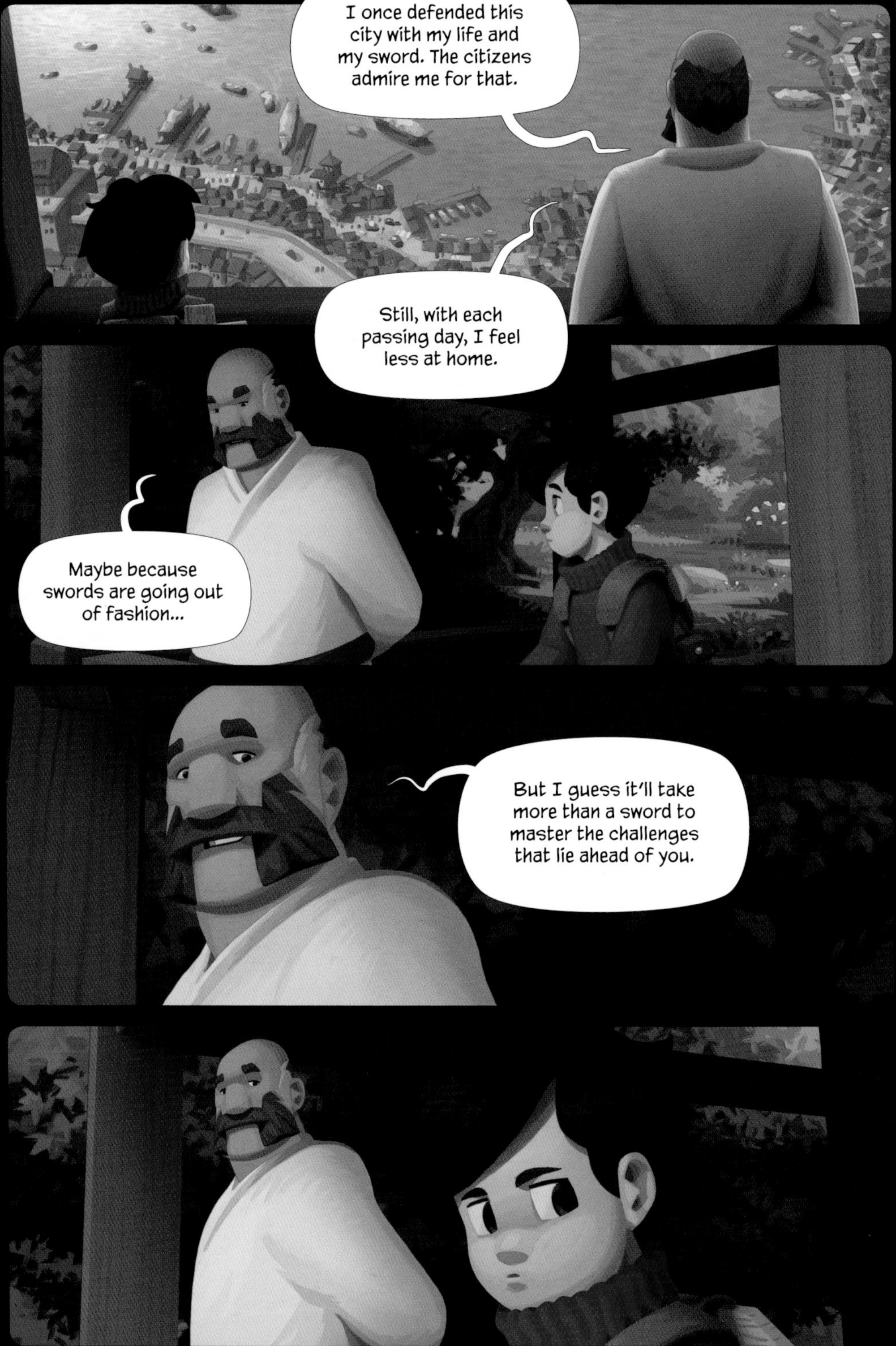
I once defended this city with my life and my sword. The citizens admire me for that.
Still, with each passing day, I feel less at home.
Maybe because swords are going out of fashion...
But I guess it'll take more than a sword to master the challenges that lie ahead of you.

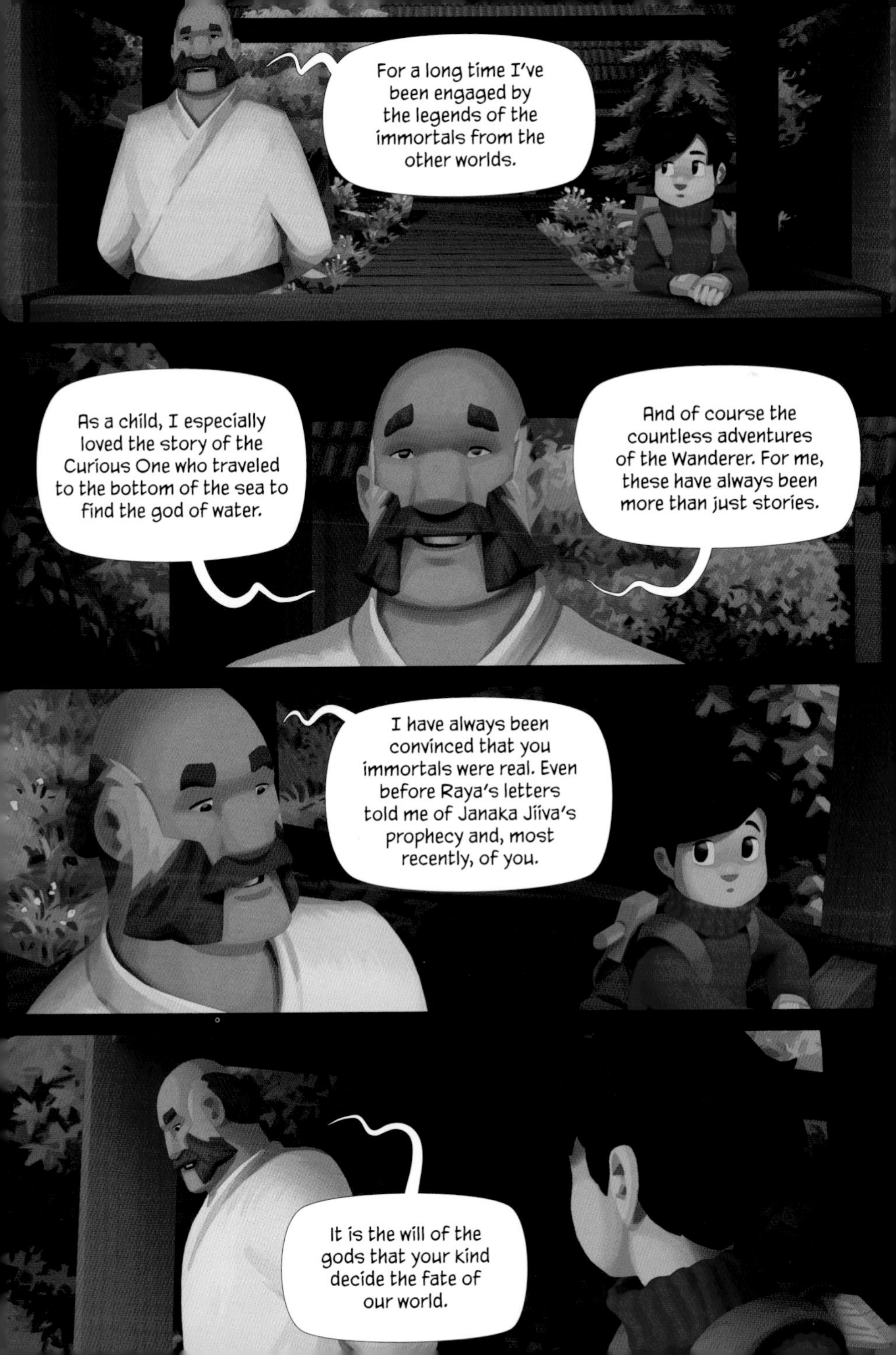
For a long time I've been engaged by the legends of the immortals from the other worlds.
As a child, I especially loved the story of the Curious One who traveled to the bottom of the sea to find the god of water.
And of course the countless adventures of the Wanderer. For me, these have always been more than just stories.
I have always been convinced that you immortals were real. Even before Raya's letters told me of Janaka Jiiva's prophecy and, most recently, of you.
It is the will of the gods that your kind decide the fate of our world.

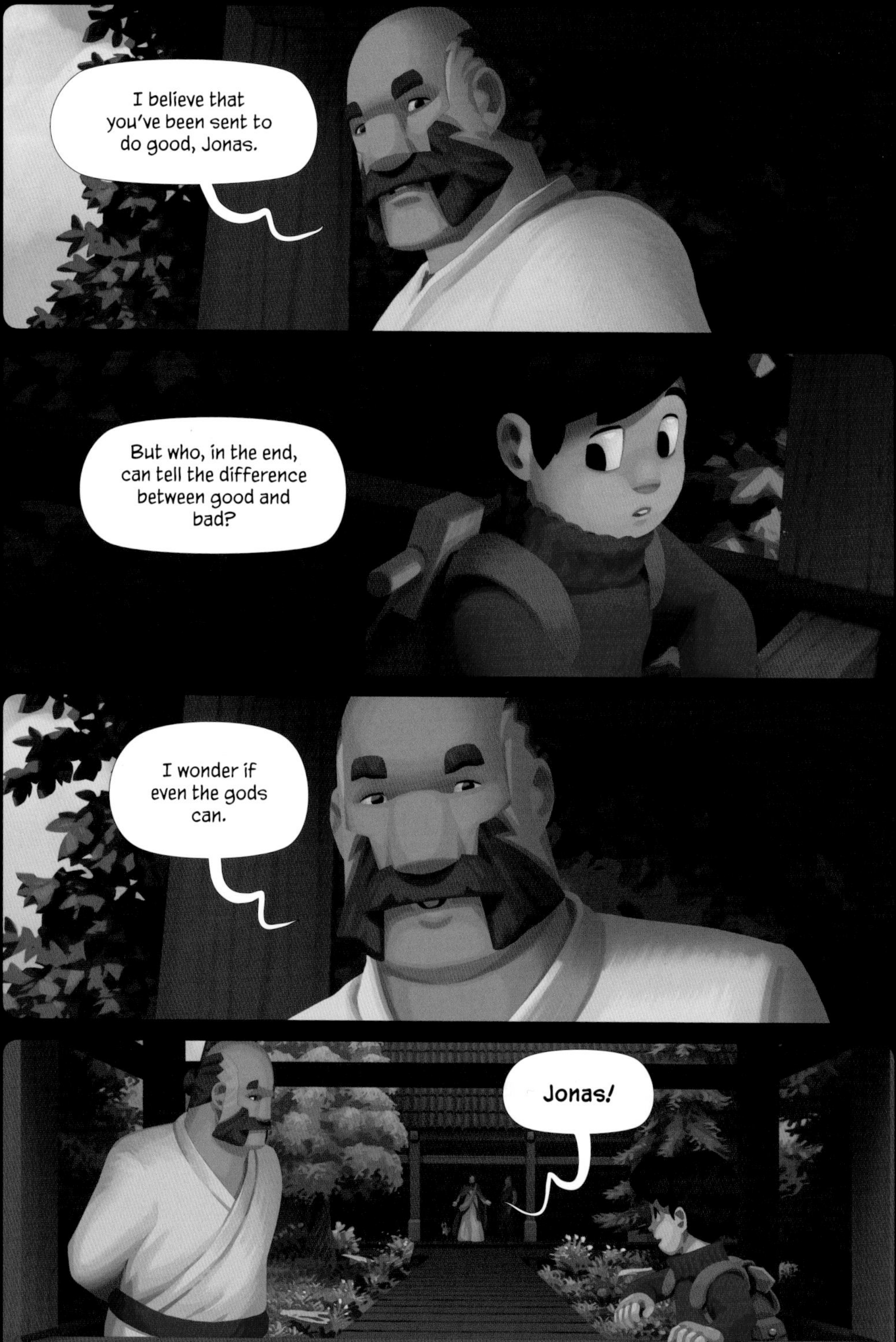
I believe that you've been sent to do good, Jonas.
But who, in the end, can tell the difference between good and bad?
I wonder if even the gods can.
Jonas!

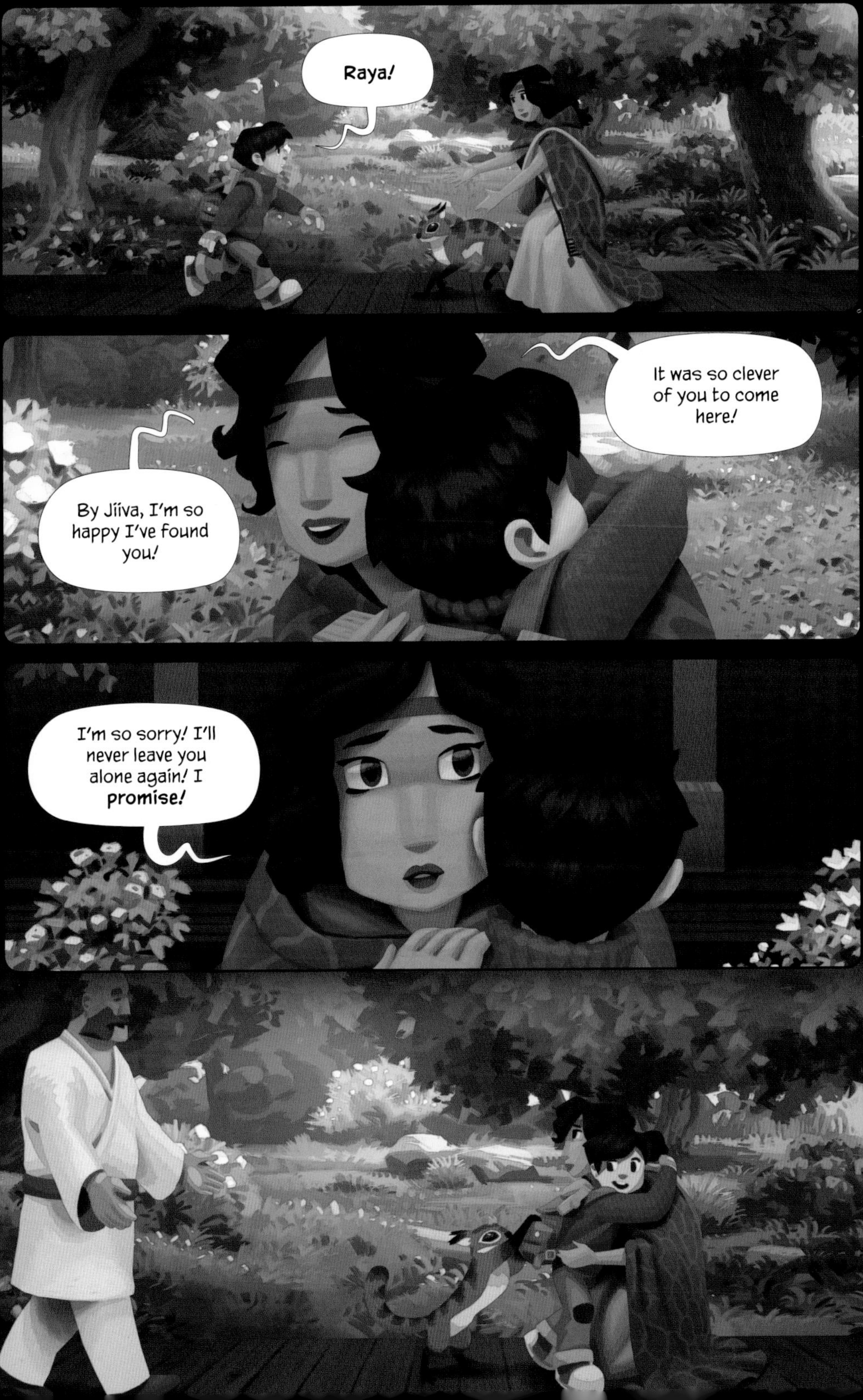
Raya!
It was so clever of you to come here!
By Jiiva, I'm so happy I've found you!
I'm so sorry! I'll never leave you alone again! I **promise!**

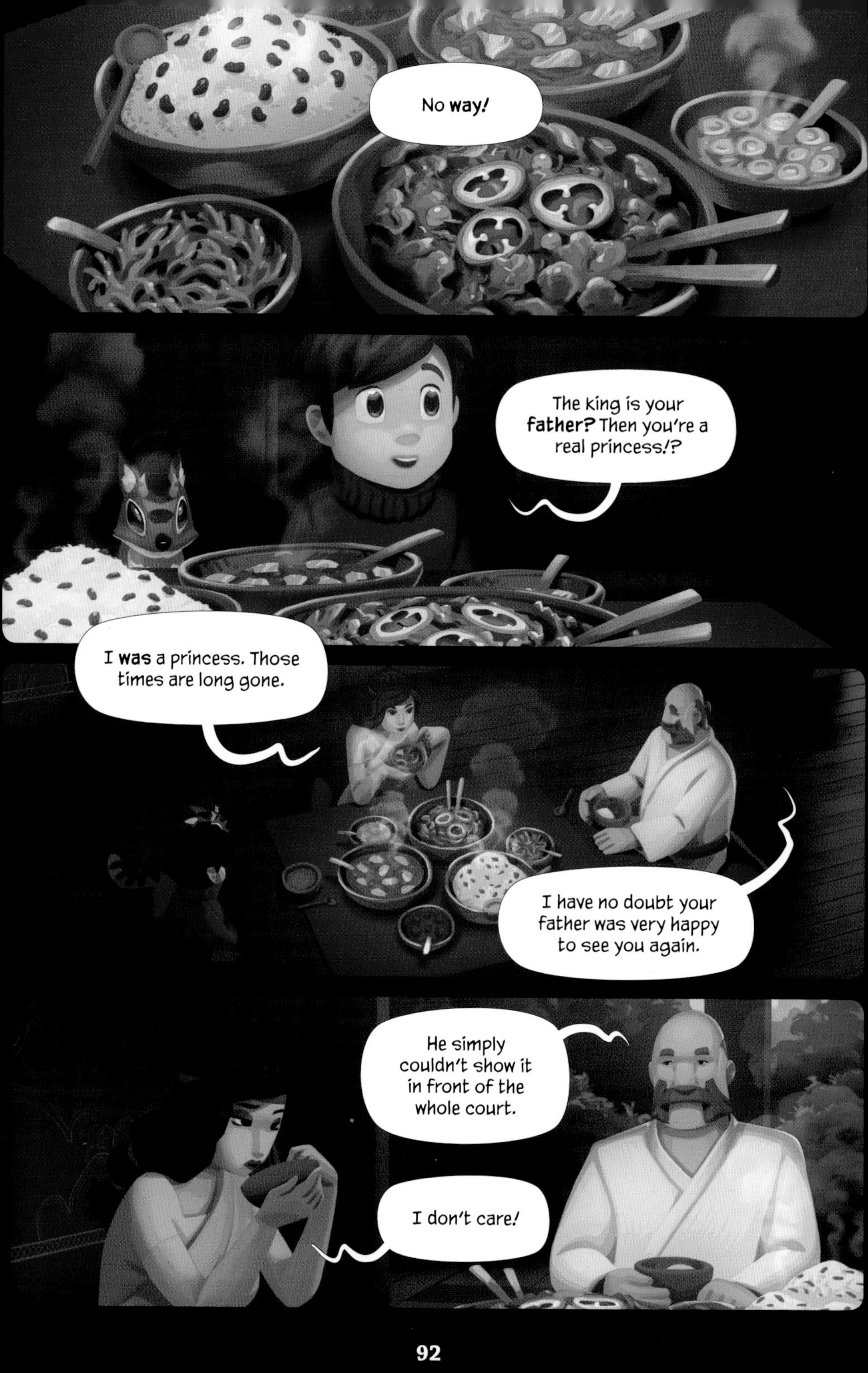
No way!
The king is your father? Then you're a real princess!?
I was a princess. Those times are long gone.
I have no doubt your father was very happy to see you again.
He simply couldn't show it in front of the whole court.
I don't care!

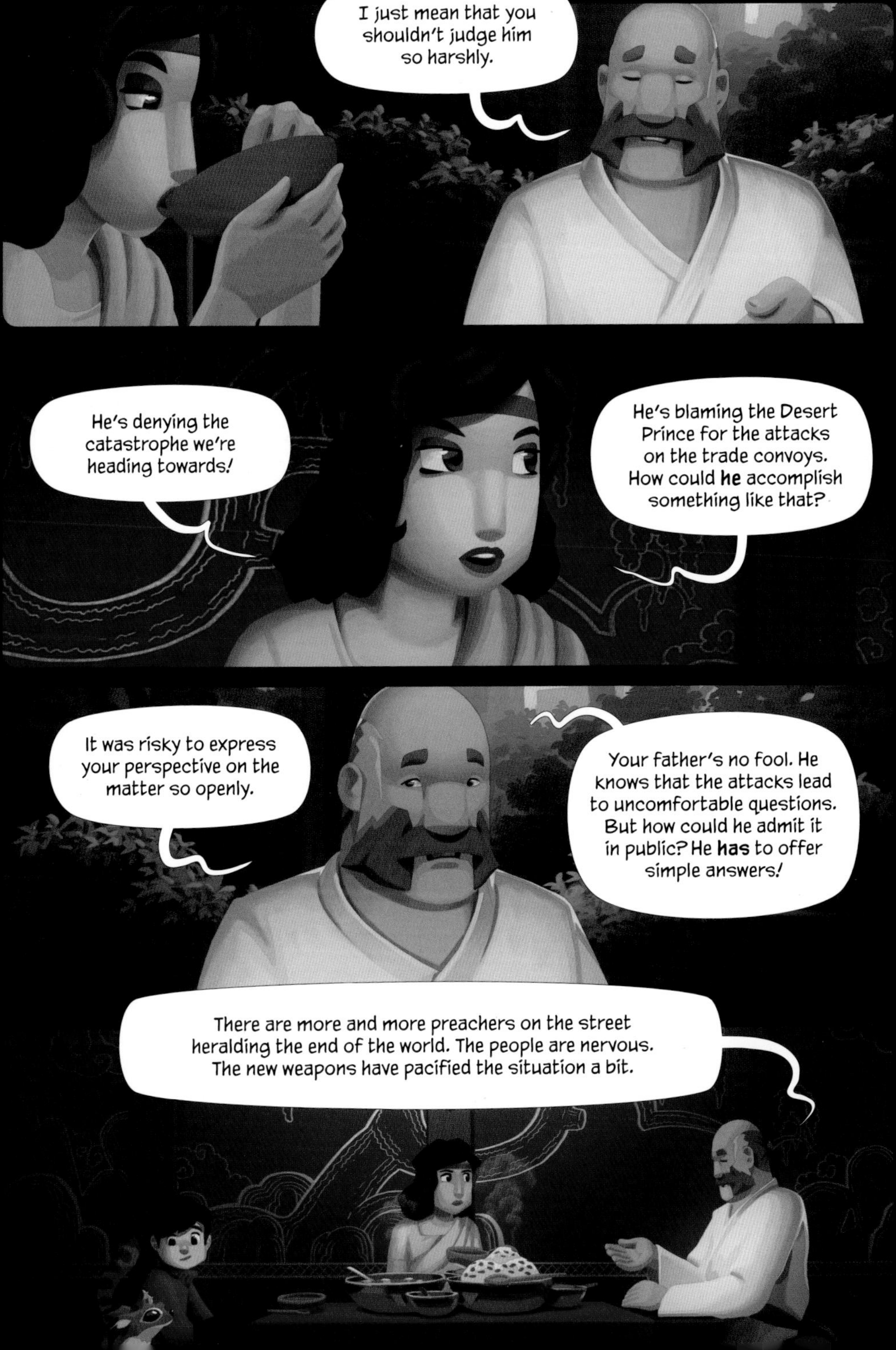

I just mean that you shouldn't judge him so harshly.
He's denying the catastrophe we're heading towards!
He's blaming the Desert Prince for the attacks on the trade convoys. How could **he** accomplish something like that?
It was risky to express your perspective on the matter so openly.
Your father's no fool. He knows that the attacks lead to uncomfortable questions. But how could he admit it in public? He **has** to offer simple answers!
There are more and more preachers on the street heralding the end of the world. The people are nervous. The new weapons have pacified the situation a bit.

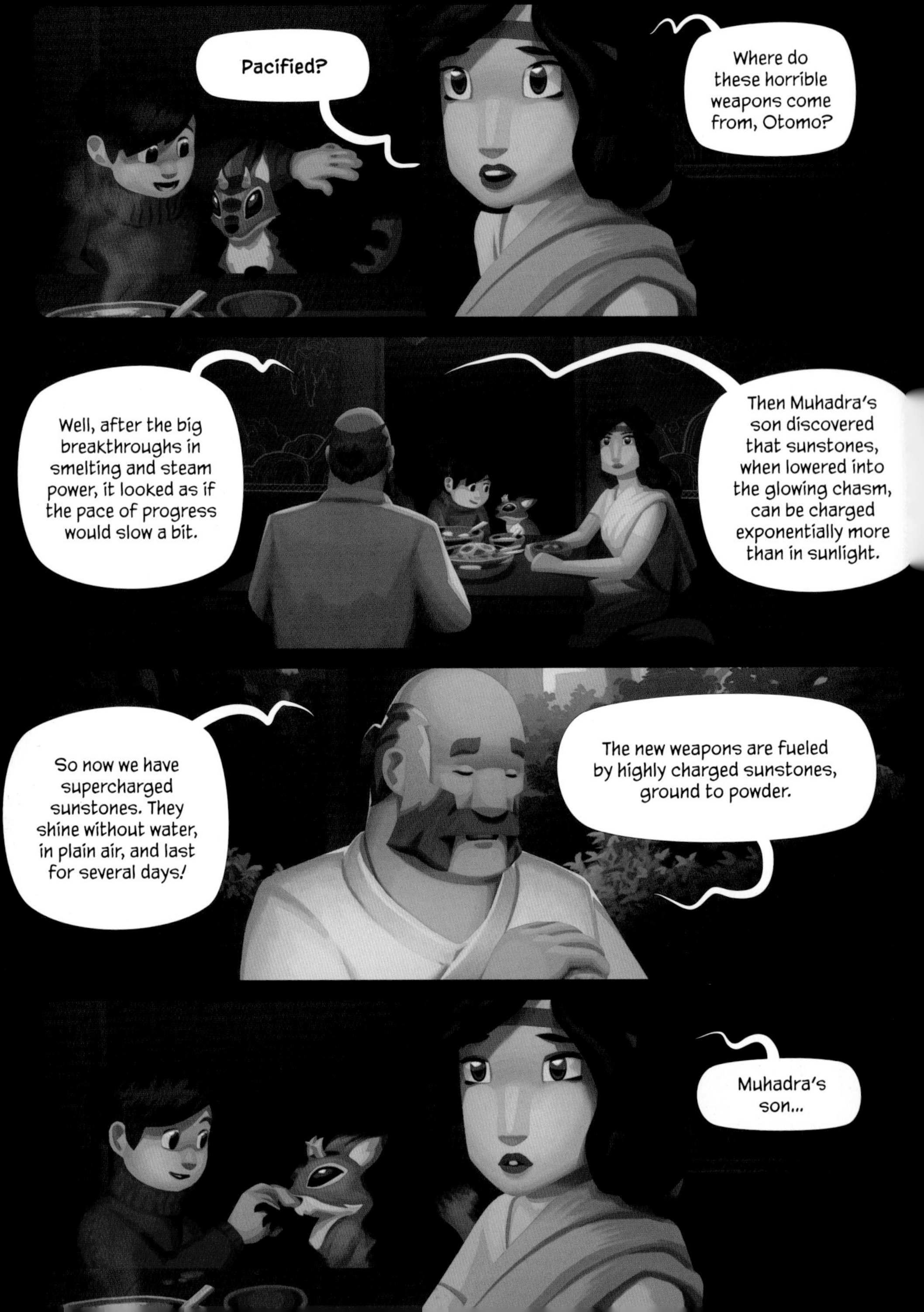
Pacified?
Where do these horrible weapons come from, Otomo?
Well, after the big breakthroughs in smelting and steam power, it looked as if the pace of progress would slow a bit.
Then Muhadra's son discovered that sunstones, when lowered into the glowing chasm, can be charged exponentially more than in sunlight.
So now we have supercharged sunstones. They shine without water, in plain air, and last for several days!
The new weapons are fueled by highly charged sunstones, ground to powder.
Muhadra's son...

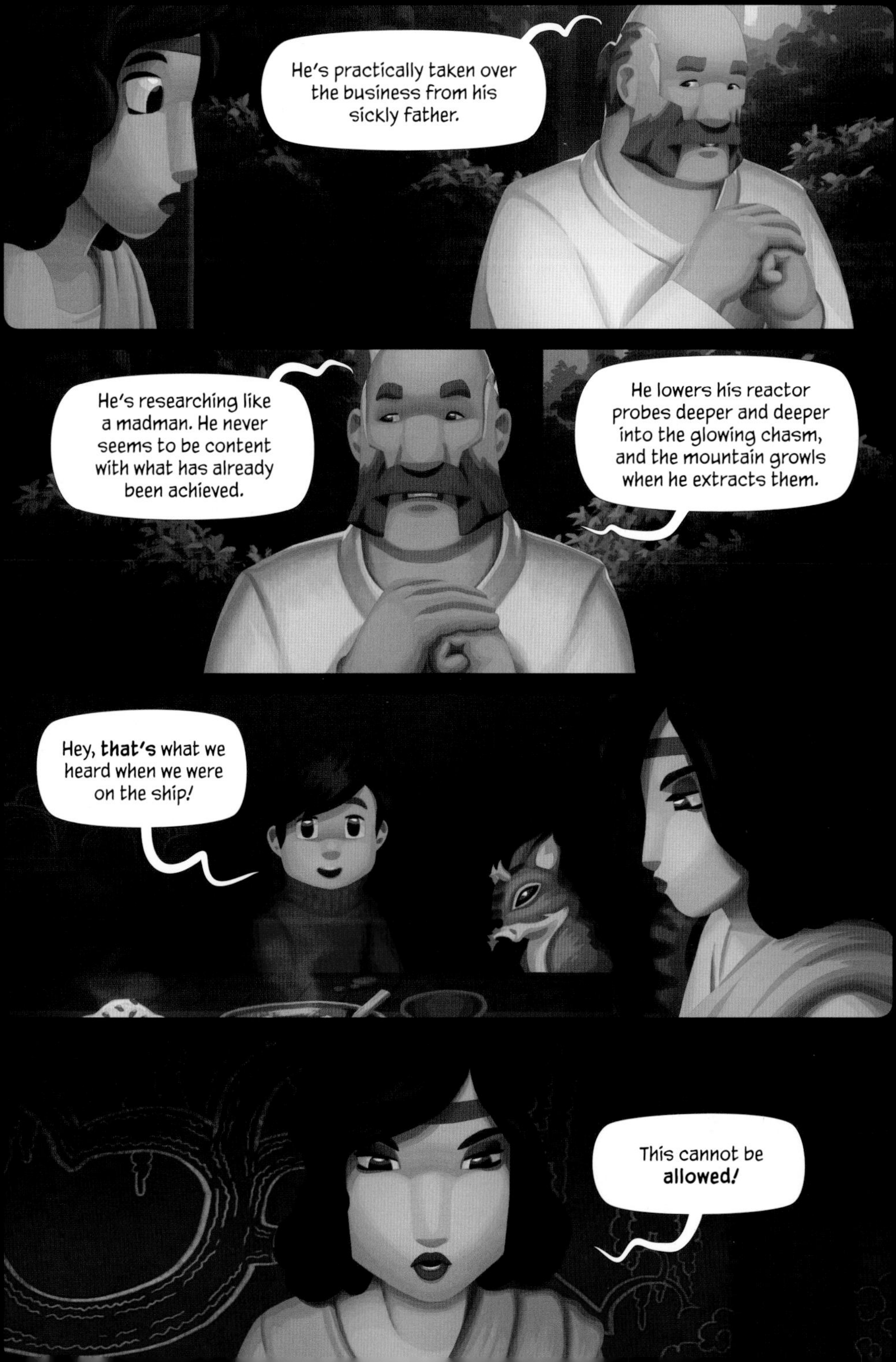
He's practically taken over the business from his sickly father.
He's researching like a madman. He never seems to be content with what has already been achieved.
He lowers his reactor probes deeper and deeper into the glowing chasm, and the mountain growls when he extracts them.
Hey, **that's** what we heard when we were on the ship!
This cannot be **allowed!**

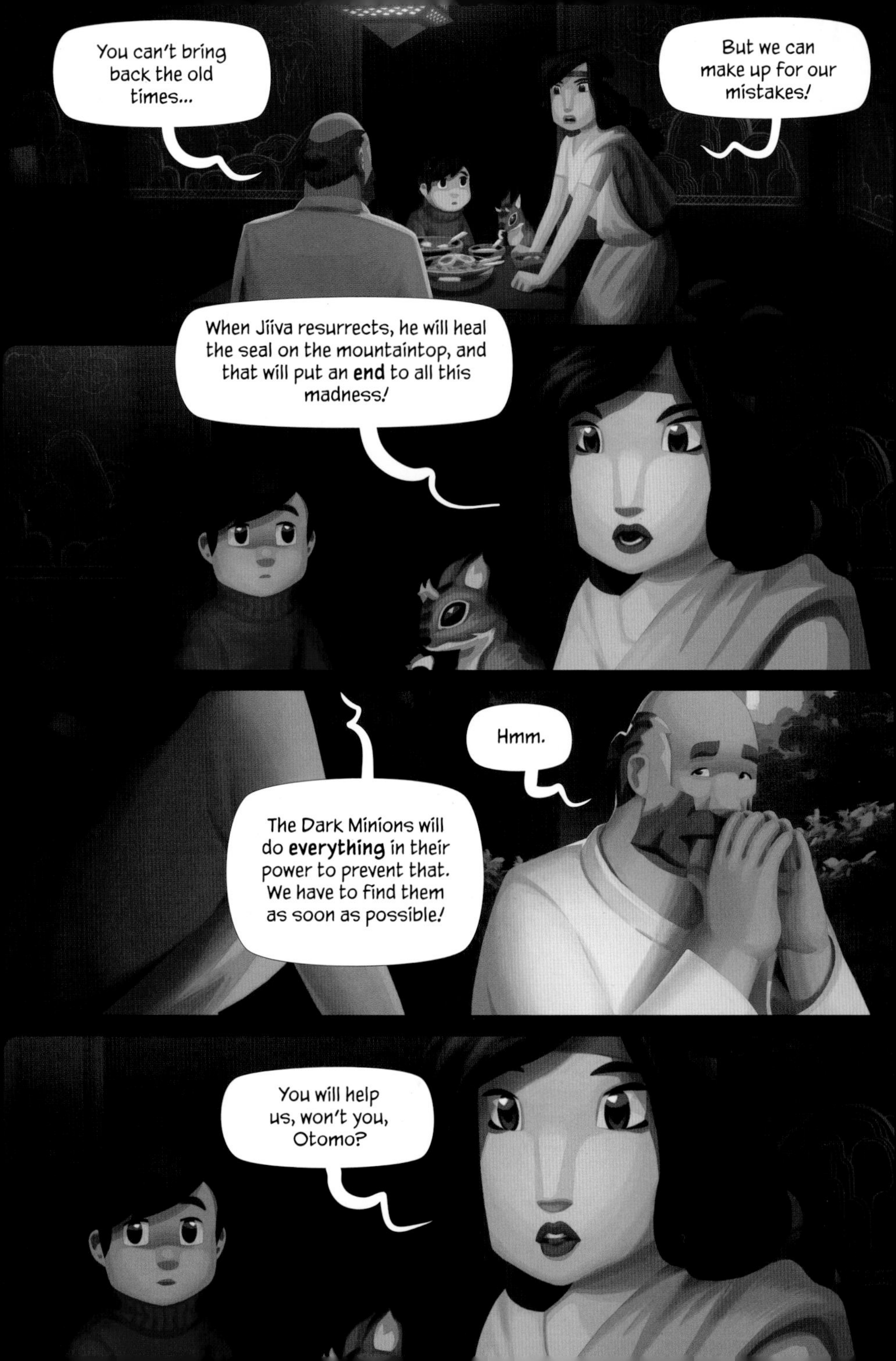
You can't bring back the old times...
But we can make up for our mistakes!
When Jiíva resurrects, he will heal the seal on the mountaintop, and that will put an **end** to all this madness!
The Dark Minions will do **everything** in their power to prevent that. We have to find them as soon as possible!
Hmm.
You will help us, won't you, Otomo?

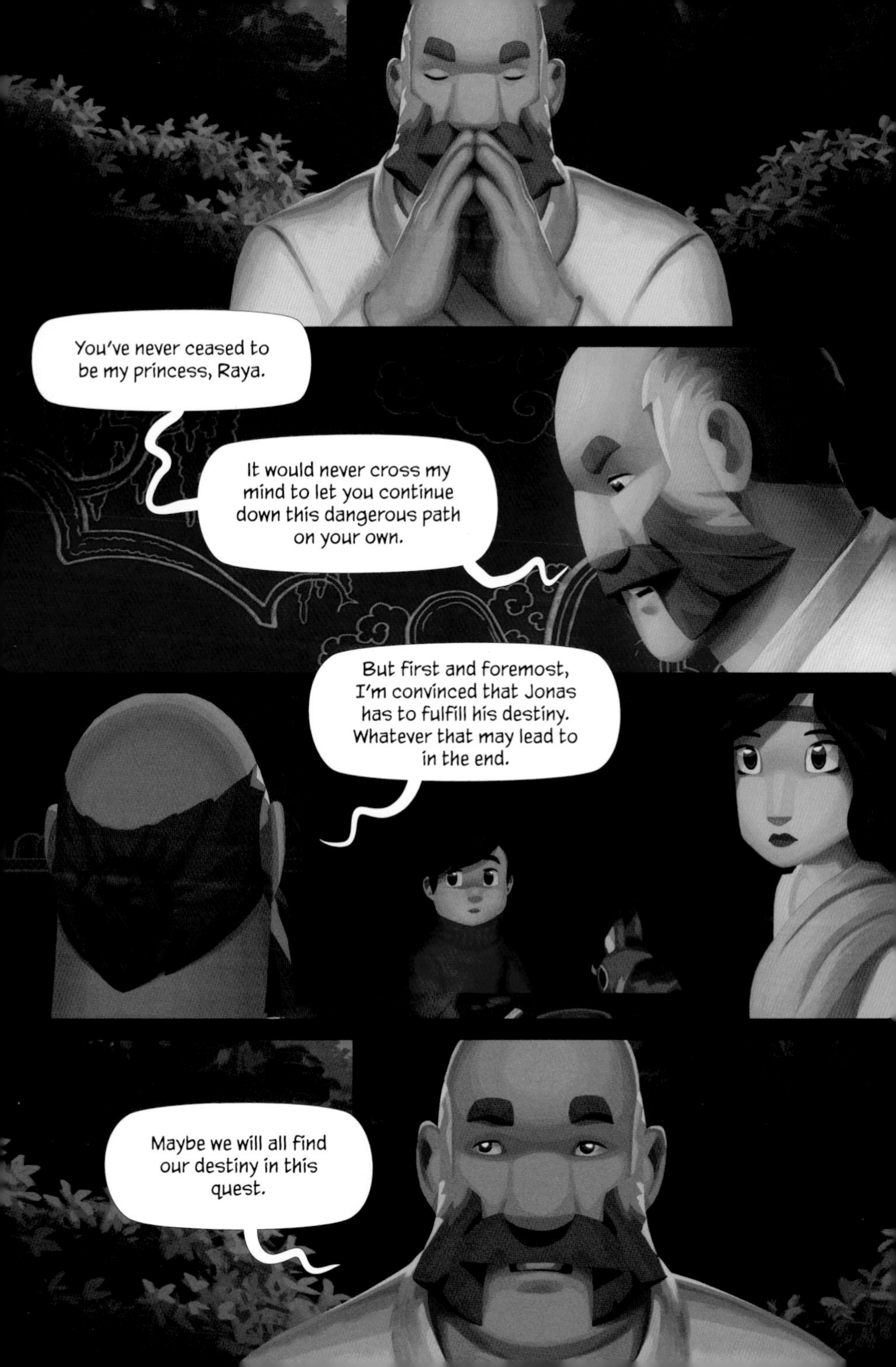
You've never ceased to be my princess, Raya.
It would never cross my mind to let you continue down this dangerous path on your own.
But first and foremost, I'm convinced that Jonas has to fulfill his destiny. Whatever that may lead to in the end.
Maybe we will all find our destiny in this quest.

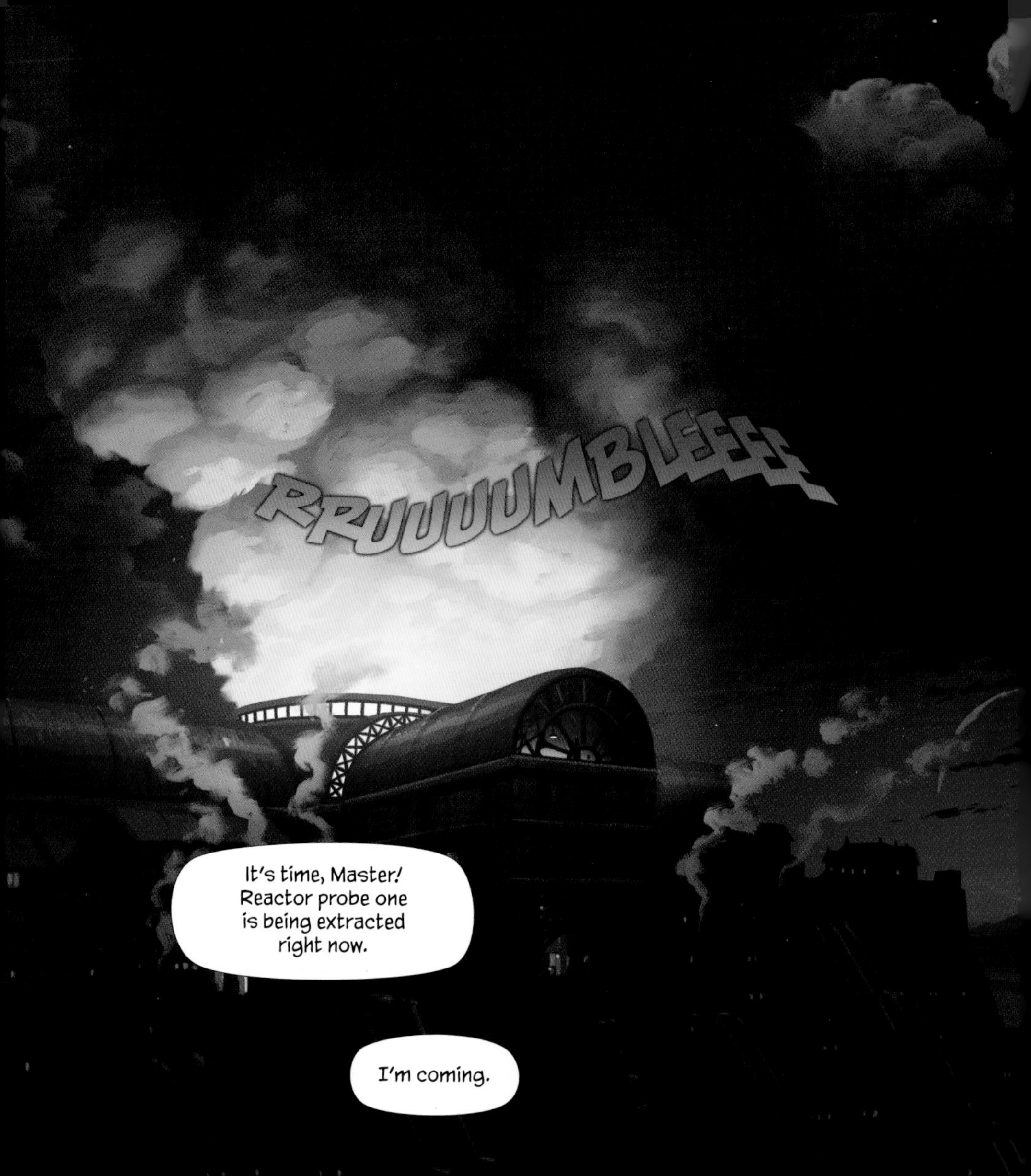
RRUUUUMBLEEEE
It's time, Master! Reactor probe one is being extracted right now.
I'm coming.

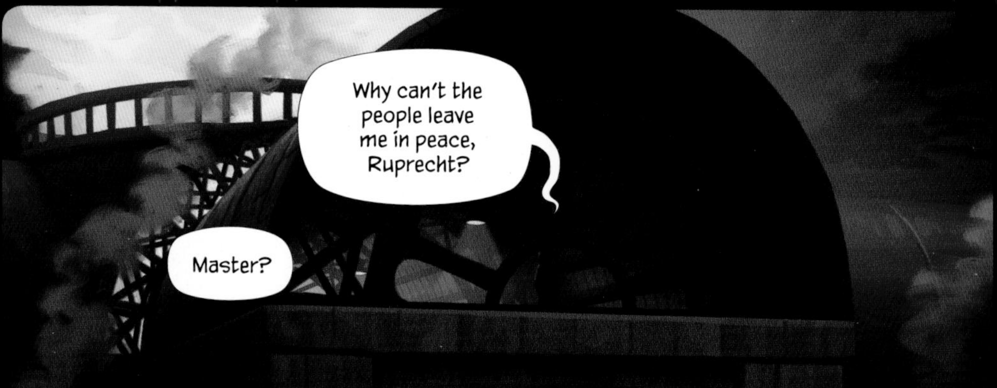
Why can't the people leave me in peace, Ruprecht?
Master?

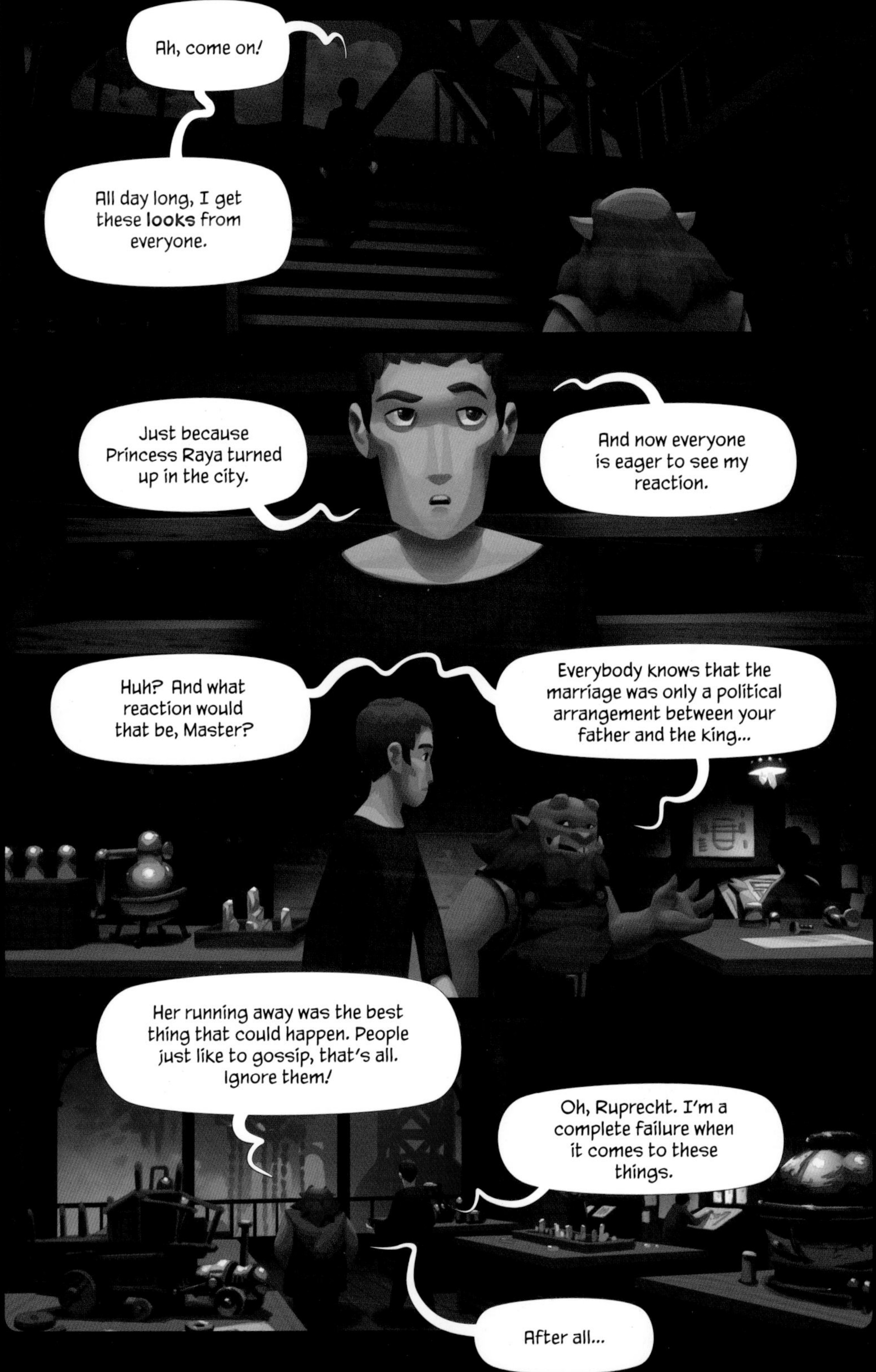
Ah, come on!
All day long, I get these **looks** from everyone.
Just because Princess Raya turned up in the city.
And now everyone is eager to see my reaction.
Huh? And what reaction would that be, Master?
Everybody knows that the marriage was only a political arrangement between your father and the king...
Her running away was the best thing that could happen. People just like to gossip, that's all. Ignore them!
Oh, Ruprecht. I'm a complete failure when it comes to these things.
After all...

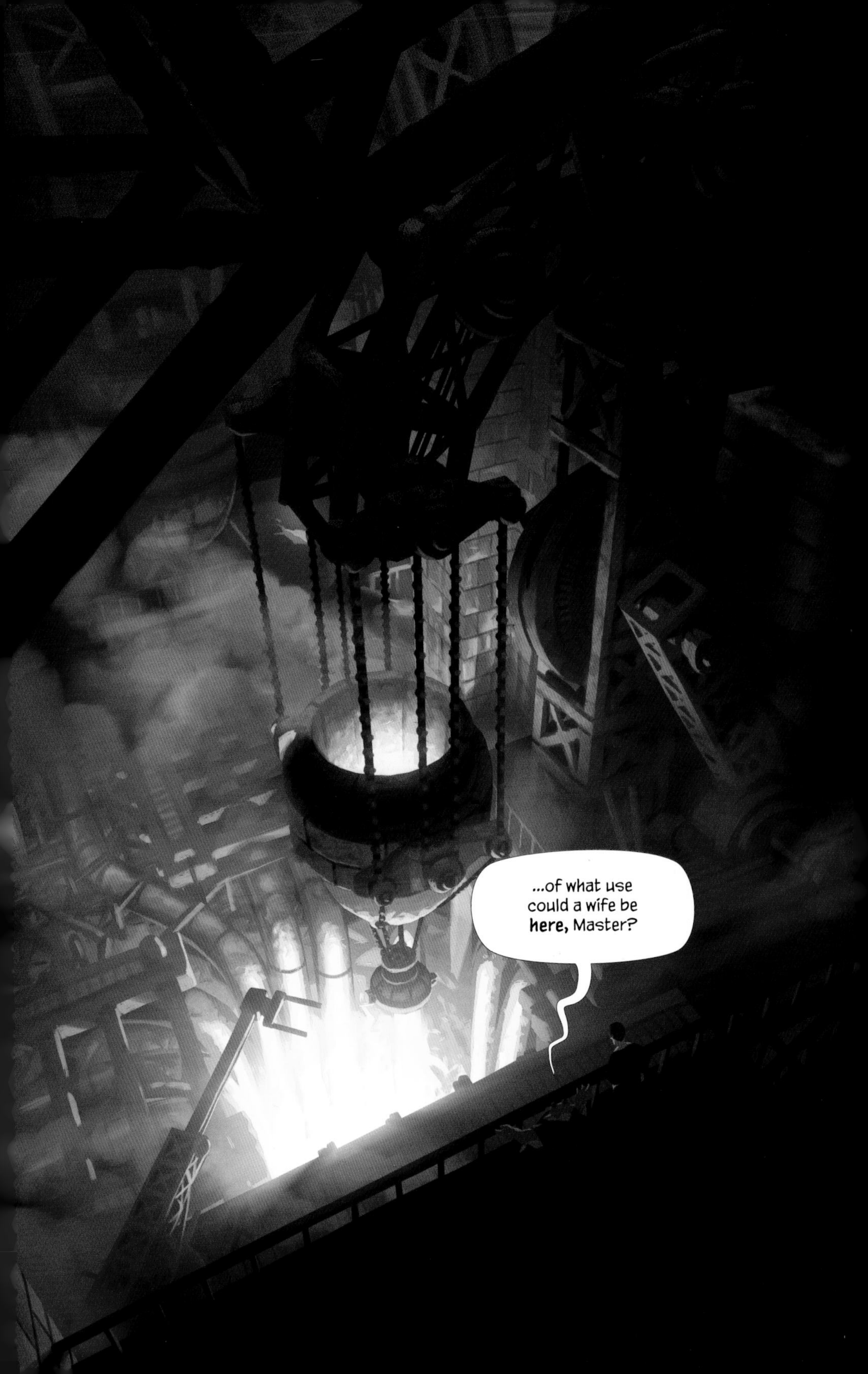
...of what use could a wife be **here,** Master?

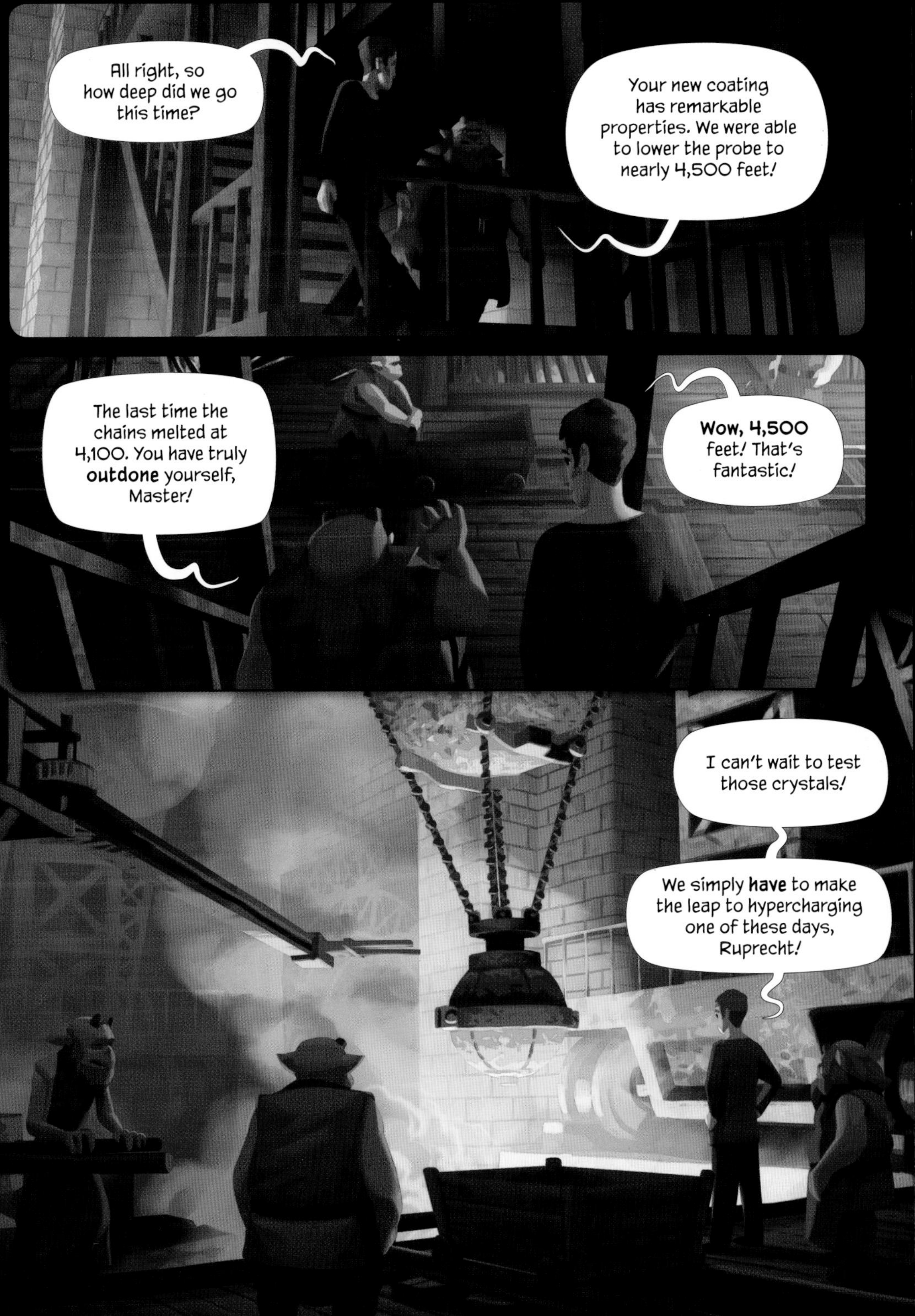
All right, so how deep did we go this time?
Your new coating has remarkable properties. We were able to lower the probe to nearly 4,500 feet!
The last time the chains melted at 4,100. You have truly **outdone** yourself, Master!
Wow, 4,500 feet! That's fantastic!
I can't wait to test those crystals!
We simply **have** to make the leap to hypercharging one of these days, Ruprecht!

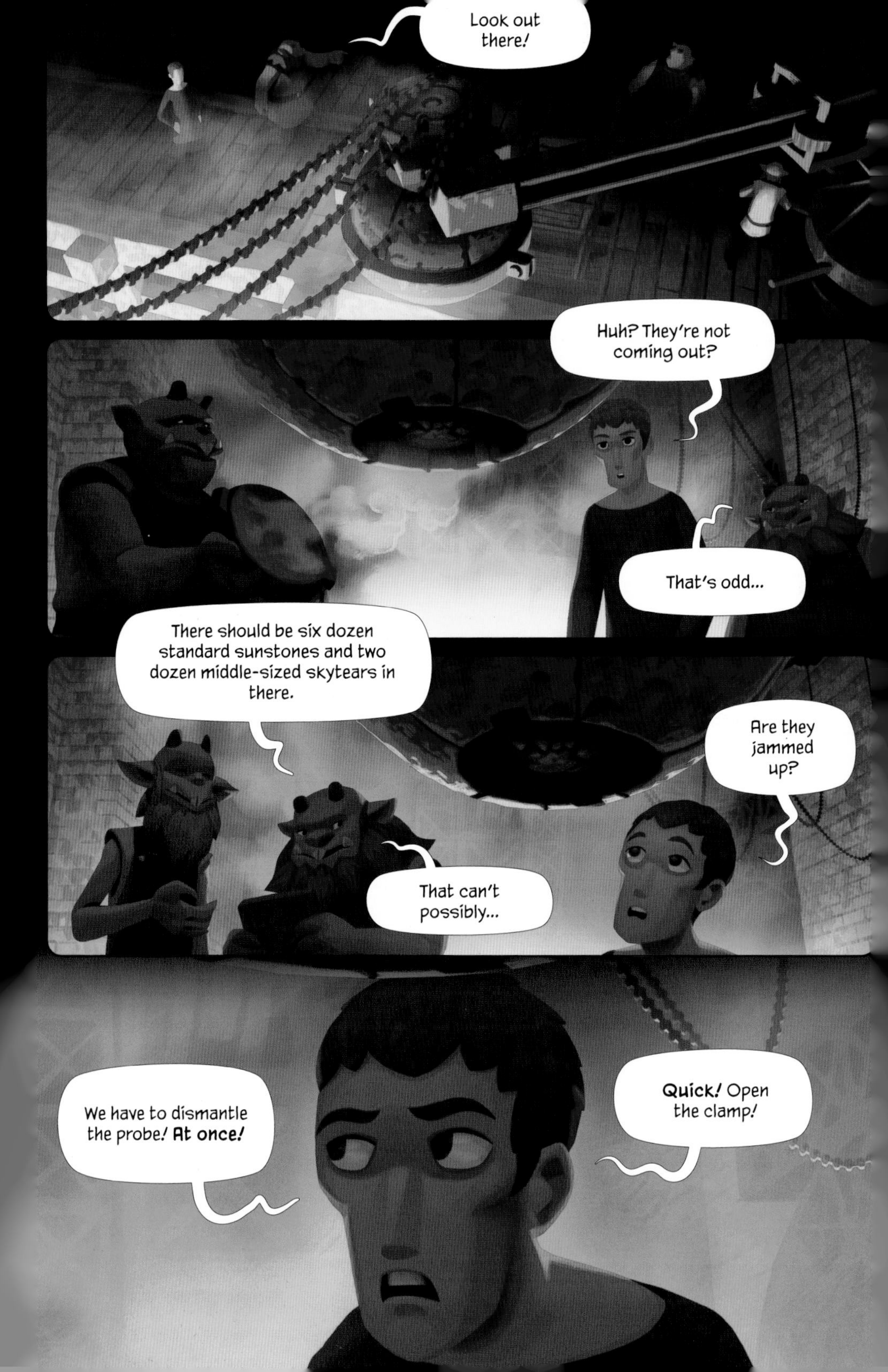
Look out there!
Huh? They're not coming out?
That's odd...
There should be six dozen standard sunstones and two dozen middle-sized skytears in there.
Are they jammed up?
That can't possibly...
Quick! Open the clamp!
We have to dismantle the probe! At once!

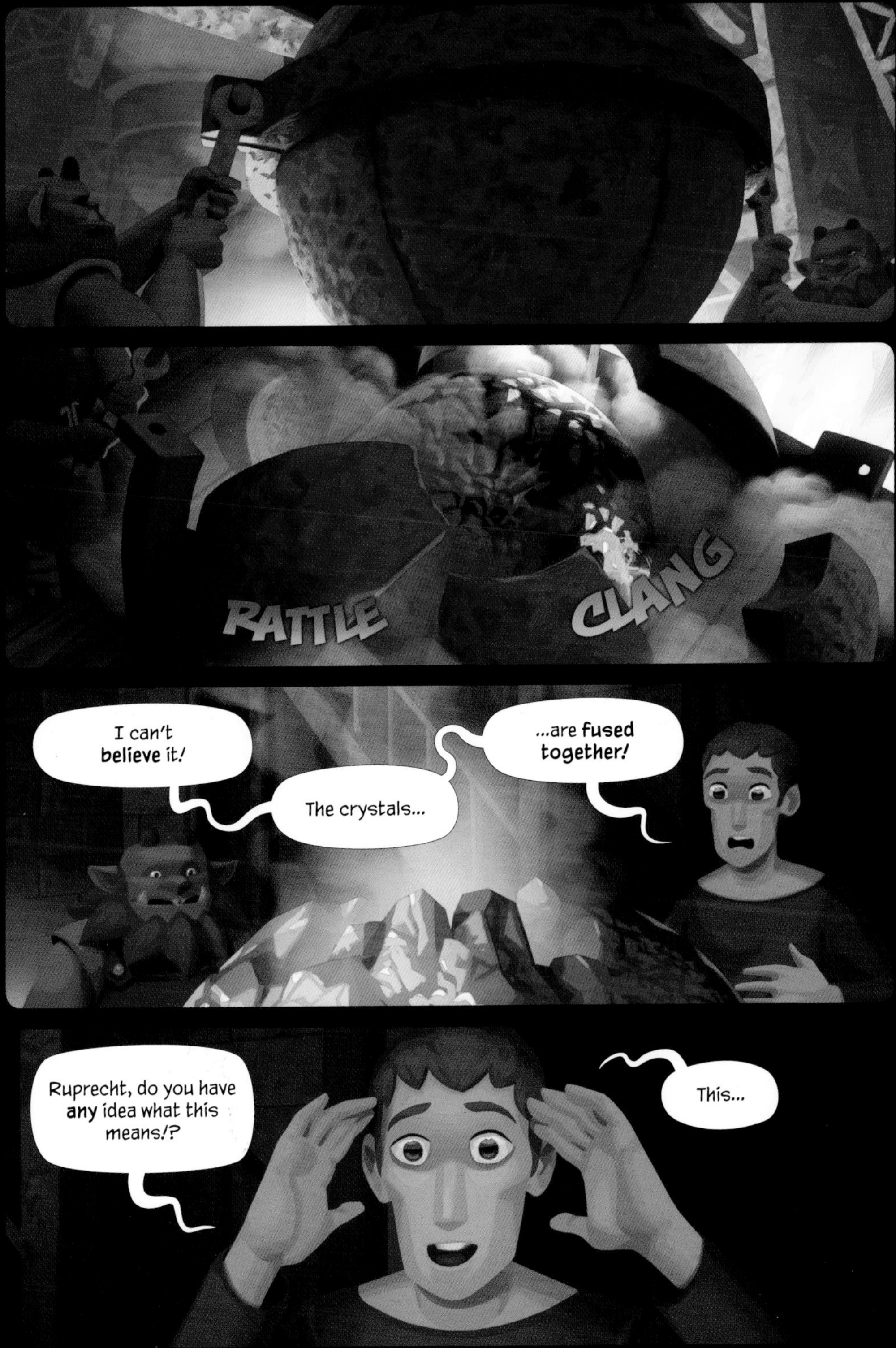
RATTLE
CLANG
I can't believe it!
The crystals...
...are fused together!
Ruprecht, do you have any idea what this means!?
This...

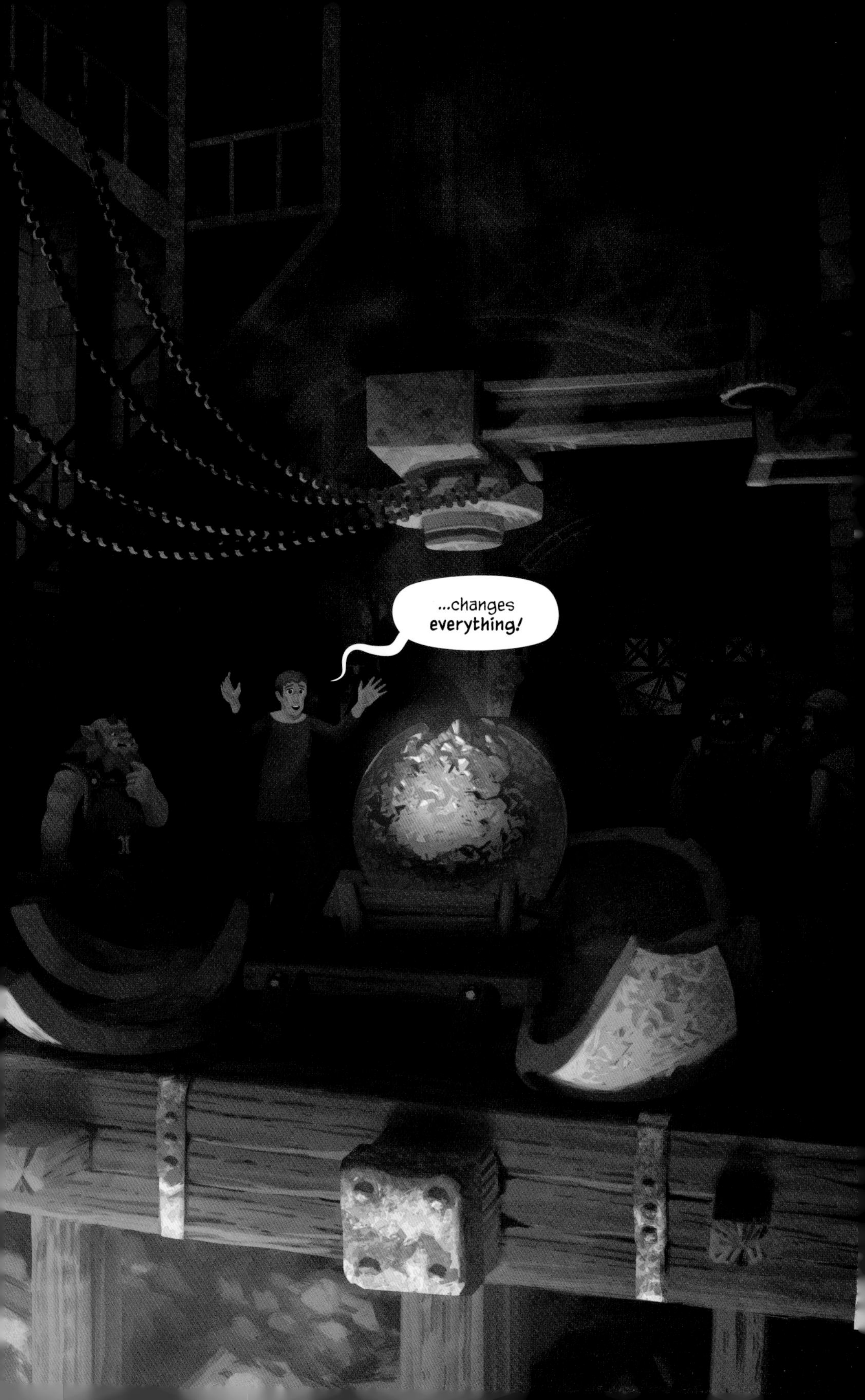
...changes **everything!**

Behind the Scenes
of *The Wormworld Saga*

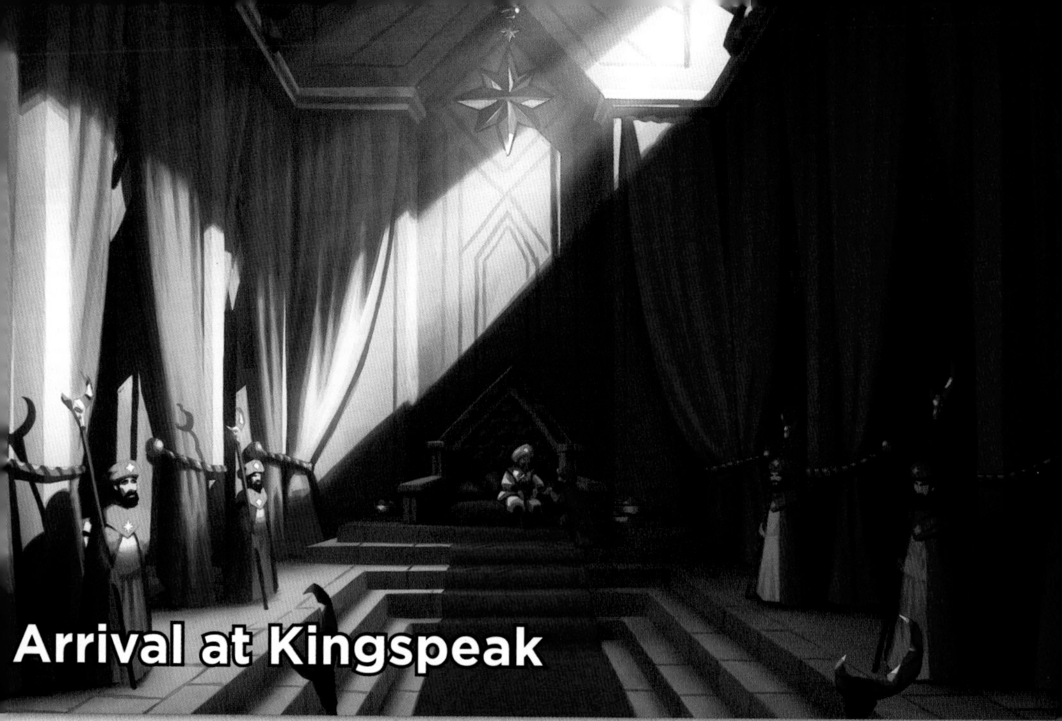

Arrival at Kingspeak

Never Look Back!

When I read the "Behind the Scenes of *The Wormworld Saga*" in the last volume, where I talked about how extraordinarily big it is and how much work it was to complete, I can't help to smile and think, "You've got NO idea!" It's true that the second chapter in volume two was a big chapter, but it's dwarfed in every aspect by the first chapter in this volume, volume three. The size is only one aspect in this comparison. What weighs even more is the subject matter of the illustrations. Volume two had a fair amount of architecture and people in it, but most of it showed jungle backgrounds and a lot of the scenes took place in the night, where the lack of light saves a lot of work. From that point of view, the only comfortable section of the first chapter of this book is the opening scene on the foggy river. As soon as we enter the city of Kingspeak, all the architectural detail and the masses of people—and everything in bright sunlight—became a really overwhelming task for me. I've never worked for so long on a single chapter of *The Wormworld Saga*, but, on the other hand, I've never been more proud of the result.

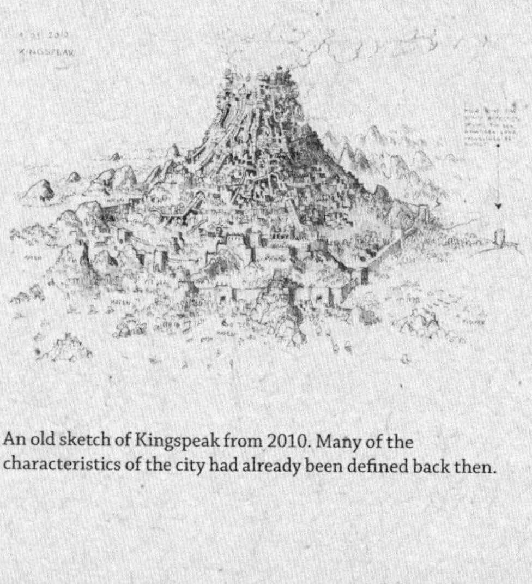

An old sketch of Kingspeak from 2010. Many of the characteristics of the city had already been defined back then.

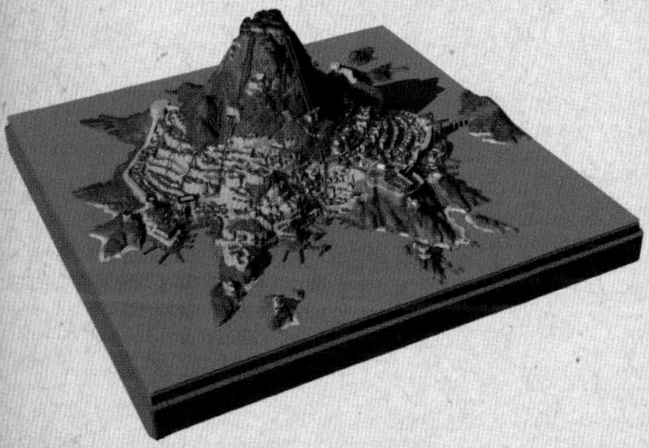

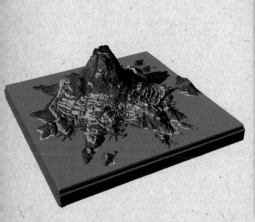

The digital sculpting of Kingspeak created in ZBrush

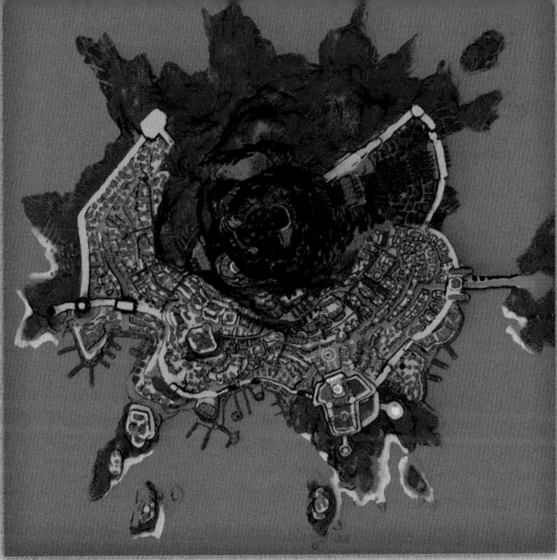

A plain top view of the city that provides something like a street map

Building the Big City

Even before I started my work on this book, I knew that the biggest challenge would be to bring the city of Kingspeak to life the way I've imagined it. I knew that it would take a lot of panoramic shots to show the vast cityscape, and that, in order to make it look really busy, I would have to paint a lot of people. But my first task was actually to get a clear picture of the city as a whole in my head. I had fantasized about the Worm Mountain and the city of Kingspeak a lot over the years, but I've never acquired a definite picture of it. The sketch from 2010 (that you can see on the previous page) was the first time I actually created a complete overview of the city. I used this sketch to build a sculpture of Kingspeak in ZBrush, which helped me a lot to find my way around this huge place. I really got hooked up by the sculpting.

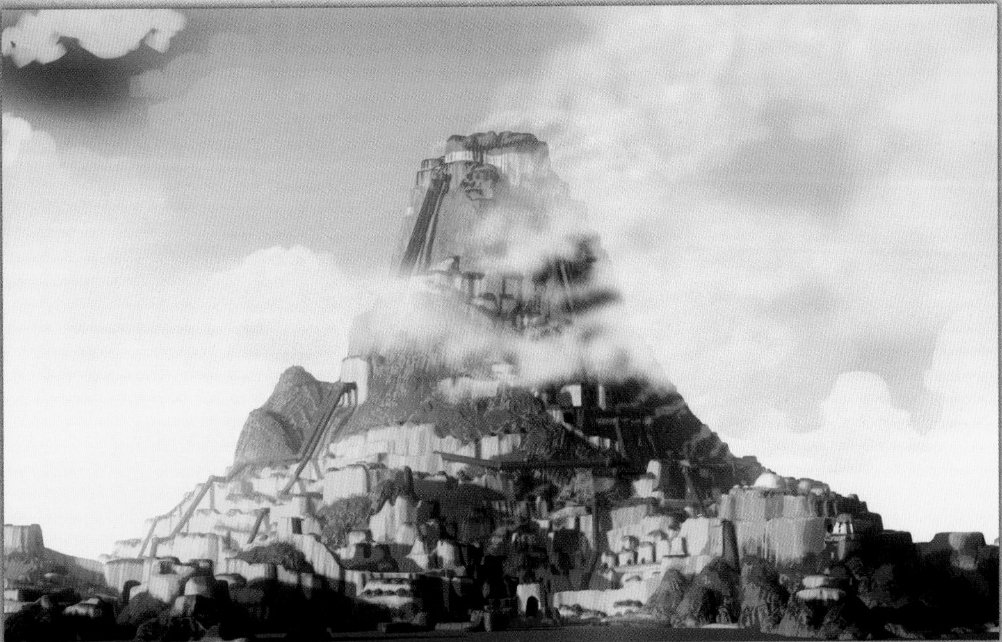

A view of the Kingspeak sculpting as seen from eye level. The ZBrush rendering has been retouched in Photoshop.

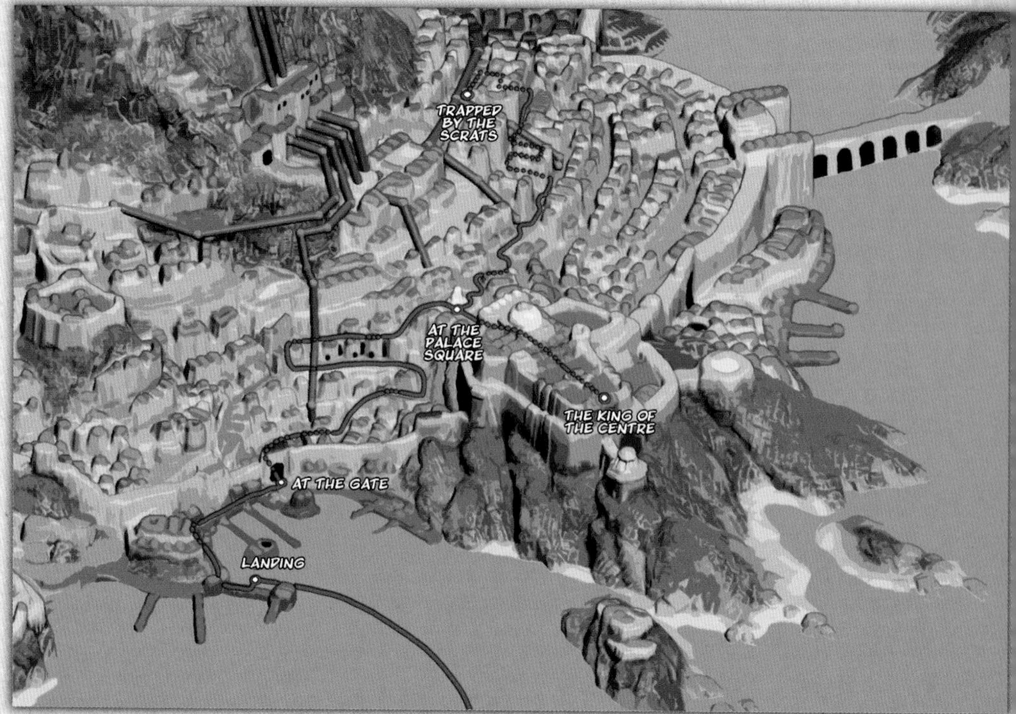
TRAPPED BY THE SCRATS
AT THE PALACE SQUARE
THE KING OF THE CENTRE
AT THE GATE
LANDING
An illustration that shows the rough path the protagonists are taking in the beginning of this book

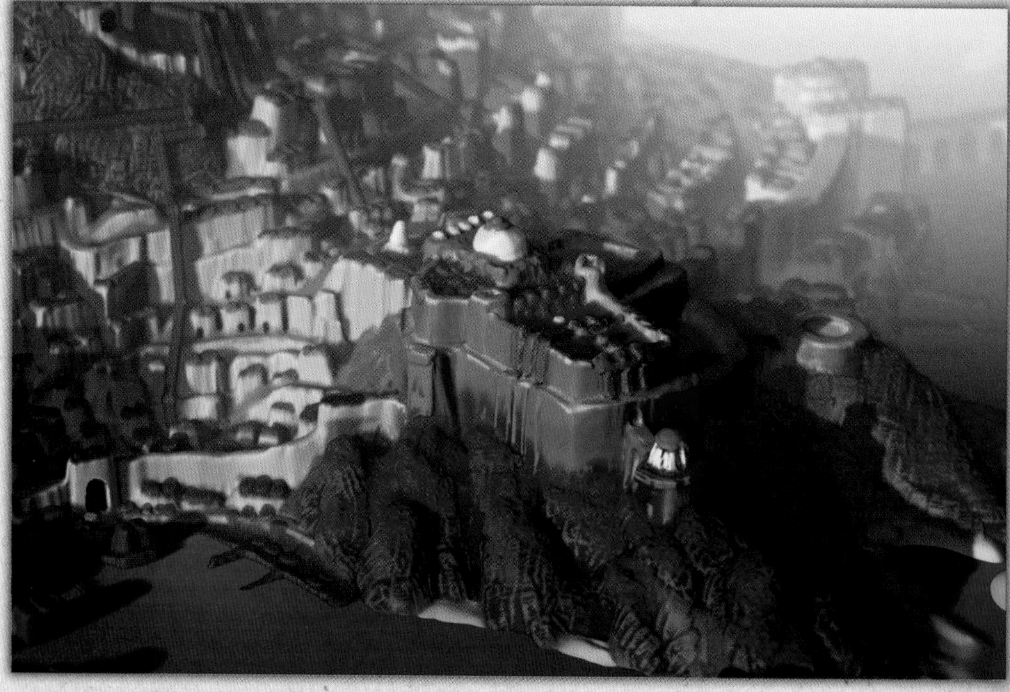
The Azure Palace in the ZBrush sculpting. Here, the rounded roofs still look more like the domes of classic European architecture.

My first idea was to create only a very rough impression of the location. I then found out that my computer was capable of handling a decent amount of detail in the sculpting, so I started to flesh out separate buildings. At some point I had to literally stop myself because I had already spent fourteen hours on the sculpting and was just getting ready to paint the roofs of the houses in different colors. However, it's important to note that the sculpting is not at all an accurate model of how the city apprears in the graphic novel. It's more of a 3-D sketch in which I put down my ideas for different parts of the city. You can see the different harbors, the Azure Palace, and the steam facility on the mountaintop. If you look closely, you can also make out different forms of houses. The rich people live in the big manors with the walled gardens, the normal people live in the multistoried houses, and in the east you find the dark and dirty alleys of the Scrat Quarter.

THE AZURE PALACE
THEATRE

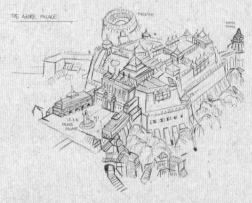

This sketch of the Azure Palace shows the pointed roofs. However, the palace is pretty small in this sketch. I actually avoided a view of the palace's full extends in the graphic novel to leave its size to the imagination of the viewer.

The Azure Palace

A central location of this book is the Azure Palace and its throne room. I have to admit that I haven't been particularly looking forward to illustrating this part of the chapter because architecture and interiors are always a lot of work. However, after drawing the first concepts, I started to enjoy the process a lot. I tried to come up with an architecture that is a mix of Western, Asian, and Indian styles. I avoided round arches completely to get away from the classic Roman look, but I used a lot of arcades, which are very popular in classic European architecture. The overall shape of the Azure Palace is heavily inspired by fortresses from India like Fort Amber and the Alhambra in Spain.

AZURE PALACE SQUARE – MAIN PORTAL

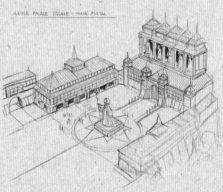

A closer view of the palace square. This is very close to the final look in the graphic novel, although there are only four statues in the final version of the facade.

The diamond shape became sort of a leitmotif for all designs around the King of the Center. It encapsulates the star symbol of the Central Kingdom; it's also very apparent in all the triangular arches and is even reflected in the quilted fabrics that

AZURE PALACE THRONEROOM

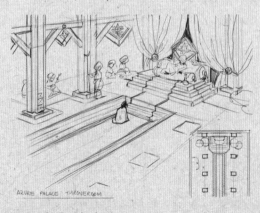

My first sketch of the throne room

are used in some of the costumes and props. For the scene in the throne room, I introduced a new workflow. I knew that for such an angular interior, the lighting would be very important to create a sense of space. I constructed a rough 3-D model of the scene and tried different lighting scenarios. In the end I settled for a sharp lighting contrast. Raya's inferior position is reflected by it, which is further supported by the fact that Raya is standing in the dark and Vena is standing in the light. With the help of the

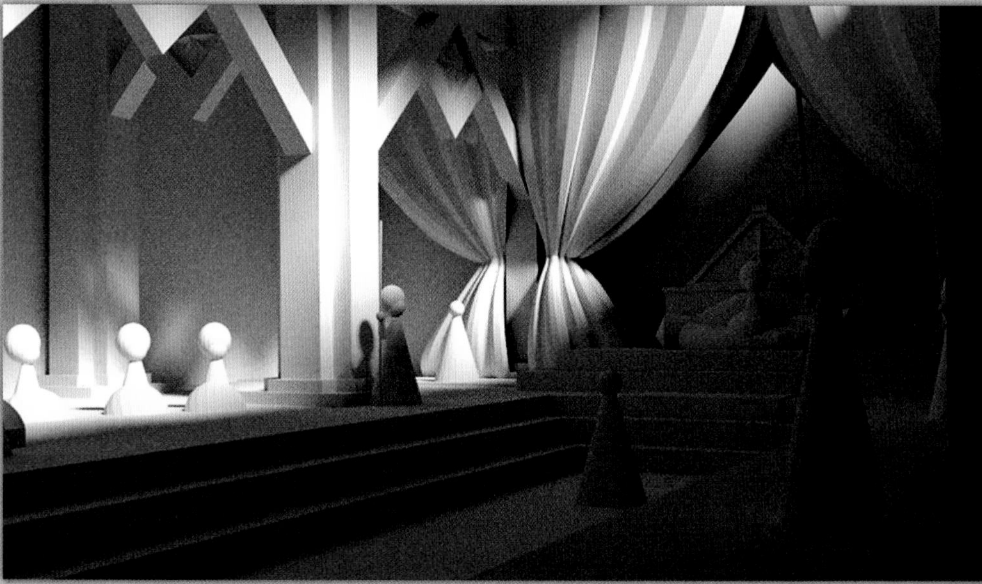

A rendering of the 3-D model with reflected light. This was a very helpful reference for the background illustrations.

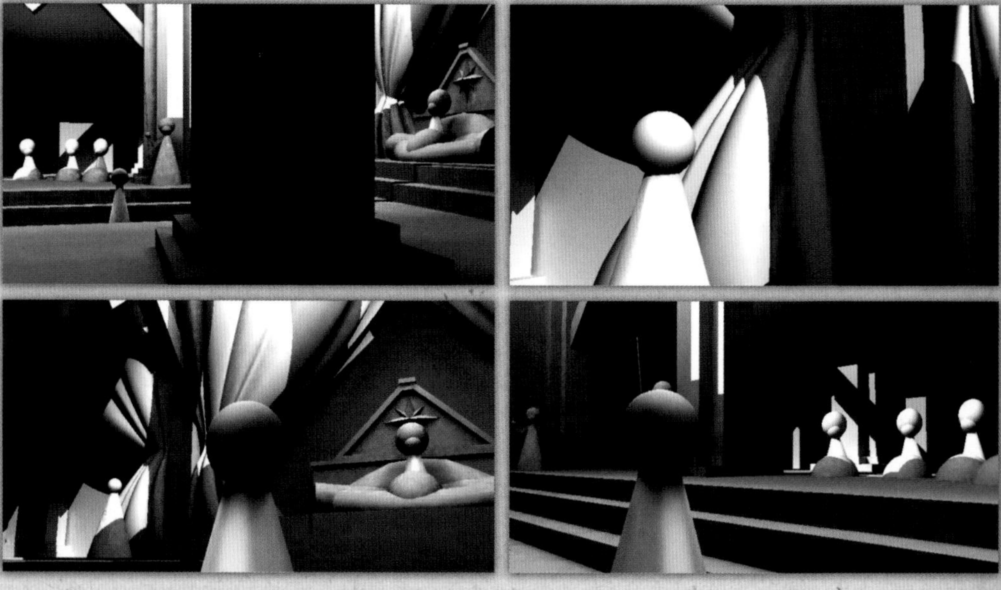

A set of different shots of the throne room. I created a lot of these in order to find good camera angles to frame the action. I especially liked the shot in the top left because of the visual barrier between Raya and her father. However, this shot became impractical when I introduced the curtains into the scene.

3-D model and the virtual camera, I could move around in it, and I was able to take full advantage of this interesting spacial arrangement. There is a streak of direct sunlight, hitting only one side of the throne room, and leaving the rest in indirect light. The only acting character in direct sunlight is Princess Vena, which creates a nice constrast between her appearance and Raya's.

The other thing I used the 3-D model for was to find working camera angles between the three characters in the scene. The problem was not only to frame three characters that were standing in quite some distance from each other, but Raya is also standing significantly lower than her dialog partners. This, however, made for some interesting subtext: the throne room is also a nice example that you can't plan for everything in advance. In the sketches and the rough renderings of the scene, the naked pillars of the throne room looked just fine. It was when I painted the establishing shot of the throne room scene that I realized how empty the room looked. I decided to put a lot of curtains into the scene to help fill out the room. This not only helped the look of the room but it also introduced a lot of diagonal lines into many of the panel backgrounds which further reflected the diamond shape leitmotif of the Central Kingdom.

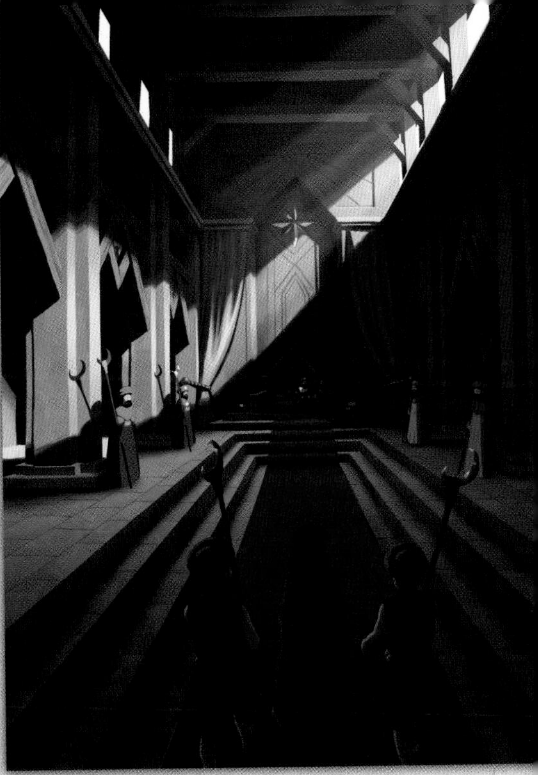

This is a work in progress of the first establishing shot of the throne room just before I realized that I'd need curtains to make the room more appealing.

Character Design

I always consider character design to be my weak spot. I almost never take the time to fully develop a character design in concept art before I take it to the page. I'm really trying to get better at this because it's much more satisfying to work with characters that are carefully designed.

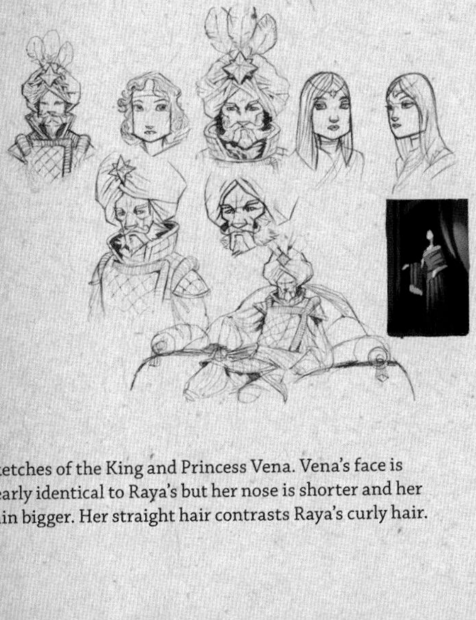

Sketches of the King and Princess Vena. Vena's face is nearly identical to Raya's but her nose is shorter and her chin bigger. Her straight hair contrasts Raya's curly hair.

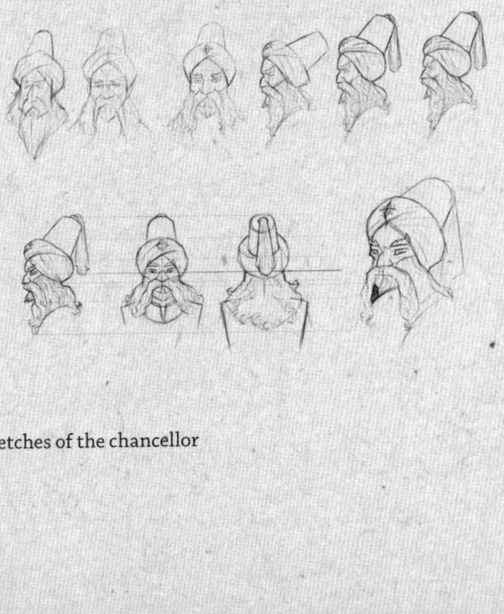

Sketches of the chancellor

However, in this chapter I improvised a lot again. There's only a couple of sketches of the king and the princess, although I especially liked how Vena turned out in the end. I spent a little more time on the chancellor because the camera is moving around him in his scene. The Black Turbans were designed in lineart only. Their color design was improvised on the page. It's interesting to note that the riflemen weren't what I was originally going for. For the longest time, I had planned that the demonstration on the palace square would feature an impressive steam weapon of some sort. I sketched a lot of walking machines, steam-powered tanks, and mechanisms, but I wasn't able to arrive at a design that would satisfy me. The problem was that all the designs seemed to be completely over the top. You can't have a society that lives without fire and then pull out a steam-powered mechanism. I started to like the idea to be more subtle. A firearm can be an awe-inspiring thing if you have never seen one before. Also, by starting with a less spectacular thing, there's more room to raise the level of tension.

I was looking forward to the Scrats the most. The design of my human characters is simplified but their proportions remain pretty normal. With the Scrats I finally have the opportunity to use exaggerated proportions and much more interesting facial features. They are simply fun to draw and I'm looking forward to having many more of these guys in future chapters. The little Scrat gang that's bullying Jonas was also improvised on the page, but the gang leader (who's name is Kralle, by the way) is heavily inspired by a goblin that appears in my painting *Trapped!* from 2007.

Sketches of the guards and the Black Turban rifleman

THE STEAM WEAPON

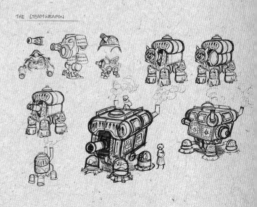

Sketches of the steam weapon that was ultimately replaced by the firearm

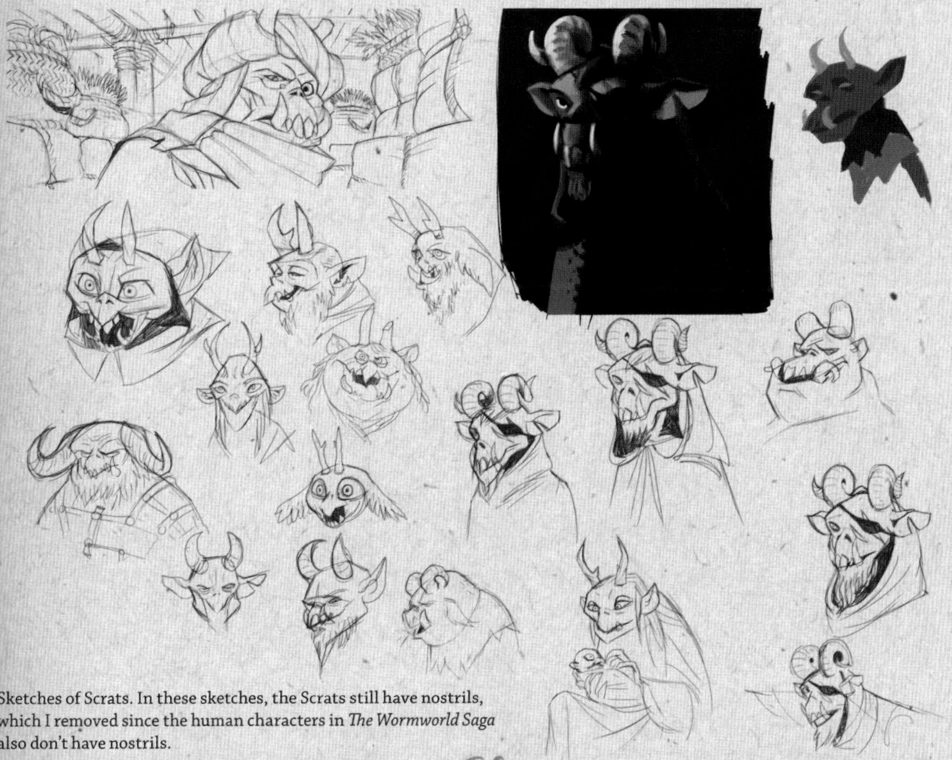

Sketches of Scrats. In these sketches, the Scrats still have nostrils, which I removed since the human characters in *The Wormworld Saga* also don't have nostrils.

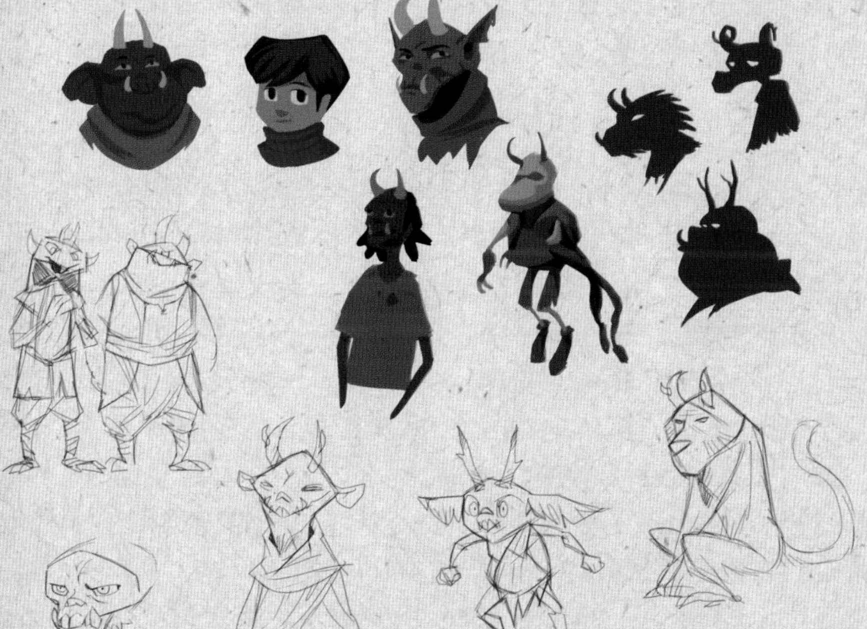

More Scrats. Here, I toyed around a little bit with shapes and color.

Back in the Big City

We already know that I couldn't afford to spend so much time on a single chapter again but I also didn't want the next chapter to feel cheap in this regard. To keep things under control, the first thing I made sure was that the length of the chapter would be much shorter than the previous one.

Fortunately the storyline called for more interior scenes this time, so that also saved me plenty of work. Knowing that these factors would play to my advantage, I decided to have at least a couple really impressive pieces of artwork in volume three. The opening shot and the big city panorama in the middle of the chapter are among the most elaborate scenes I've painted for *The Wormworld Saga* so far. And then I was especially looking forward to the final sequence of the book, in which we enter Muhadra's facility at the top of the Worm Mountain. I made extensive use of 3-D modeling in the production of this sequence, which you will see below. All in all, I feel that chapter two of this book turned out to be a worthy successor to the first chapter (and without driving me insane).

Fleshing Out Kingspeak

In chapter one, we've already seen a lot of places in Kingspeak: the harbor, the bazaar, Azure Palace, and the Scrat Quarter. All these locations can be considered to be the old or traditional Kingspeak. Later in the book, I wanted to introduce more information about the modern Kingspeak as it is shaped by the genius of Muhadra and his son. We learn more about the metal production process that starts with the ore wagons coming into the city from the northern mountains. They are unloaded at the elevator station and then the ore is transported in railway wagons to the mountaintop into Muhadra's facility. Inside the facility, we see how the metal is molten inside the huge reactor probes that are lowered into the glowing chasm.

Sketches for the opening shot of chapter two
It turned out very different in the end.

Muhadra's facility is a huge complex of buildings with four main wings that radiate from the center, where the glowing chasm is located. The southern wing is where the elevator brings the ore in. Muhadra's studio is located at the top level of the southern wing. The other three wings are occupied by the three movable cranes from which the reactor probes are lowered into the glowing chasm. These three wings are flanked by numerous smaller halls that contain workshops in which the molten metal is processed.

For the first time, I used a very detailed 3-D model to create a location of *The Wormworld Saga*. I had already used 3-D models before for Janaka's tower and the throne room. But these models were very simple and just provided me a general guideline for the design of the panel artwork. The model of Muhadra's facility is detailed enough so that, in many cases, I didn't even have to create a drawing for the background artwork because I simply based my paintings on the 3-D geometry. I invested about two days into creating the 3-D model and that time investment payed off greatly in the production process later.

The 3-D model of Muhadra's facility didn't just serve as a substitute for preliminary drawings. I was looking for a very specific lighting situation inside the facility, and

Excerpt from the big panorama in the middle of chapter two of this volume, on which I have worked twenty-one hours.

the 3-D model helped me a lot to set this up properly. I created lighted 3-D renderings of the facility setting as a base for my paintings. These renderings were often very raw and noisy, but that generally was enough to give me a hint on light intensities and shadow placement in the scene. I never planned to just retouch the 3-D renderings, so I didn't put much effort into optimizing the rendering quality. Although I've created renderings for all panels of the facility sequence, in the end the panel artwork was all painted from scratch.

ORE WAGON

Design exploration for the ore wagon

ORE WAGON - NOW WITH BREAKS!

A more detailed drawing of the ore wagon

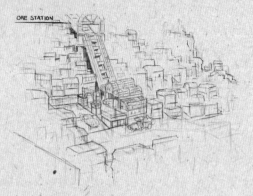

ORE STATION

A sketch of the elevator station at the foot of the Worm Mountain

MUHADRA'S FACILITY

A complete view of the facility

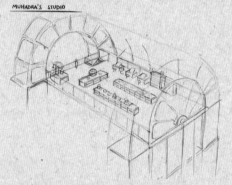

MUHADRA'S STUDIO

A sketch of Muhadra's studio

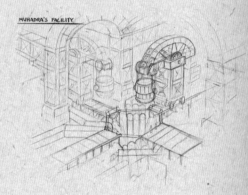

MUHADRA'S FACILITY

A sketch of Muhadra's studio

Two New Main Characters

This book introduces two new important characters: Master Otomo and Muhadra. Master Otomo will be joining Jonas and Raya on their quest to find and destroy the Dark Minions. And actually a third character was originally planned to be introduced: Otomo's son. This is an interesting case study about storytelling. My original idea of the party that will face the Dark Minions consisted of four characters: Jonas, Raya, Otomo and Hiro, Otomo's son. I struggled with bringing all these things together in the dinner scene and realized that it would just get completely cluttered and unfocused. I tried many different variations but with no result that I would be happy with. Then it occurred to me that Hiro was a superfluous character. I took his main character functions—the skepticism and love for science—and gave it in accentuated form to Otomo. Otomo does not love science. But I planned for him to be the loyal warrior type and his son was going to be

the skeptical, science embracing counterpart to Raya. Even when I started to write this book, this constellation was still intact. When I reached the scenes in Otomo's house, I realized that it would be a very complicated situation between the four characters: Raya insisting on the evil of technology, Hiro challenging this perspective, Otomo trying to hold his son back out of respect for his princess, and Jonas being irritated by this clash.

Also, Otomo shows moderate skepticism towards religious beliefs. This all doesn't hinder him to be loyal to Raya though. His character becomes much more rounded that way. As is often the case, this example shows clearly that editing a story means making it simpler. If fewer characters can transport the same ideas, you should get rid of those that you don't need.

The second character introduced in this volume is Muhadra. Muhadra has always been a mysterious character to me. His role in the story changed quite a bit over the years. My initial idea of him was that of a ruthless inventor who eventually would become an antagonist to Jonas and his friends. Later, I came to the conclusion to make him an introverted character who is obsessed with his inventions but doesn't intend to use his power in evil ways. The idea of his introverted nature first led me to a gloomy character design with long hair. At some point, I decided that he would be such a pragmatist that he would cut his hair short. His understated clothing reflects the non-fashion attitude of Silicon Valley icons of our time. His look is at the brink of being anachronistic next to the turbans and beards of the other male characters in the Wormworld, but so are his inventions. Muhadra is clearly ahead of his time.

The Bottom Line

When I started this book, I had already been mentally prepared for a lot of work. The enormous size of the first chapter alone was intimidating, and I anticipated that the vast cityscapes with its countless buildings and people in it would call for quite some extra work. I was relieved when the first milestone took me only seventy-six hours, which actually was not the longest time I've ever spent on a milestone up to that date. The devastating blow came with the second milestone, which proved impossible no matter how much time I was putting into it. I went over the seventy-five-hour mark and wasn't even half finished. I worked close to one hundred hours and there was still no end in sight. When I reached the 150-hour mark, I really got nervous. This thing had clearly gone out of control. In the end, it took me 162 hours to reach the second milestone. To put this in perspective: the entire first chapter of *The Wormworld Saga* took me only 159 hours to paint. From that point on, I knew that I was dealing with a monster of a chapter.

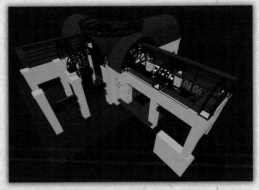

A view of the 3-D model of Muhadra's facility in the 3-D software Blender.

The 3-D-model from Blender, a 3-D computer software. In the distance you can see the dismantled probe of the last panel of this book.

The first sketches of Master Otomo, dating back as far as 2010

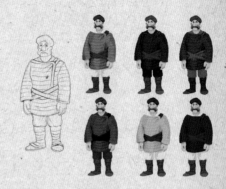

Different color variations for Otomo's costume

Initially, Muhadra had much longer hair in my design sketches

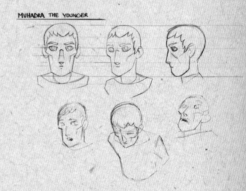

MUHADRA THE YOUNGER

The character turnaround of Muhadra

The following milestones all took close to or over one hundred hours, and when I finally finished the illustration of chapter one of this volume, I had spent over seven hundred hours working on it. I swore to myself that the next chapter would be shorter. However, I started this article laughing at myself because I thought that the last book had been a lot of work. You never know!

I'm pretty happy with how the production of chapter two of this book turned out. I planned for three months of production as soon as the prelim was ready, and I was able to stick to that schedule. This was especially reassuring after the messed-up production schedule of the first chapter of this book. I worked 462 hours on chapter two, which is thirty hours longer than my work on the last chapter of volume two, but only sixty percent of the time it took me to create chapter one of volume three. I think that I might finally have found a good length for upcoming *Wormworld Saga* chapters, and that lies somewhere between the lengths of the last chapter of volume two and the last chapter of this book. However, I think there will always be room for an outlier. If I need the space to tell a chapter properly, I will claim it.

From the Sketchbook of Daniel Lieske

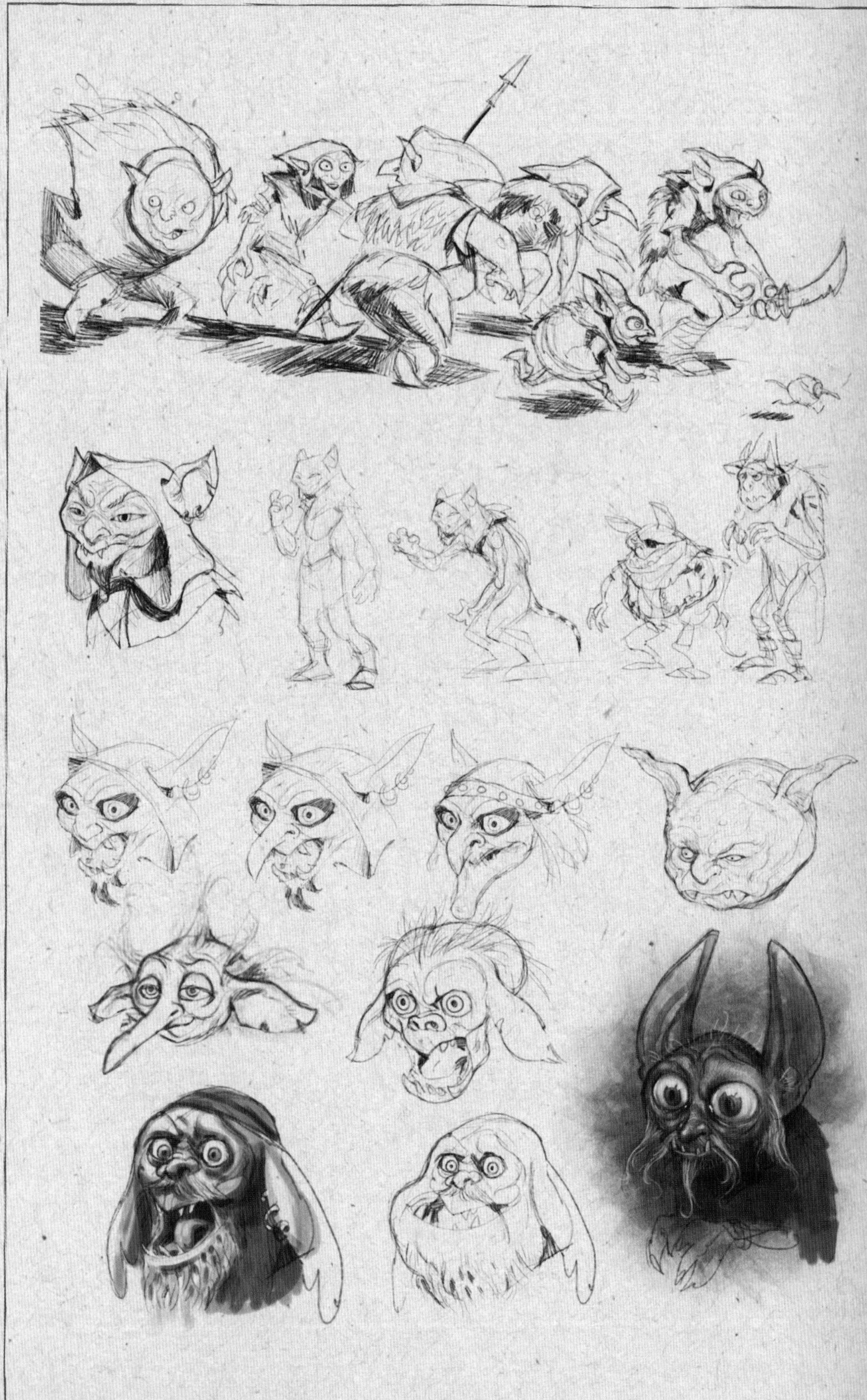

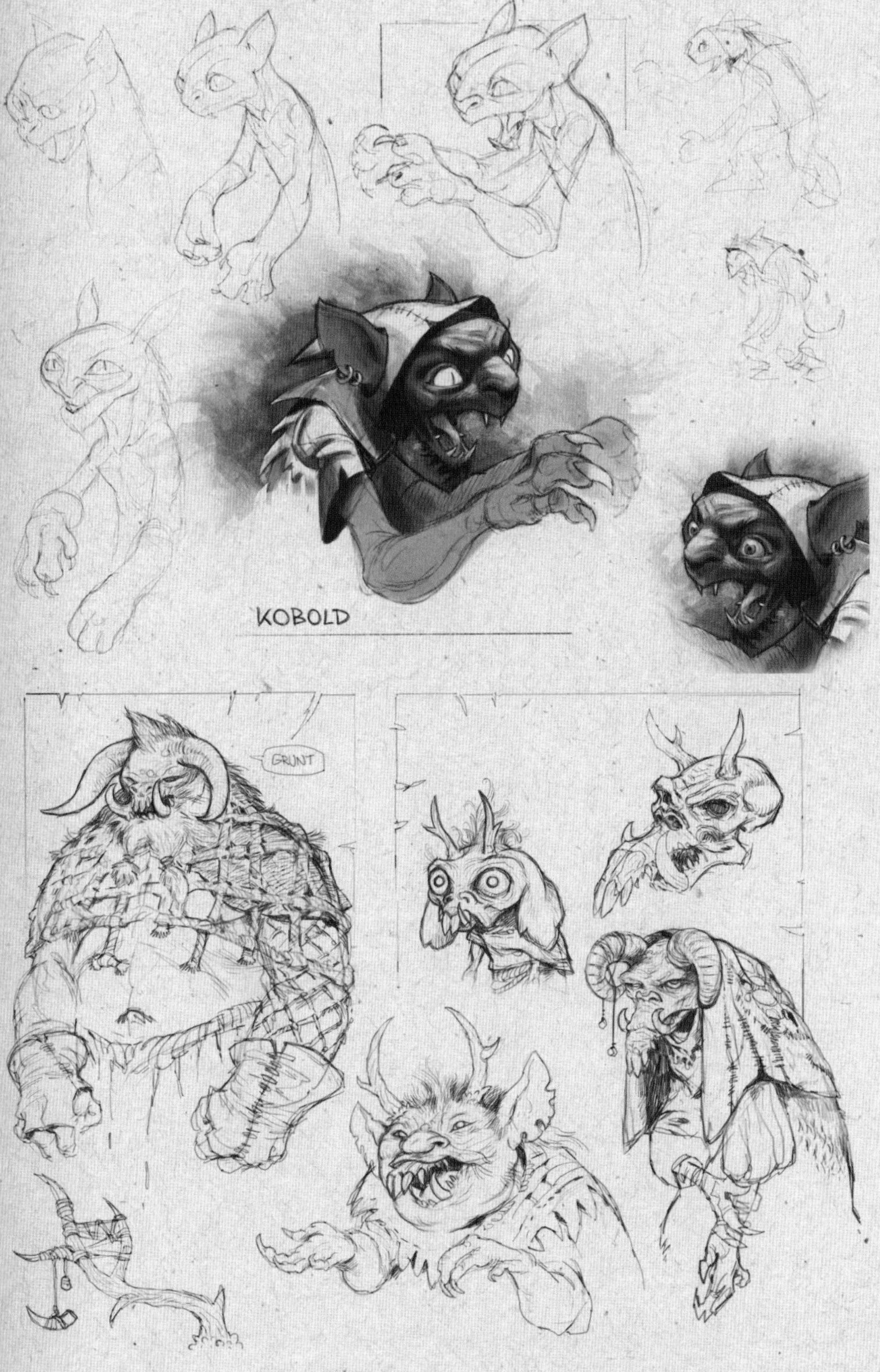
KOBOLD
GRUNT

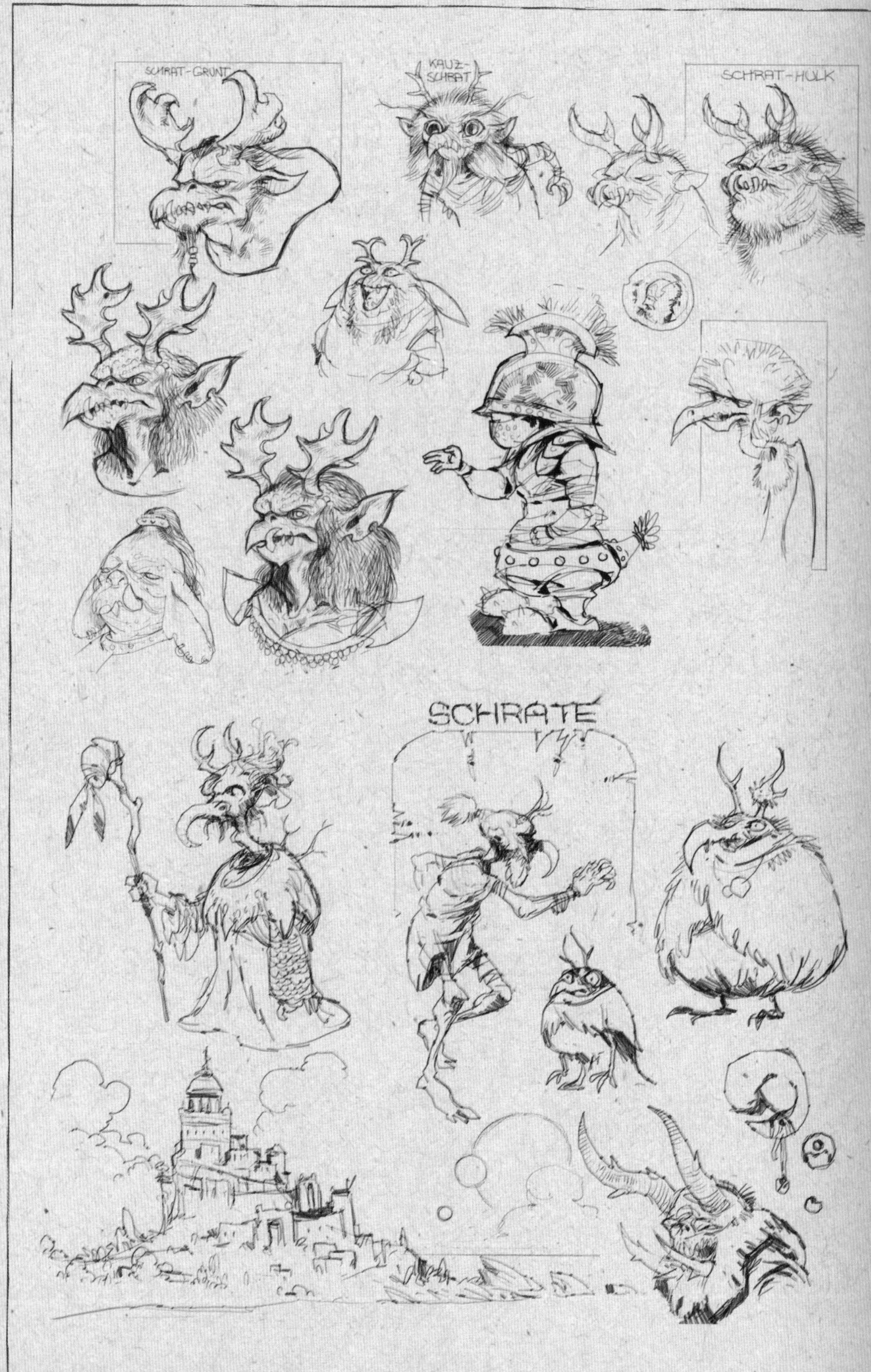
SCHRAT-GRUNT
KAUZ-SCHRAT
SCHRAT-HULK
SCHRATE

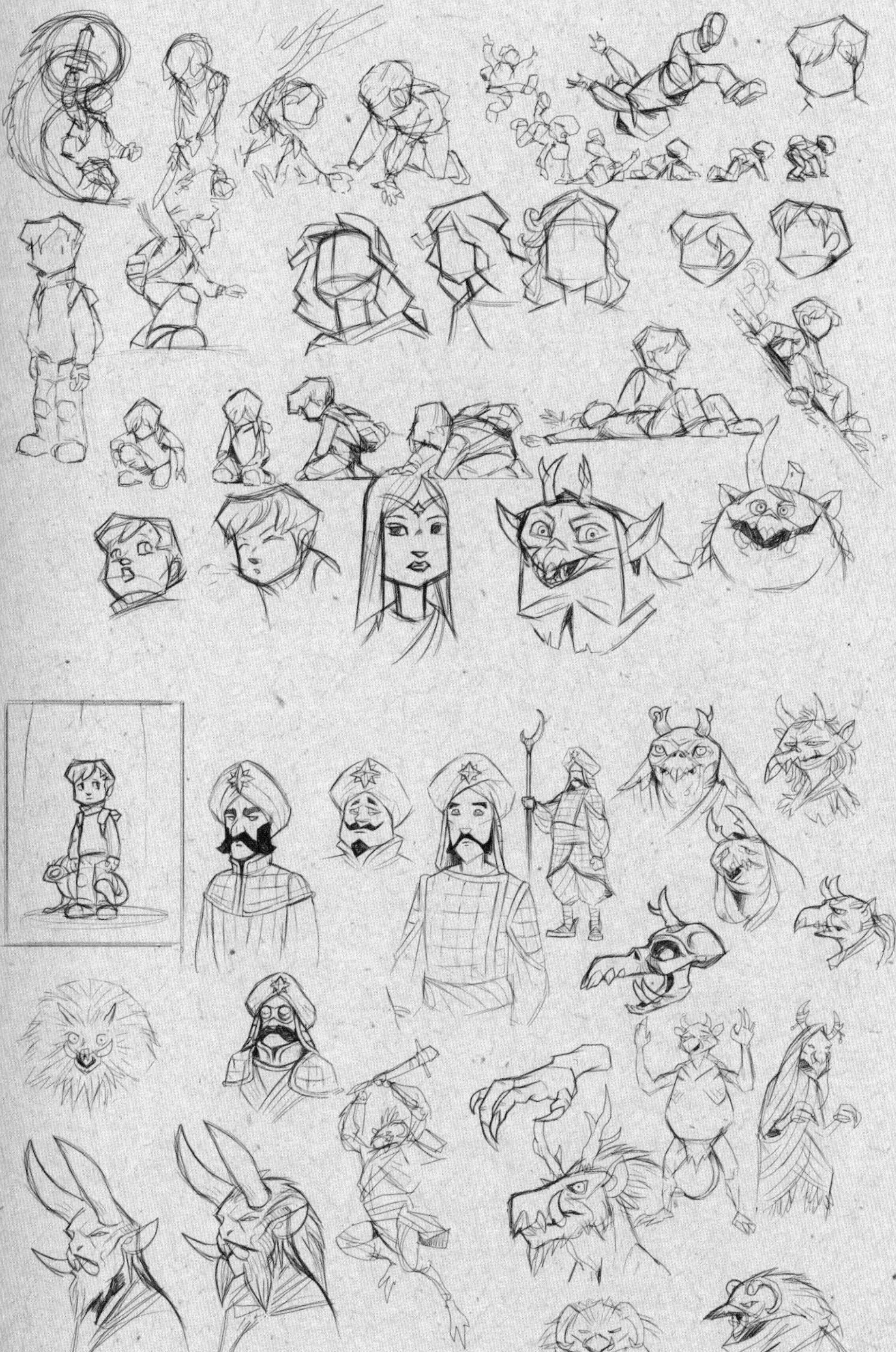

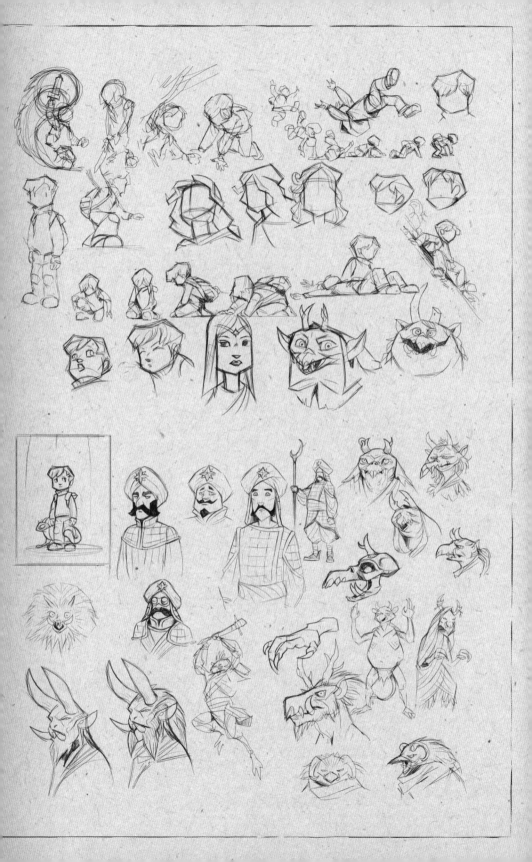

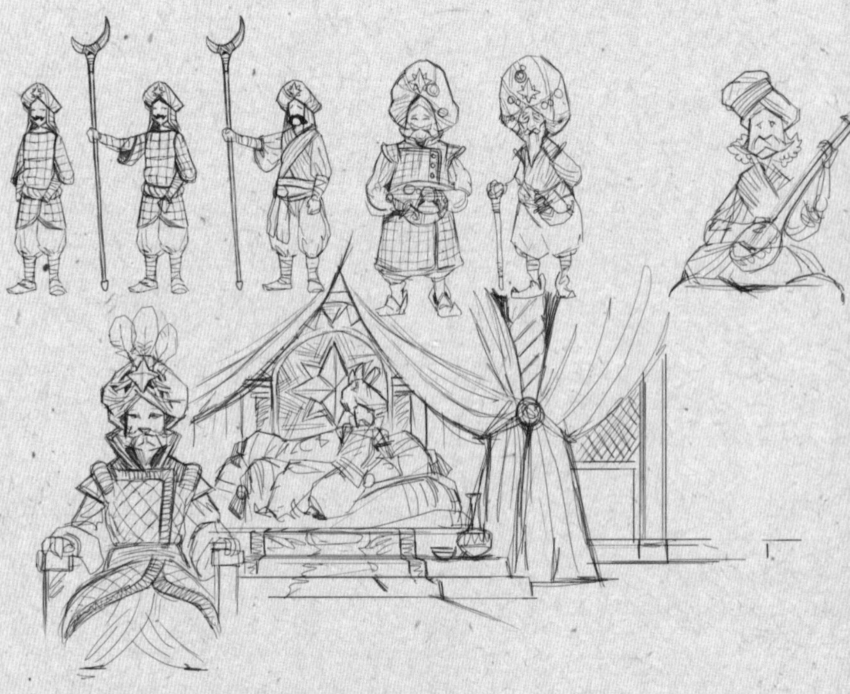
1.

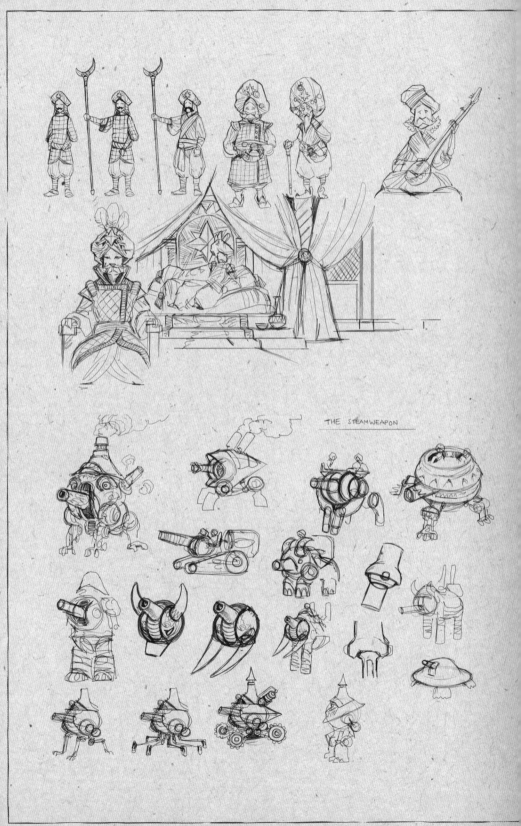

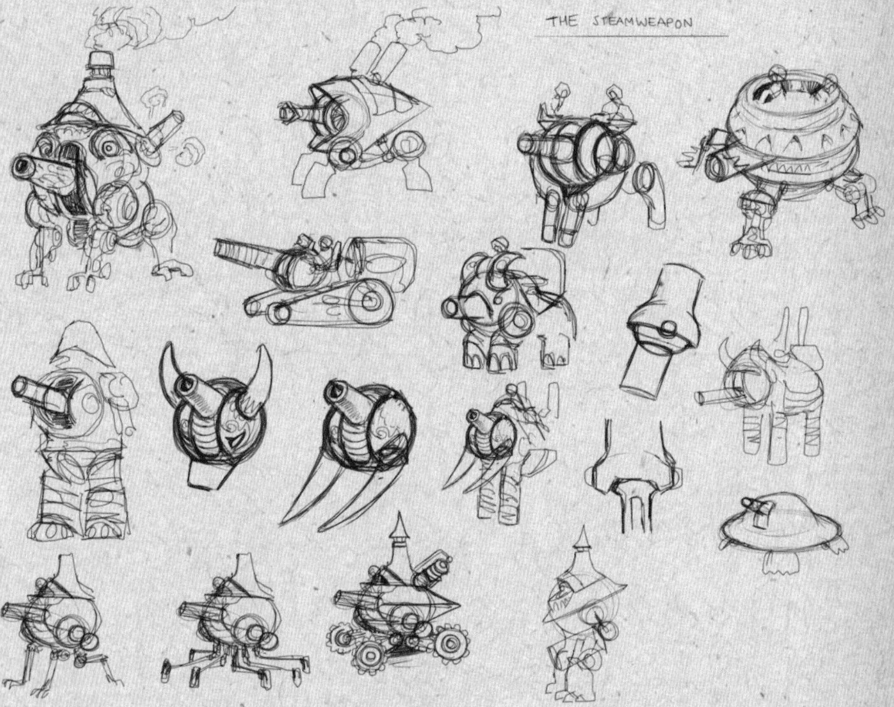
THE STEAMWEAPON